**"You wish to discuss surrender?"** he asked.

"I do."

Captain Rose approached her with long strides, and Cassandra shifted back until she hit the side of one trunk and could go no farther. She braced herself, waiting for him to knock the pistols aside and press his wide body against hers. He didn't, but clasped his hands behind his back, the stance stretching his shirt tight across his massive chest. If she pulled the trigger, she couldn't miss him. If she killed him, his crew would set on her and the others like rabid dogs.

He swept the length of her with an appreciative look.

"Imagine what a surrender it could be." His low voice reverberated through her, cutting through the heat of the cabin and adding to it. If he weren't a rogue, and she a lady in danger of losing more than her valuables, she could well imagine it. To hear such tones in her ear in the dark of night, with jasmine scenting the air, his warm hands on her moist skin. A temptation even the devil could not create stood before her.

# GEORGIE LEE

—

*Captain Rose's*
*Redemption*

HARLEQUIN® HISTORICAL

Recycling programs
for this product may
not exist in your area.

ISBN-13: 978-1-335-52275-7

Captain Rose's Redemption

Copyright © 2018 by Georgie Reinstein

Printed in U.S.A.

www.Harlequin.com

A lifelong history buff, **Georgie Lee** hasn't given up hope that she will one day inherit a title and a manor house. Until then, she fulfills her dreams of lords, ladies and a Season in London through her stories. When not writing, she can be found reading nonfiction history or watching any film with a costume and an accent. Please visit georgie-lee.com to learn more about Georgie and her books.

### Books by Georgie Lee

#### Harlequin Historical

*Engagement of Convenience*
*The Courtesan's Book of Secrets*
*The Captain's Frozen Dream*
*Captain Rose's Redemption*

#### The Business of Marriage

*A Debt Paid in Marriage*
*A Too Convenient Marriage*
*The Secret Marriage Pact*

#### The Governess Tales

*The Cinderella Governess*

#### Scandal and Disgrace

*Rescued from Ruin*
*Miss Marianne's Disgrace*
*Courting Danger with Mr. Dyer*

Visit the Author Profile page at Harlequin.com.

To the little one
who was with me through much of this story.

# Chapter One

*Off the coast of Virginia—1721*

'**O**pen the door or we'll break it down.'

Lady Cassandra Shepherd flexed her fingers over the butts of her father's matched duelling pistols and remained silent. Dread and the humid air of the mid-Atlantic nearly smothered her and made the mother-of-pearl handles stick to her skin.

'What'll we do, my lady? What'll they do to us if they get in here?' asked Jane, the young nurse, her weak whisper nearly lost beneath the pounding boots, screaming and gunfire overwhelming the small cabin from the pirates pouring on to the *Winter Gale*.

Cassandra could answer the question, but didn't. 'Don't worry, Jane, all will be well. I promise.'

Cassandra smiled at Dinah, her two-year-old daughter, who clung to the nurse's skirts, her eyes wide with concern. Innocence made her braver than Jane, but not immune to the panic of the adults. Dr

Abney stood beside Cassandra, clutching his old sea service pistol. All four of them watched the door from behind the trunks where they'd barricaded themselves inside the Captain's cabin at the outset of the attack.

No further demands were made. Beyond the door, the air cracked with blunderbuss fire and the continued commands and hollering of the pirates on deck, their voices much closer and more commanding of the crew than before. The pirates on the other side of the door didn't repeat their demand.

'Perhaps they've gone away,' Jane choked out.

'They won't be put off so easily.' Dr Abney exchanged an uneasy look with Cassandra and cocked his pistol. His ball wasn't for the pirates, but for her. Hers were for Jane and Dinah, to spare them from slavery or a worse fate at the hands of these brigands if Cassandra couldn't think of a way to save them all. The reality of it almost shattered her nerves and she prayed, if the time came, she'd have the courage to do the unthinkable.

*No, it won't come to that.* She gripped the weapons tight and focused on the door. There was still a chance they might survive, no matter how slim, and she would seize it. She must.

Everyone jumped when a blow rattled the flimsy door along with the narrow and spindly desk and the low trunk they'd shoved against it. The hit shook the iron hinges loose in the jamb and the wood bowed under the pressure. It was clear the rusted hinges wouldn't hold against another assault and the desk and trunk would only delay and not stop the intruders.

A final strike wrenched the hinges free and sent the door crashing down to crush the desk and see-saw across the top of the trunk. Filthy men squinting to see in the dim light stumbled into the cabin, tripping over the broken wood.

Cassandra raised the pistols, demanding her hands remain steady. She didn't have enough lead shot to send these dogs to hell, but she wouldn't give up, not before she tried to save herself and her daughter.

'How dare you enter here,' she scolded loudly.

The pirates jerked to a halt and their grimy jaws fell open at the sight of her.

'Pardon us, lady, we weren't meaning to intrude,' a slim man with weasel-like eyes over a pointed nose replied, his hands slipping one over the other in their eagerness to be on her. 'If you'll be puttin' down the pistols, we'll be gettin' to business.'

'Mr Barlow, 'tis Captain's orders no woman is to be forced and no passengers molested,' a man in a red Monmouth cap, his grey hair sticking out from beneath it, warned, more interested in the contents of the damaged desk than Cassandra. He searched through the papers that had been scattered about when the door had broken it, probably searching for any gold or jewellery the Captain kept there.

'I don't give a fig for Captain's orders,' the weasel spat. He turned back to Cassandra and licked his lips. 'I'll be tastin' a little of the finery he keeps for himself.'

Mr Barlow took a menacing step forward, and Cassandra cocked the pistols. 'Come closer and you'll regret it.'

'Don't go givin' orders, missy. There are twelve of us and only two shot.' His lascivious smile revealed a mouth of yellow and missing teeth.

A shudder slid down Cassandra's spine, but she kept her stance strong. 'Then you'll be the first to die.'

The weasel exchanged an uneasy glance with the other men who took a step back, willing to let the weasel take the first ball before they attacked.

'Thar be no need for anyone to die.' Mr Barlow held out his hands in a forced friendly way, but Cassandra didn't relax.

'Then fetch your Captain. I'll discuss the terms of my surrender with him.'

'No need to fetch him. He's here.' The deep voice rolled through the room from the doorway, the Virginia accent drawing out the vowels sounding familiar, like a hummed song she couldn't remember the words to.

Mr Rush jerked to his feet, still clutching a handful of papers, while the other pirates hustled to shove aside the broken desk and door and make way for their Captain.

The sheer mass of the man blocked the light from outside when he crossed the threshold, his presence shrinking the already tight quarters. He stood above six feet tall with shoulders like a thick yoke draped in a white shirt open at the neck. Perspiration soaked the linen, making it cling to the dark tan of his chest and each ripple of his taut stomach. Dark breeches tucked into high boots covered the solid muscles of his legs. A Spanish sword swung from a belt at his hip and a leather sash slung across his torso held two pistols fine enough to make Lord Chatham, her great-uncle, jealous. The butts of the pistols clanked together when he jerked to a halt at the sight of her. From behind the thin black half-mask that swept the bridge of his nose, leaving his cheeks and mouth free, his rich blue eyes with a hint of yellow near the irises widened, his shock striking Cassandra harder than the cannonball that had shattered the *Winter Gale*'s mainmast.

*He didn't expect to find a lady on board*, she thought. And yet there was more to his shock than her sex, station or even her weapons, especially when he glanced to the side, avoiding her eyes the way Giles, her late husband, used to do whenever Cassandra had confronted him about his mistress.

Something in the slight tilt of the pirate Captain's head while he studied the rough floorboards shifted an old memory deep inside Cassandra, of Virginia pine trees and warm fields, and sitting on the porch at Belle View reading Greek myths aloud with her former fiancé in the days before he'd gone to sea and then died. Anger rushed in with the memory and, when the Captain met her gaze again, she stepped back, stunned to find the same indignation blazing in his deep blue eyes.

*He's angry at me for resisting.* She ran one finger down the curve of the trigger, afraid her act of defiance might have placed her, Dinah and the others in more peril. She tensed, waiting for him to yell or lunge at her the way Giles had whenever she'd defied him. Instead, the Captain swept into a deep bow, his posture concealing the confusion in his eyes. 'Captain Rose, at your service, Miss—?'

Captain Rose straightened, his brow above the mask rising a touch while he waited for her answer. However, his lips moved slightly as if he already knew it and was about to say her name.

*Impossible.* He didn't know who she was and she shouldn't enlighten him. It risked him taking her hostage, though he'd get nothing for her. Lord and Lady Chatham would probably answer a ransom letter with a request for the rogue to dispatch her. It would spare them and London society further embarrassment. Her solid aim slackened at the memory of their betrayal, but she made her arms rigid again, keeping the pistol fixed on the pirate Captain. She still had the shots and command over however many minutes remained of her life. 'Lady Cassandra Shepherd.'

He ground his jaw, and she wondered if it was a pirate's grudge against the King and nobility that made him tense at the mention of her name instead of smiling with delight at the grand ransom a prisoner of her station might bring. He rested one hand on the hilt of his sword. 'Cassandra, the mythic Greek woman doomed to be ignored by men?'

'Most of whom perished for not heeding her warnings.'

'Are you a goddess, sweet lady?'

She cocked one pistol hammer. 'I'm as mortal as you are.'

'And tempted like me by the weaknesses of the flesh.' He rubbed his square chin with his thumb and forefinger and watched her with an admiration she'd not seen in a man's gaze for far too long. 'You wish to discuss surrender?'

'I do.'

Captain Rose approached her with long strides, and Cassandra shifted back until she hit the side of one trunk and could go no further. She braced herself, waiting for him to knock the pistols aside and press his wide body against hers. He didn't, but clasped his hands behind his back, the stance stretching his shirt tight across his massive chest. If she pulled the trigger, she couldn't miss him. If she killed him, his crew would set on her and the others like rabid dogs.

He swept the length of her with an appreciative look, lingering on the round mounds of her breasts as they rose and fell with each of her anxious breaths. She rolled her shoulders in a feeble attempt to raise the neckline of her floral-print cotton dress.

'Imagine what a surrender it could be.' His low voice reverberated through her, cutting through the heat of the cabin and adding to it. If he weren't a rogue and she a lady in danger of losing more than her valuables, she could well imagine it. To hear such tones in her ear in the dark of night, with jasmine scenting the air, his warm hands on her moist skin. A temptation even the devil could not create stood before her. 'I see you agree.'

'No, not at all.' Cassandra gripped the pistols tighter, horrified not only by her scandalous thoughts but that he'd seen them in her eyes. Now was no time to lose her head like some ridiculous servant girl wooed by her manor lord. She needed her wits. Whether he was strangely charming or not she had no desire to be ravished by this man. 'I will kill you first.'

He tilted closer to her, so she could see the shadow of his beard and the small drop of sweat sliding down his chest in the V of his shirt. 'And deny yourself the pleasure of my company?'

Cassandra swallowed hard, horrified and intrigued all at once by this man. 'It would be no pleasure.'

'It could be.' Something familiar lingered in the curve of his full lips as they drew to one side in a wry smile, as though she'd seen the expression before in a painting viewed in low light, although she couldn't recall when or where. It couldn't have been in London. None of the fops there possessed the sheer presence of this man, nor the grace laced with a lethal edge. 'Tell me, what brings such a classical lady to these waters?'

'I'm on my way to Virginia and I should very much like to reach it.'

'I'm not a man to stand between a lady and her *desires*.' He drew out the word like an invitation, making it sound as wicked as a curse and as tempting as an inheritance.

'You're a wicked man,' she spat out, as irritated with herself as she was angry and wary of him.

'Yes, I am.' His eyes turned from languid to hard and he flexed his fingers over the silver hilt of his sword. Judging by the reverence his crew had paid him at his entrance, Captain Rose wasn't used to being spoken to like a common seaman and didn't take lightly to being upbraided in front of his men by a woman.

The slosh of waves against the hull of the ship and the rough voices of pirates shouting orders on the main deck filled the drawn-out quiet in the cabin while everyone waited for Captain Rose's response.

'Name your terms and we'll see if they're agreeable to us both,' he said at last.

The man in the Monmouth cap let out a relieved sigh, but Cassandra, too aware of the danger, could barely exhale. 'No harm is to come to me, my child or her nurse.'

Cassandra nodded for Jane to come out from behind her and she did, hugging Dinah close. Dinah watched with wide eyes while Jane trembled so violently she could hardly stand.

Captain Rose ignored the young and comely nursemaid and focused on Dinah. 'I hope we haven't frightened you too much.'

Dinah, more curious than afraid, clutched her doll to her chest and shook her head, making the light curls near her cheeks bounce.

'Good. It was never my intention to scare a child.' The unexpected remorse in his voice echoed inside Cassandra. It was the same one that coloured her words whenever she spoke of her troubles in England, the ones driving her back to Virginia.

'Dr Abney must be under your protection, too,' Cassandra added, recapturing the Captain's attention. The rogue didn't deserve her sympathy and he should be ashamed of his conduct.

'Granted.' Captain Rose turned to address his men. 'No man is to touch the women, the child or the good doctor. Anyone who does will sing falsetto.'

'It ain't right, you saying what men can and can't have for a prize when it should be laid out in articles signed by us all.' Mr Barlow sneered at the Captain. 'On any other pirate ship, the crew would overthrow you for acting so mighty and thinkin' yourself above them.'

'You're not on any other ship but mine.' Captain Rose brought the back of his hand down hard across Mr Barlow's cheek, knocking him to the ground and making Cassandra gasp in horror. Captain Rose towered over the weasel who clasped his face and shrank back against the hull, a line of blood dripping from his cracked lip. 'I'll brook no mutinous talk from any of my crew. If you don't like how I run my ship, then you're free to leave it at the next port, or sooner if I deem it necessary. Do I make myself clear?'

'Yes, sir,' Mr Barlow whimpered.

'Good. Then find some work on deck and get out of my sight.'

Mr Barlow stumbled to his feet and pushed through the men still clogging the cabin door to watch the drama between their Captain and Cassandra, no doubt wondering when she would receive the same treatment for her defiance. Cassandra feared it, too, thinking this man's patience already at an end, but when he turned back to her he laid one wide hand over his heart, as sincere as a magistrate.

'I'm sorry you had to see such a thing, Lady Shepherd. My apologies.' Before she could tell him what she thought of his despicable behaviour, he fixed on Dr Abney. 'Sir, are you a man of the cloth or one of those useless physicians who know nothing more than to bleed and purge a man?'

'I'm a physician and a surgeon.' Dr Abney's voice carried a slight warble of fear.

'Then would you be so kind as to assist our surgeon in treating the wounded?' It was an order dressed up in a request.

Dr Abney exchanged a hesitant glance with Cassandra. After what they'd witnessed, it was clear they were in no position to refuse. Even if he did, and despite being a spry man of fifty with a thick chest leading down to solid arms, Dr Abney couldn't protect her against this mob and they both knew it. It was better for him to co-operate and hope for the best than to fight. He placed his pistol on the top of the chest he stood behind. 'If it means the continued safety of the ladies, I will.'

Captain Rose turned to the slender man standing

next to the one in the Monmouth cap. 'Mr O'Malley, take Dr Abney to Mr Perry.'

'Yes, sir.' Mr O'Malley motioned for Dr Abney to follow him and, with hesitant steps, Dr Abney complied, as reluctant to leave as Cassandra was to see him go.

'Everyone else, back to your stations.' Captain Rose's thundering command strained Cassandra's already tense nerves. Despite his manners, he was mercurial and she wondered when he'd finally turn his temper on her. 'The lady and I have a great deal to discuss.'

The pirates scrambled to obey, exiting the cabin as quickly as they'd entered it, except for Mr Rush and one other man who picked up the legless desk and the scattered papers and carried them out.

When they were gone, a quiet louder than the battle settled over the cabin, broken by the creak of the rigging and the snapping of sails. Cassandra nudged Jane and Dinah back behind the trunks, then stepped forward to face Captain Rose, unwilling to relinquish her weapons. 'When you're done plundering the ship, will you let us go, unharmed?'

He strode in a semicircle around her, once again eyeing her like the hungry tiger did its prey. 'What are you willing to offer me in return for your safe passage?'

She swallowed hard against the thick heat in the cabin and his expression, taking small comfort in the door lying on the floor instead of on its hinges. Though she doubted anyone would rush to her aid should she cry out. 'Anything not on or of our persons.'

He stopped in front of her and raked his hand through the thick tangle of his ebony hair hanging loose about his shoulders. 'A tall order for one with so little to bargain with.'

'I have two guns pointed at you.'

'Do you intend to aim at me all the way to Virginia?'

'If I must.'

'Then let me propose another solution, one more pleasurable for us both.' He straightened and fixed her with a smile charming enough to make him the toast of every bawd in the Bahamas. 'I will allow you, the Captain and the crew to continue on your journey in exchange for two favours. First, you will honour me with your presence at dinner in my cabin aboard the *Devil's Rose*. Cultured dinner partners are difficult to find among seafaring men. I miss the pleasures of a well-set table, of hearing London gossip and the delight of dining with a charming and beautiful woman.'

Cassandra's arms ached from holding the guns, but she didn't lower them, their slight protection offering her some comfort. If she dined with him, alone, aboard his ship, she'd be entirely at his mercy and the restraint he'd shown with her might finally vanish. 'Drawing-room prattle won't interest you.'

'Perhaps, but I can't help but be captivated by anything spoken in your melodious voice.'

'It isn't conversation I'm concerned about.' She cursed the slight tremble in her words and her hands.

He shifted closer until the barrel of the pistols touched the white of his shirt. The smell of man, leather and sea cut through her like lightning until she couldn't tell if it was the ship or her that rocked.

'You have nothing to fear, Lady Shepherd. I assure you, you will be safe with me.' A change came over him, so subtle it was like a shadow seen along the periphery of her vision. The planes of his face softened and he reached up behind his head to where the strings of his mask were tied, as if his true identity would vouch for his trustworthiness. She held her breath, waiting for him to undo them and reveal what it was about him he believed would comfort her. She couldn't imagine what it might be but she waited, curious to see the man behind the mask. A breeze drifted in through the narrow pane of open glass in the window, heavy with the tang of salt air and fading gunpowder. Then he dropped his hands. 'Do you agree to my terms?'

She shouldn't trust her life or her sanctity to this rogue, but the depths of his blue irises and the softness of the lines at the corners told her he would honour his word. She slid her fingers off the warm metal triggers and rested them on the cool mother-of-pearl handles. If agreeing to his terms meant the freedom and safety of those aboard the *Winter Gale*, then she must do it. 'I will dine with you, as long as Dr Abney is allowed to remain with my child and her nurse while I'm gone.'

'Granted.'

'And the second favour?'

'I'll explain that when we dine.' He laid his hands on the barrels of the pistols and, with a subtle pressure, lowered them, leaving nothing between them to protect her. He slid his hands off the silver, his fingers never touching hers although she was keenly aware of how close his skin was to hers. 'I'll send Mr Rush for you in an hour. Bring both pistols when you come. Unloaded.'

'Why?'

'You'll understand in an hour.' He shifted back into a bow worthy of a courtier, then turned and strode out of the cabin.

Cassandra sagged against the crate beside her in brief relief before the next wave of tension gripped her. She laid the pistols on top of the trunk, dropped to her knees in front of Dinah and clasped her close. Dinah and the others were safe, for the moment, but she didn't know how long it would last. She might trust the Captain, but it was clear the rest of his crew weren't as honourable as him. If one of them decided to sneak in here while she was gone… No, she couldn't think about it. Dr Abney would be here to watch over them.

'Everything all right now, Mama?' Dinah asked in her little voice and wrapped her arms around Cassandra's neck.

'Yes, honey. It is.' Cassandra inhaled her daughter's clean scent tinged with the salty damp and almost wept. They were so close to Virginia and the safety of Belle View. As in London, before her husband's death, the peace of their lives was dangerously close to being stolen from them. It all rested in the hands of yet another disreputable rake.

Richard stepped out of the Captain's cabin into the sunlight and took a bracing breath of sea air, but it failed to ease the tightness in his chest. He'd seen numerous female passengers quake with fear while he'd assured them no harm would come to them and been proud afterwards to have kept his word. He'd patted their crying children on the heads and offered them treats, confident their ordeal would end the moment his men finished loading the stolen cargo. Not once in all that time had he been forced to face the ugly, twisted thing he'd become as he had through Cas's wide, terrified eyes today.

He rubbed the back of his hand where it'd cracked against Mr Barlow's cheekbone, a bruise forming there beneath an old scar. Richard's presence had made her winsome voice tremble with fear and the sound of it had cut him deeper than the edge of a cutlass. In it had been the echo of everything Vincent Fitzwilliam had stolen from him five years ago, including the man he'd abandoned to become Captain Rose and the woman he'd loved.

Richard stormed across the deck, adjusting the sash across his chest. It was yet another reason why he must destroy the man.

'Your report, Mr Rush,' Richard demanded of his old friend and first mate when he approached the shattered mainmast. The deck surrounding it was a tangled mass of rigging and sails. Beside the mess, a few of his men guarded the *Winter Gale*'s crew, knives and blunderbusses at the ready. The seamen were the usual riff-raff the Virginia Trading Company hired, the toughness of their lives etched on their scarred and gnarled hands. Their dubious pasts and need for regular pay made them indifferent to the numerous maritime crimes their employer committed but it didn't mean they wouldn't strike at or kill Richard and his men if given the chance.

'The *Winter Gale*'s cooper says there's rumours some Virginia Trading Company ships are trading with pirates.'

'We'll have to find out if they're true and, if so, put a stop to it. Vincent can't be allowed to recover from our strikes.' The owner of the Virginia Trading Company had stolen everything from Richard and his crew. Richard would make sure he took everything from Vincent, including his company, his standing in Williamsburg and some day, his life.

'Perhaps we should press the cooper into service in exchange for Mr Barlow. He'd certainly be more use to us than that bilge rat,' Mr Rush suggested.

'As tempting as it is to get rid of Mr Barlow, I won't force any man into this life or invite more trouble than we already have.' After their cooper had died of a fever, they'd needed a new one to build and repair the fresh-water casks. Mr Barlow had been the best they could find and his presence made their complicated lives even more difficult.

The men didn't trust him enough to tell him their real names, or the reason behind their piracy, and Richard made sure he never saw him without his mask. He felt certain the rat, when faced with the lure of coin or the threat of the gallows, would betray them all. They didn't need to add another questionable man to their ranks and risk more danger. 'Have you found anything?'

'I searched the papers I pulled from the Captain's desk. Nothin' official there where they should be. Captain probably hid them before we boarded, like the last one did on your Mr Fitzwilliam's orders.'

'Then let's ask the Captain.' Richard marched up to where two of his men held the Captain and his first mate a short distance from his crew. The wiry first mate stepped back, but the Captain, a round man with a leathery face full of deep lines, stood firm against Richard's approach.

'Where are the ship's papers?' Richard demanded.

'The papers?' the thick man snorted. 'You're taking our cargo, what need can you have for our papers?'

'I don't have to explain my reasons. Tell me where you're hiding the shipping passes and whatever else the Virginia Trading Company gave you before you set sail.'

'There aren't any papers.' The Captain threw out his wide hands in feigned innocence and glanced at his first mate to reinforce his claim, but the first mate, silenced by his cowardice, stared at the deck.

'Bollocks there aren't.' Richard snatched a pistol

from his sash, then grabbed the Captain by the back of his thick neck and jerked him close. The stench of rum and dirty clothes engulfing the man was more pungent than rotting fish and so different from the faint scent of roses that had surrounded Cassandra. 'Where are they?'

'I don't know,' the Captain sputtered, struggling against Richard's grasp.

Richard cocked the pistol hammer with his thumb and jammed the muzzle beneath the Captain's chin, determined to find the documents. 'Is hiding them worth your life?'

The man's small eyes widened with the same fear Richard had witnessed in Cassandra's and guilt tripped up Richard's spine. At one time he'd been an admired and respected gentleman who only had to ask politely to receive things, not a brigand willing to kill a man over flimsy pieces of parchment. 'Where are they?'

The Captain raised a shaking hand to point at something behind Richard. 'There, in the cask by the mizzen mast.'

Richard shoved the man back to his first mate, holstered his pistol and stormed to the cask. He knocked aside the lid and reached inside. His fingers brushed nothing but a rough twist of rope before, near the bottom, he touched the smooth leather of a folio. He pulled it out and flipped through the air-dampened and watermarked contents, his hope fading with each turn of the vellum. He removed a shipping pass and held it up to the sun.

'Anything?' Mr Rush examined the pass over Richard's arm.

'I can't tell. Either it's real or Vincent is hiring more talented forgers.' Richard laid it on top of the other papers in the folio and snapped it shut.

*Curse the bastard.* Vincent would pay for all his sins. Richard would make sure of it, but it wouldn't be because of what they'd found on this ship.

'Maybe we should search the Captain's quarters?' Mr Rush suggested. 'Might be something more damning in there, something we missed.'

Richard looked at the Captain's cabin and the crooked door which had been returned haphazardly to its jamb. Cassandra sat inside, preparing for their meal. He could almost see her dark blonde hair arranged in soft rows of curls framing her face, with the long curls at the back just brushing the nape of her neck when she tilted her face up to his, her eyes the same rich green and brown he used to lose himself in during those spring evenings in Williamsburg.

*What the hell is she doing here?* She should be in London, the grand lady of the manor like she'd always wanted to be in Virginia, not aboard one of Vincent's ships complicating Richard's plans and threatening his peace of mind. The accusations of selfishness she'd flung at him before he'd set sail from Yorktown five years ago came back to him like a punch in the gut. She'd gloat if she knew how right she'd been and still was. She might yet get the chance. 'No. We've unsettled the lady and her child enough. I won't disturb them again.'

Mr Rush hooked his thumbs in the belt of his breeches. 'You'll risk letting good evidence go because of the nerves of some titled woman?'

Richard folded the folio in half and used it to motion Mr Rush to join him at the balustrade, out of hearing of the others. 'The lady in the cabin isn't simply a titled passenger. She's Walter Lewis's niece.'

Mr Rush let out a low whistle. 'Did she recognise you?'

'No, and there's no reason she should. Like everyone in Virginia, she thinks I'm dead.' He tapped the folio against his palm, thinking of Cas and the odd opportunity that had all but landed in his lap. 'I may resurrect myself before we leave. Walter's a mere solicitor. He doesn't have the connections in Williamsburg to collect information or wield influence, but a woman whose family used to be among the finest in Williamsburg might. Arrange for a meal in my cabin in one hour. I'm going to dine with the lady.'

'And try to win her to our side, to have her risk the hangman's noose for helpin' pirates after you lied to her and attacked her ship?' Mr Rush crossed his arms in disbelief. 'I don't care how skilled you are with the ladies of Port Royal, no man is that good.'

'I am.' He tapped the folio against Mr Rush's chest with an arrogance he didn't feel. If Richard revealed himself to her, Mr Rush was right, she would despise him for having lied to her, but he'd seen the faint flashes of recognition in Cas's eyes and the desire that had clouded them when he'd teased her. Her mind might not have allowed her to believe he was still alive, but her heart had recognised him. It had been there in the faint blush that had coloured her cheeks when he'd stood close to her. It was wrong to play on this, but he'd long since stopped caring about right and wrong. All he wanted now was justice. Revenge. 'See to the meal.'

Richard grabbed a hold of the rigging and swung himself up on to the planks connecting the two ships. He strode across the wood and dropped down on to the deck of the *Devil's Rose.* Men stepped aside to allow him to pass as he bounded up the forecastle stairs. 'Progress, Mr O'Malley.'

'Another excellent haul, Captain,' Mr O'Malley congratulated from where he stood at the helm while the rest of the crew continued to load the *Winter Gale*'s cargo into the hold. There it would stay until the next time they careened the ship at Knott Island when they'd bury it with the rest of their seized wealth.

'It is.' Richard clapped the helmsman on the back. 'We've struck another well-deserved blow. There'll be more to come before we're through and we won't stop until the Virginia Trading Company is wrecked.'

Richard's triumph faded at the sight of Dr Abney watching him. Dr Abney knelt beside one of Richard's men, treating the gash on his forearm. He looked away the moment he caught Richard's eye, but there was no mistaking the accusation and disgust in his expression. Justice for his men was what

Richard had sought since the beginning, but in Dr Abney's aged eyes Richard caught a shadow of the darker man beneath the mask, the one who didn't care about wealth or the future. Only bringing Vincent down.

He wondered if this was what Cassandra would see, too, when she dined with him.

He snatched up a map and rolled it out with a quick flick.

It didn't matter what Cas saw or thought so long as she agreed to help him.

## Chapter Two

'It isn't wise to dine alone with him, Lady Shepherd,' Dr Abney cautioned from where he stood guarding the door. She and the Virginian surgeon had become friends during the crossing. He was one of the few people who'd heard the rumours about her in London and chosen not to believe them. Cassandra appreciated his fatherly attitude and the many pieces of advice he'd offered her about returning to Williamsburg since they'd set sail.

'I have no more choice in whether to join him than you did in assisting his surgeon.' Cassandra sat on the edge of Dinah's bed, stroking her daughter's dark hair and watching the child's eyelids flutter while she slept. Jane stood on the other side, her small face with the snub nose still white with fright.

'I understand, but others may not see it the same way and think you went to him willingly. It might bring you more heartache than you left behind in London.'

Cassandra paused in her stroking of Dinah's hair. She *was* going to him willingly because he'd asked her to in exchange for the crew and the passengers' freedom, not because he'd demanded it, but it didn't change her lack of choice in the matter. Her daughter was her most prized possession and the only good to come from her marriage and she would do anything to protect her. 'If I have to meet privately with Captain Rose to ensure we reach Virginia, and Dinah has a real home and a future, then I will.'

'What future will she have if you are ruined?'

She leaned down and kissed Dinah's chubby cheek, then rose to face Dr Abney. 'Belle View plantation is mine and nothing, not rumours, my reputation or any man, can take it away from me.' Though heaven knew what condition she'd find it in once she reached it. 'Besides, if there's one thing that can always be counted on, either in London or in Williamsburg, it's the English love of titles and land. Thankfully, I possess both.' It was money she lacked. She had enough fine gowns and jewellery to give the illusion of wealth so necessary for securing one's place in society, but it wouldn't last for ever. She hoped it worked in Williamsburg long enough for her to succeed for it was the only card she had to play.

She wandered to the window, desperate for a cool breeze to ease the heat. On either side of the open pane, the swirled leaded glass distorted the view of the water. The cloying humid air sat heavy over the ship and she dabbed her sweat-soaked chest with a small handkerchief, unable to find relief. The prospect of facing all the old ghosts waiting for her in Virginia unnerved her as much as the man she was about to dine with. 'Captain Rose gave me his word that no harm will come to any of us and so far he's kept his promise.'

'Then for your sake, I pray he continues to do so.'

'Me, too.' She smoothed her hands over the light blue silk of her robe *à la française*, trying not to let Dr Abney's concerns increase hers. If the Captain proved as untrustworthy as Giles, it would add another salacious story to the ones from London already trailing her like a wake behind a ship and make everything she hoped to regain in Williamsburg that much more difficult.

A knock at the door tightened the already strained air of the room.

'Enter.' Cassandra faced the door, lacing her hands together in front of her. She'd changed from her simple cotton day dress to a deep maroon silk one, with lace along the half sleeves and silver embroidered flourishes on the skirt and bodice. Although it was heavier and hotter than the other, it was thicker in the front and wider at the hips, revealing less of her narrow waist. The bodice was a touch higher, but it still emphasised a good deal more of her décolletage than she would have liked. Witty conversation was how she intended to charm Captain Rose into keeping his promise to send them on their way, not the more carnal assets Giles had once accused her of using to ensnare lovers. As loathsome as her late husband's touch had been, there hadn't been anyone but him. It no longer mattered. By wearing the fine gown, she'd give Captain Rose the cultured dinner partner he'd asked for. Besides, if he proved to be a rogue, none of her gowns, no matter how high the bodice or how wide the skirt, would stop him from taking what he wanted.

The man with the Monmouth cap entered, tugging at the dirty red scarf tied around his neck while he struggled to keep his eyes on hers and not her chest. 'Mr Rush, milady. I'm to escort you to the *Devil's Rose*.'

Cassandra took a steadying breath. She must be brave for Dinah's sake and for everyone else aboard the *Winter Gale*. 'Then let's be off.'

Mr Rush offered her his arm. 'Milady, if I may?'

She slid the slender walnut pistol box off the table and tucked it under her arm, wondering why Captain Rose had asked her to bring it. There were more valuable items he could take from her, though two fine weapons were probably of more use to a pirate than jewellery. She placed her free hand on Mr Rush's coarse, sea-spray-stiffened coat and allowed him to lead her on deck and to an unknown fate.

The *Winter Gale* crew, guarded by the pirates, watched Cassandra and Mr Rush walk side by side to the wide planks laid between the ships. Pity filled a few of the older men's eyes, but she ignored them as she'd ignored the vicious stares and whispers of London society. The plank bobbed and rolled while the two ships, held together by grappling hooks and lines, tossed about on the sea. Captain Rose stood on the other side, some of his men flanking him at the balustrade, the change in him from earlier remarkable.

He wore a black frock coat without facing. A row of silver buttons curved down along the front and decorated the bootleg cuffs folded back to reveal his large hands. A red waistcoat hugged his trim torso, the line of it broken by a wide belt pulled down on one side by the weight of his sword. Black breeches tucked into tall cuffed boots covered his long legs. The severity of his dark attire was lightened by the white shirt beneath his waistcoat and the silver embroidery about the edge of the tricorn he wore low over his forehead to meet his mask. His exposed cheeks and jaw beneath the mask revealed a smooth face freshly shaved. If she hadn't seen him an hour ago, his shirt wild and loose about him, his hair hanging to his shoulders, she might have mistaken him for any gentleman in a ballroom in Mayfair.

When she approached the plank, he examined her with a gaze intense enough to ignite every cask of gunpowder on the ship. Panic gripped her harder than when the pirates had first burst through the door, and her hand tightened on Mr Rush's arm. She wanted to rush back to the cabin and reload the pistols, but she held her ground, refusing to reveal her fear to everyone, especially Captain Rose.

'You needn't worry,' Mr Rush offered when they stopped before the plank. 'Captain Rose is a gentleman. No harm will come to you.'

The older man's faith in his Captain bolstered hers and her courage. With Captain Rose and both crews watching, she couldn't turn back or betray her word and risk placing the ship, herself and Dinah in danger. 'Thank you for your concern, it's very much appreciated.'

'I'll hold the box while you cross.'

She handed Mr Rush the pistol case, then took his hand and stepped up on to the plank. The timbers of the ships and the thick ropes lashing them together groaned and creaked with the movement of the swell and every once in a while the hulls banged together, sending up a small spray of water.

Captain Rose stepped up on to the plank on his side. He clutched the rigging in one hand and offered Cassandra the other. She ignored it and took hold of the sides of her dress and began to walk regally across the splintered wood. She didn't look down, aware that if she fell between the ships they might slam together and crush her. She was halfway across the boards when the *Winter Gale* lurched, throwing her off balance.

In a flash of black fabric, Captain Rose caught her about the waist and whirled her around to set her on the deck of the *Devil's Rose*. He held her close, his arm tight about her waist, his wide chest hard against her stomach. The potent smell of sandalwood shaving soap and leather surrounding him made her dizzier than the near fall. He'd been imposing in the confines of the cabin with little more than the distance of the pistols between them. With his body pressed against hers, the fine wool of his frock coat brushing her bare chest above her bodice, he was overwhelming.

'The trick is to move quickly.' His husky voice rumbled deep inside her. She peered up at him, her breath stolen by his closeness. His suntanned skin showed no evidence of the weathered grit of a sailor too long at sea and the fine colour of it heightened the black of his hair. She shouldn't think a rogue striking, but she did.

'Thank you.' She inhaled the spice of wood and salt emanating from him and another memory, faint like the fading scent of smoke, rose up in the back of her mind. It was of Uncle Walter's Williamsburg garden and the flowering dogwood tree in the centre of it. Beneath it stood Uncle Walter's young apprentice solicitor waiting to steal a kiss from her. That young man was dead, but this one was very much alive, his chest hard beneath her fingertips, his thigh firm against hers.

She tucked her fingers in against her palms, resisting the urge to slide them up over his stoic chin, across his angled cheeks and under the silk to reveal his face. She wanted to see the gentleman beneath the pirate, to view the full effect of the sharp, straight nose covered by the black silk and the intense blue eyes making her recall so many things she longed to forget.

She lowered her hands and his grip on her eased. She stepped out of his embrace, steadying herself against the roll of the ship and the enticing power of him. He wasn't a curiosity, but her enemy, and she must remember it and remain on guard.

Mr Rush crossed with the box and handed it to his Captain.

Captain Rose tucked the pistol case under one arm and offered her the other. 'Shall we?'

'Yes, please.'

The supple wool of his dark jacket shifted beneath Cassandra's palm with each sure step of his boots during the walk to his cabin. She matched his stride, holding her head high as if they were parading across Hyde Park and not a pirate ship. The crew stood at respectful attention, with only the weasel Mr Barlow leering as though he expected Captain Rose to ravish her in plain view. She should have shot the nasty man, but heaven knew what repercussions his death would have brought down on her, Dinah and the crew of the *Winter Gale*. Even now she couldn't say what fate awaited her. Alone, with the door to Captain Rose's cabin firmly closed, she would be at his mercy. However, the lives of many depended on her being a pleasant and charming guest, so with purpose she swept across the threshold and into the semi-darkness of his cabin.

A bank of diamond-shaped glass windows made up the far wall of the narrow cabin situated at the back of the ship. A faded, red-velvet curtain graced the top of the window, cascading down each side and edged with faded gold tassels. One end hung next to a small desk, the other end pooled near the head of the narrow bed built into the hull. Her attention

darted from the sumptuous pillows and fine coverlet
to the small, square table in the middle of the room.
A woven rug lay beneath it and two sturdy nail-
head-trimmed chairs flanked either side. An assort-
ment of exotic fruits including pineapples covered
the well-set table. Everything from the silverware
beside each plate to the books arranged on the desk
spoke of the refined tastes of a gentleman, not the
vulgar clutter of a hardened sailor new to comfort.
It was a strange contradiction. He was commanding,
but he hadn't forced her; charming and yet violent;
a scoundrel and at the same time a man of station.
She wondered what had driven him to this life. Perhaps through witty conversation and grace of manners she could bring out more of the gentleman she
was sure he'd once been and appeal to him for her
and the *Winter Gale*'s freedom.

'Do you approve?' He set the walnut box down
beside a pewter service at one end of the table, then
pulled out a chair.

'It's far more refined than I expected.' She sat
down, conscious of how close he stood, his hands
near her shoulders, the cuffs of his coat brushing
against her skin when he slid the chair in until the
seat touched the back of her thighs. She glanced over
her shoulder at him towering above her, dark and impressive, her curiosity giving her more to consider
than her worries that he might turn on her at any
moment, and a reason for her to be brave and bold.
She sensed he would respect her for it. 'Though it's
ill-gotten.'

* * *

Richard trilled his fingers once on the chair, then gripped the leather tight. The delicate curve of her bare shoulders above the bodice of the dress was so close that if he reached out one finger he could touch it. The skin would be warm, but not her reaction. The uncertainty in her eyes when she'd stepped out of his embrace on deck had undermined her defiant crossing of the planks. She was afraid of him, but determined to show otherwise. He could remove the mask and prove that she had nothing to fear, but he didn't. Despite her having upheld her end of the bargain, being a charming partner at dinner was one thing. Colluding with a pirate in a place as hostile to them as Virginia was quite another. Until he was sure he could win her to his cause, he would remain Captain Rose. A woman scorned could be a lethal enemy in Virginia at a time when he needed all the allies he could cultivate.

'Not as ill-gotten as the way the Virginia Trading Company obtained it through the misery of slaves, seamen and countless other ruined lives.' He let go of the chair and took his seat across the table from her.

She raised her rich eyes framed by dark lashes to meet his. 'You dislike the Virginia Trading Company?'

He opened and closed his hand beneath the table, thinking he should have stayed behind her and not faced her. The white mounds of her breasts were supple and smooth against the dark fabric of her gown, tempting him to break from her gaze and admire them. 'I do. Their ships are the only ones I attack. The others I let go.'

'Why?' She tilted her head to view him, making the teardrops of her earrings brush the line of her delicate jaw. 'Were you an officer on one of their ships and the Captain disciplined you too harshly?'

He tapped the chair's arm, wishing he could taste a little of her discipline again. 'No.'

'Then a rival perhaps, a gentleman of some means who had his own company but couldn't keep it in the face of competition?' She speared a piece of pineapple off her plate with the fork and set it between her lips, using her teeth to draw it off the tines.

Richard, his pulse racing in his ears as well as places lower down, took hold of the thin neck of the wine decanter and reached over to fill the crystal goblet in front of her. Its red depths danced with the candlelight from the chandelier above the table, the heady vintage as tempting as her. 'No.'

She set down the fork, rested her elbows on the table and steepled her fingers beneath her chin. The delicate lengths of them almost begged Richard to take them in his calloused hands and kiss the tips of each one the way he used to do during their afternoons in the Belle View barn. How beautiful she'd been beneath him then, her languid body curled around his, eager and ready for him. 'Then tell me why?'

The amethyst jewels around her neck winked with the candlelight and the largest of the descending teardrops rested between the swells of her full breasts.

One close to her throat had turned over, hiding the gem. He reached across the table and righted it, his fingers lightly brushing her neck and bringing a chill to her skin and his. 'Because not all scoundrels sail under a black flag.'

She didn't lean away despite the nervousness flickering through her eyes, but met his steady gaze. 'How unfortunate I chose one of their ships for my passage.'

'If you hadn't, we may not have met.' He raised his wineglass to her. She held up her goblet before taking a sip, watching him over the rim of the crystal, except it wasn't her sparkling eyes that held his attention, but the gold wedding band sitting like an ugly scar on her finger. It killed the desire for her coursing through his body. 'What does your husband think of you sailing by yourself?'

He nearly choked on the word *husband* and everything it meant. She was not his to enjoy and tease, she hadn't been for a long time and all because of the choices he'd made. It didn't matter—nothing did except securing her help. She'd be no use to him if her lord and master put a stop to things.

She set down the wine and glanced at the ring as if she wanted to snatch the cursed thing from her finger and hurl it into the sea. 'He thinks nothing of it. He's dead.'

Richard sat back in shock, her reason for being at sea and on her way home suddenly clear. He'd despised the man who'd taken his place, but he didn't want Cas to suffer in mourning. She didn't deserve it—however, the man's being gone would make many things so much easier. 'I'm very sorry for your loss.'

'I'm not. He did nothing but make my life miserable.' She stared at the reflection of the candles in the surface of the wine, the shape of them widening and narrowing with each tilt of the ship making the liquid sway. The teasing, alluring woman from a moment ago was gone, revealing the wounded one she'd hidden so well with her bravery and her charming words, the one he'd failed to recognise because he'd been too intent on getting what he wanted.

Just like when he'd left her at Yorktown five years ago.

Richard picked at the nail head on his chair, a guilt washing over him such as he hadn't experienced since the first time he'd taken a ship what seemed like a lifetime ago. He was quickly proving to be as big a bastard as his enemy. 'I'm sorry things did not turn out as you would have liked.'

'It's been a long time since anything has.' Defeat draped her like a sail cut loose from a mast. It was the same futility he'd experienced when word had reached him of her marriage and then of his father's death. Regret crept along the back of his mind, resisting all his efforts to kill it. He'd worked hard for so long to dampen those emotions because there was nothing he could do to change what had happened. He could change things today. He'd done nothing to earn the right to ask her for any favour, especially one that might cause her more grief than Richard's selfishness had already visited upon her. Let Walter tell her the truth in his own time, if at all. It would keep her untarnished by the hate enveloping Richard and grant her some peace of mind.

He rose, ready to escort her back to the *Winter Gale*, to bid her goodbye as he had five years ago, except this time she was ignorant of who he was and he was all too aware that they would not meet again. 'I hope you find solace with your family in Virginia.'

She slowly spun the amethyst bracelet she wore around her delicate wrist, then spoke in so low a voice he almost didn't hear her. 'I have no family in Virginia.'

Every sense that told him when an enemy ship was approaching on the horizon raised the hairs along the back of his neck, and he pressed his fingertips into the top of the table. 'What?'

'My uncle, my only family, was sick with a fever,' she choked through heavy words. 'He died three months ago.'

Richard worked to steady himself as everything around him came apart like a ship in a hurricane. Walter Lewis, his only ally in the colonies, was gone and with him went Richard's greatest chance of seeing himself and his men exonerated, and Vincent ruined. Panic filled him, and he struggled to keep it under control.

Before Richard could speak, Cassandra jumped to her feet, making the plates on the table rattle. 'I've entertained you at supper as you asked. Will you let us go now?'

Her plea didn't move him this time and neither

did the anguish in her eyes. Everything Richard had spent the last five years working to accomplish teetered on the edge of ruin and he would not see it go over the side. He balled his hands into fists. Vincent had defeated him once before. He wouldn't allow Walter's death to let him do it again. 'No, Cas, I'm afraid I can't, not yet.'

Cassandra gripped the side of the table as the ship tilted. 'What did you call me?'

He reached up and untied the strings of his mask, allowing the silk to slide down his face and drop to the floor.

'Richard!' It couldn't be, but it was. 'You're alive!'

Hard work at sea had broadened his chest and arms and everything else about him. The sun had lightened his hair, making some strands near red, and turned his skin tawny. His eyes were almost the same except for the small lines about the corners and the steel of experience hardening them. She wouldn't believe it was him if it weren't for the small scar beneath his left eye formerly hidden by the mask. It was a reminder of a wherry accident from when he was a boy, a tale his father had laughingly recounted to her once when she and Uncle Walter had dined at Sutherland Place in the early days of their engagement. Tears blurred her vision. During too many lonely nights Richard's memory had haunted her and made her wail over their lost future. She'd cursed the sea for luring him away and when the strangling weight of her marriage bonds had chafed,

Richard's memory had fed the faint hope she might some day find happiness again. It had all been a lie, like Giles's love during their courtship and Lord and Lady Chatham's concern for her. 'When they said you'd turned from privateer to pirate, I thought they were mistaken. I told everyone you were innocent. I lost friends and was ridiculed because of my faith in you and all along they were right.'

'No, they weren't.' He banged his fist against the table, overturning a bowl and sending the oranges inside it rolling across the table and on to the floor. 'I was innocent. I *am* innocent.'

'You aren't. Look at you. I wish you had died, then I could remember the man who loved me and not this…' she flapped her hand at him, no name black enough to describe what he'd become '…pirate.'

'I didn't choose this life,' he hissed with a fierceness to make her shift further behind the chair. 'I and my crew were forced into it by Vincent Fitzwilliam and I have no choice but to live it until either he's ruined or I'm dead.'

'How can that be?'

'The ship we attacked was a Virginia Trading Company sloop shipping cargo under Dutch colours and a forged Dutch pass. We attacked it because the Dutch had joined the war and their ships were fair prizes. I didn't realise what Vincent was doing until I saw the Captain's papers. By then it was too late. The Captain escaped in a launch and made it to Virginia before I could. To protect himself, Vincent had me and my men declared pirates and bounties placed on our heads. His company was foundering under the weight of his father's gambling debts and when the embargo was issued against the French, shipping cargo illegally under a Dutch flag was the only way he could maintain his business. He sank me, his oldest friend, to save himself.'

'If you had the fake papers, then why didn't you fight the charges?'

'Vincent had the Governor's ear—he still does—and his Captain's testimony. I had nothing except my ship, my men and my disgraced word.' He pressed his fist into his hips, his fury easing, but not the tightness along his shoulders. 'I renamed the *Maiden's Veil* the *Devil's Rose* and we've plundered Virginia Trading Company ships in search of evidence and to destroy Vincent's business ever since. What little evidence I've found I've sent to your uncle, hoping it would one day be enough for him to take to Lord Spotswood and see the man convicted and me and my men pardoned of all charges, but it hasn't been enough.'

He bent his head in a frustration she could feel because like him, she knew what it was to fight and struggle and to keep failing. But she couldn't comfort him, not with the realisation of the truth behind his words cruelly dawning on her.

'Uncle Walter knew you were alive? He lied to me about your death?' She dropped into the chair, her legs no longer able to support her and the grief weighing her down. Uncle Walter had been a steady rock for her to cling to in the midst of the storms of her life in Williamsburg after her parents' deaths and again in London when his letters had offered advice and affection when no one else would. All the while he'd been lying to her, and in the cruellest of ways, like almost everyone she'd ever cared for including Richard, Giles and the Chathams.

*Why am I not worthy of love and honesty?* She longed to bury her face in her hands and cry, but she couldn't. All she could do was continue on, as she always did, adding this new grief to the old ones already bruising her.

'He lied to you and to my father because I didn't want either of you to see what I was forced to become in order to destroy Vincent.' He righted the bowl, his fingers lingering to trace the engraving on the edge of it. 'I was aware of the dangers when I went to sea, how it could kill a man. I didn't think it could destroy the very essence of who he is, or was.'

The pain of his strained words made her heartache slide away. The man she'd once loved was suffering in a way she understood and longed to ease. She laid a comforting hand on his and curled her fingertips to press against his palm. His muscles tensed, but he didn't pull away. He clutched her hand in a firm embrace which reached deep into her soul. 'Then leave this life. Take the money you've made from it and go to the islands and establish yourself as a planter. Many have done it before.' *And I could come with you.* London, Williamsburg and all the torment of her past and the uncertainty of starting over at Belle

View could be set aside. She would no longer be alone and he no longer a faded dream.

He brushed the back of her hand with his thumb, as tender as he'd been during all the evenings they'd spent together in the garden. She wasn't foolish enough to think he would walk away from his ship and crew at her mere suggestion, but still she wished it might happen, as she'd done so many times since he'd first set sail, until she'd learned he was dead.

Then, he slid his hand out from under hers, drawing away like he used to when he'd tire of her arguments against his becoming a privateer. 'Not until Vincent is ruined.'

She stepped back, fighting the urge to sweep the dishes from the table. He was choosing the sea over her again and not caring whether it destroyed them both. This wasn't the Richard she used to cherish and, for the first time since she'd seen him come up the walk at her uncle's house, she wondered if she'd been as wrong about him as she'd been about Giles. 'It's just like when you left before. All you care about is what you want and you don't care who it hurts, not innocent travellers, yourself or me.'

He snatched the mask off the floor and gripped it hard in his fist, holding it out to her. 'You don't know what it's like to be accused of something you didn't do and to have everything, your family, your property, your life, your very identity, stolen from you because of it.'

'Yes, I do,' she shot back, twisting the gold band on her finger. 'Giles stole almost everything from me, my meagre dowry, my good name, my belief in his affection for me. He even tried to take Dinah away before he killed himself riding home drunk from his mistress's house in the rain, but not even his death spared me from more pain and humiliation. Without a son to inherit, the estate went to a cousin and I was turned out and left with nothing except a reputation blackened by his mistress and her catty London friends. I'd never done anything wrong and it didn't matter because he still ruined my life.'

Tears stung her eyes, and she wiped them away with the backs of her hands, refusing to appear more desperate and lonely than she already did. She still had her pride and the chance to rebuild her life. She had to believe in that for there was nothing else. She raised her chin to Richard in defiance, but her stiffness eased at the change in him.

His fury dimmed and he lowered his hand, opening his fist to let the silk drop to the floor. The man who'd stood beside her at her parents' graves and listened to her wail over their loss and how it had irrevocably changed everything stood before her again. The life of a brigand had altered him almost beyond recognition, yet echoes of the old Richard remained in the softness of his expression while he studied her.

'Your husband was a fool. He should have loved you and worshipped you, not cast you aside. He should have been faithful to you, not left you to be torn down by society.' He brushed her cheek with the back of his fingers, the delicate touch burning her skin. She should knock his hand away, take up the knife beside her plate and stab him for what he'd done to her and countless others, but she didn't, she couldn't. His caress disturbed places long forgotten in her marriage and widowhood. It had been too many years since anyone had spoken to her of love and here it was on Richard's lips, just as it had been in the Williamsburg garden a lifetime ago. They'd both been wounded, their innocence torn from them by the machinations of others and their own mistakes, but with his warm skin caressing hers, she could almost believe that if she pressed her lips to his she might regain everything they'd once meant to one another. She wouldn't have to face the trials of life by herself and he wouldn't be a rogue, but the man to help and protect her, to love her as he'd once vowed he would.

As if hearing her silent longing, he slid his fingers behind her neck and drew her to him. She closed her eyes and five years fell away when their lips met. She was sixteen again, her life and heart filled with love and promise. He was no longer a privateer captain turned pirate, but an apprentice to her uncle with a passion for the sea and eager to make his fortune so they could marry. Her tongue tasted his, the spice of wine still lingering on his lips. In the strength of his kiss there existed traces of the honourable Richard she'd loved, the one who might live again if he abandoned Captain Rose. It wasn't possible, but with his arms around her, his hands firm against her back, she could almost imagine it was.

* * *

Richard broke from her kiss and rested his forehead on hers, the press of her against him like touching his old life. Except all of it was gone and there was no gaining it back. His father, Sutherland Place, his life in Virginia were only memories, just like Cas had been. Except she was here in his arms. For the first time in five years the possibility that there might be more for him in this world than revenge teased him like her fingertips did the back of his neck. Maybe he could reclaim something of what he'd lost, let his men go on to enjoy the treasure they'd collected, to raise families and own land and be free of the threat of the hangman's noose. He could take his share of the money and become something more than an outlaw driven by hate, but a respected planter once again.

He rested his cheek against hers and over her shoulder caught sight of the desk and the folio with the Virginia Trading Company papers lying on top of it. Bitterness flooded in to kill his hope. If he walked away from this life to chase some dream, he would have to live every day with the knowledge that Vincent was out there, enjoying the very things he'd stolen from Richard, and all the misery Richard had brought on himself, his men and countless others would have been in vain.

'Captain!' Mr Rush called from outside, making the door rattle with a frantic knock. 'Mr Tibbs has spied a Royal Navy ship. We must set sail at once.'

'See to it, Mr Rush,' Richard ordered, jerking back from Cas.

'Aye, sir.' Mr Rush's voice faded as he hurried off, shouting orders to the men.

'Our time together is over.' Richard slid his arms from around Cas, addressing her with the same sharpness he did the passengers on other ships he'd taken—except she wasn't like them. He dismissed the thought and the slight prick to his conscience. 'I asked you for two favours in exchange for your freedom. I must insist on the second one.'

'You can't.'

'With Walter dead, I have no choice.'

'Of course you do. You always have a choice and, now that I see the kind of decisions you prefer, I thank you very much for sparing me from making the worst mistake of my life by marrying you.'

He ignored her jibe as he removed a pouch of money from the desk. He deserved her scorn, but it wouldn't stop him from securing her help to bring Vincent down. This was why he'd brought her here and not for any other reason. 'You will soon have control of the evidence I sent Walter. You must promise me you'll safeguard it and help me when I request it.'

'I won't! Do you know what they'll do to me if they discover I'm colluding with a pirate? I'll be hanged and my daughter left an orphan with no one to care for her.'

He stamped out the guilt scratching at him the way he did every time he boarded a ship and faced the terrified souls on board. What he was doing was wrong and might cause her more heartache than anything he'd done before, but she was his only link to Virginia and he needed her help. 'There are risks, but I will make it worth your while.' He held up the leather pouch between them, the bottom sagging beneath the weight of the coins.

'That's blood money.'

'If anyone's hands are tainted, it's Vincent. At least a small portion of it will finally go to good, to help you start over in Virginia.' He gently encircled her wrist with his fingers and raised her hand to lay the sack in her palm. Her pulse raced beneath his fingertips and he waited for her to throw the money back at him along with a parcel of curses, but her fingers curled around it instead and he knew he had her. 'I will only call on you if I absolutely have to and, when I do, there will be more.'

'I don't want it, or anything to do with you.' She dropped the money on the floor.

He scooped it up and set it on the table beside the pistol box. He lifted one pistol out of its velvet bed and held it up between them. 'This will be our signal. When I send this to you, you'll follow the man who bears it and he'll provide you with further information about what is required.'

He slipped the weapon into the deep pocket of his coat, binding her to him in a most dangerous way. He laid the money in the empty space in the case and closed and locked the lid.

'The Richard I loved wouldn't have done this.'

He pressed his fingers into the smooth surface. 'That Richard is gone. Vincent killed him.'

'No, you did!' She snatched the case out from beneath his hands and clutched it to her chest, pinning him with a look more filled with hate than any captain or passenger he'd ever captured at sea.

He flashed her a wicked smile to conceal the remorse making her harsh words sting. 'Take heart, Cas, I could be killed long before I ever call in my favour.'

'I hope you are.'

Cassandra swept around him and out the door, marching across the deck and to the plank joining the two vessels. The pirate crew paid her little heed while they rushed to disengage the grappling hooks and ready the ship. Overhead, the large sail filled with wind and pulled the rigging taut. Over the noise, she caught the faint clink of the coins inside the case. She should open it and throw the money overboard, but to do so would mean revealing something of their conversation and the fact that she'd accepted money from a pirate.

*I did it for Dinah.* The money was significantly more than she presently possessed and it would help them start over in Virginia.

She hurried to the balustrade, ready to cross to the *Winter Gale.* No activity marred its deck where the sails and rigging lay torn and shattered. They needed the Royal Navy ship to reach them and help the sailors repair the mainmast before they could continue.

Dr Abney stood in front of the mess, anxiously waiting for her, his full cheeks sagging with relief when he saw her approach the rails. He'd warned her about going willingly to Richard, but she hadn't listened. She wished she had, then Richard would have remained a treasured part of her past instead of another person who'd betrayed her.

In a few long strides Richard was beside her, his mask fixed over his face, his tricorn settled low over his forehead to further shade his eyes. They stopped at the plank and he took the box from her and tossed it across the gap to Dr Abney. Cassandra held her breath, hoping the lock didn't break open and scatter the money about the deck. Dr Abney caught the box without reaction, unable to hear or feel the weight of the coins shifting inside over the noise of the sea and the pirates.

Cassandra gathered up the sides of her skirt, ready to rush across when Richard held out his hand to help her. She peered up at him, loss consuming her as it had when she'd watched him climb the gangplank to the *Maiden's Veil* in Yorktown. He'd left her with promises that he'd return to her and she'd lived off their hope for so long, until there hadn't been any more.

'If things had been different, would you have come home to me? Would we have been happy together?' she asked, desperate for something in her life to have been real and good.

He closed his fingers over his palm, then opened them again, still holding it out to her, silently urging her to accept it and his help. 'Yes.'

The wind whipped at her, making her eyes water

as much as her desire to weep. She despised what he'd become, but it pained her to let him go again. It was like learning of his death for a second time, except he wasn't dead, but achingly beyond her reach. Beneath the black silk, in the touch of yellow about his irises, there lingered something of the man who'd almost become her husband, the one she'd been willing to wait for until he'd lied about his death.

*I don't believe in that man any more.*

She brushed past him, stepped up on the plank and rushed across. On the other side, Dr Abney took her hand and helped her down, staying close beside her as she wiped the moisture from the corners of her eyes.

'My lady, are you all right?' Concern made the lines of his face deepen. 'He didn't take liberties with you, did he?'

'No. He was a perfect gentleman.' Until he'd changed into a rogue and made it clear he wanted nothing more from her than her word.

She took the pistol box from Dr Abney and made for the Captain's cabin and Dinah. Behind her, Richard called out orders to his crew, his voice reverberating across the water even as the growing distance between the ships swallowed it. The sound of it called to her, but she didn't look back. She refused to mourn him a second time.

Richard marched to the opposite side of the ship, unwilling to watch the *Winter Gale*, and yet another thing torn from him, disappear over the horizon.

He gripped the rigging and leaned out over the rail to take in the salty air. Even in the stiff breeze the echoes of Cassandra's rosewater-scented skin continued to torture him.

'Captain?' Mr Rush approached him. 'We've caught a good wind and should outrun the Navy vessel. Mr O'Malley wants to know what course to plot.'

Richard stared out at the whitecaps breaking over the tops of the wind-driven chop, ignoring the weight of the pistol in his coat pocket. The news of Walter's death and Cas's appearance had hit him broadside like a wave, but he wouldn't let it capsize him, nor would he pine for her like some abandoned dog. Let her return to Virginia cursing him. It made no difference as long as she helped him. He couldn't be certain she would until the moment came to send her the pistol. Until then, like the rest of his past, his time with her was over. With the evidence in jeopardy, he must find another way to ruin Vincent. He'd promised his crew they'd clear their names and have a future free from the threat of the gallows. It was a promise he would damn well keep. 'Set a course for Nassau, Mr Rush. Let's find out if those rumours of Vincent trading with pirates are true.'

# Chapter Three

*One month later*

'Milady, scrubbing floors is no task for a titled lady!' Mrs Sween, the Belle View housekeeper, gasped from the dining-room door. She'd come up from the cellar and the underground passage leading to the kitchen building in the garden. The earthy scent of the lavender she'd hung in the cellar clung to her and it filled the dining room where Cassandra knelt on the floor with a bucket of warm water and a scrub brush. Cassandra's arms burned from her effort to make the old floorboards shine again. Over the years, Uncle Walter had given little thought to the house, focusing instead on rents and the annual crops, neither of which had ever brought in enough money, as Giles had complained every quarter when her meagre payments had arrived.

'I'm afraid I'm not much of a titled lady.' There were few young ladies who'd left Virginia as an impoverished orphan and returned a dowager baron-

ess. At one time the achievement had seemed like
the pinnacle of success, a finger in the eye of everyone in society who'd abandoned her after her parents died and her family's fortune was lost. It hadn't
been the triumph she'd hoped for. 'Mother would've
been ashamed at the way I used to sit idle at Greyson
Manor. Giles never let me do more than decide on
the dinners.' Even if she'd been able to work beside
him, she doubted he could have taught her much.
He'd driven the estate deeper into debt than when
he'd inherited it, caring more for his mistress than
the careful management of his income. 'Mother always insisted I take a hand in the affairs of Belle
View. I intend to teach Dinah to do the same thing.'

Dinah played next to her with a small brush, a
wide smile on her cherubic face, making more of a
mess than a difference in the condition of the floors.
Cassandra's efforts hadn't achieved much either. The
scrubbed boards stood out against the surrounding
dull ones, many of which were in need of repair.
The carpenter was too busy fixing the barn to see
to something as trivial as the unused dining room.

She glanced about the room and sighed at the
faded and dusty furnishings, the best pieces having
been sold off years ago to pay debts. What was left
would have made her mother cry to see it. It almost
made Cassandra weep, too, when she recalled the
many family dinners she'd enjoyed here. Some day,
Dinah would enjoy them, too.

*If I can continue to make something of Belle View
and to cultivate Williamsburg society.* She thought

of the money from Richard hidden upstairs and how much of it she'd already spent to purchase seed stock, hire labourers and pay for the carpenter's work on the barn. She shouldn't spend it, but hoarding it away didn't free it from the taint of piracy or do anyone any good—not her, not Dinah, not the workers who relied on Belle View for their living. Not spending it would also make maintaining the illusion of wealth more difficult, especially if she had to go begging for loans to keep the plantation from sinking into debt.

'Lady Shepherd, I don't mean to trouble you...' Mrs Sween's brogue muddied by a Virginia twang interrupted Cassandra's thoughts '...but I heard one of the field hands say Mr Marston quit this morning.'

'He did.' Cassandra snatched up the brush and started scrubbing again. 'He insisted I evict the tenant farmers and commute the tenure of the indentured servants and replace them with slaves. I refused and, because I failed to "see the future", he felt he could no longer remain as overseer.'

'He was also being paid far less than most of the overseers around these parts.'

'It did make his decision to leave a little easier.' Cassandra sat on her heels and wiped her forehead with the back of her hand. Belle View's numerous windows and doors stood open, allowing the breeze coming off the James River to move through the rooms and the main hallway, but it did little to lessen the oppressive humidity.

'What will you do without him?' Mrs Sween tucked an escaping wisp of grey hair beneath her white cap. She was stout and shorter than Cassandra with a ruddy face like a farmer's wife. She'd come to Virginia from Scotland as an indentured servant to Uncle Walter twenty years ago and had helped raise Cassandra after her parents' deaths. Cassandra wished Mrs Sween had been with her in London. She would've seen through all of the Chathams' lies and Cassandra's ignorance.

*What about Richard's lies?*

Cassandra studied the matronly woman standing before her, wondering if she knew the truth about Richard. She was desperate for someone to speak with about him, but if Mrs Sween was ignorant of the truth, then asking her meant inadvertently revealing what had happened on the *Devil's Rose.*

She glanced at the burled-wood pistol box resting on the mantel across the room. Inside, the missing weapon marred the beauty of the presentation of the pewter against the red velvet. She twisted the gold band on her finger, her stomach tightening with worry. Every day she thought about his pistol, both anticipating and dreading its return.

She plunked the scrub brush in the bucket, sending a wave of soapy water cresting over the side. She refused to live in fear here as she had in London with Giles. She'd turn Richard in before she'd allow his bargain to threaten her or Dinah. 'I'll manage the farmers as best I can until I can engage a new overseer. Heaven only knows how I'll pay one.'

'Better find a way. A place like this is too much for one person to run alone.'

Cassandra stood and wiped her hands on her old plain cotton dress, one of many she'd left in trunks in the attic before her trip to England, thinking she'd return within the year. She'd never expected such a long and heartbreaking delay. 'At present, I don't have a choice but to do it myself. Besides, I enjoy the work. It takes my mind off so many things.' *Like Richard.*

Learning he wasn't dead had been like having fabric pulled off a dried wound. She'd cursed him for weeks after coming home, but in the still of the dark nights, with the cicadas singing their old familiar song, his resurrection had created another, more startling feeling in her heart—hope. He was still alive and perhaps, like her place in Williamsburg society and the grandeur of Belle View, the future they'd once imagined could be reclaimed. She had no idea how it might come about but, with the memory of his lips still vivid on hers, a small part of her believed in it and him, even if he no longer wanted her and she should want nothing to do with him. Emotion had led her to make a grave mistake with one man. It was a mistake she couldn't afford to repeat, but surrounded by the humid aroma of dirt and trees, the smells of her childhood, it was hard not to believe in the old dreams again.

'Don't worry, my lady, all will be well. You'll have this place soon set to rights and Belle View will be one of the finest plantations on the James River.' Mrs Sween rested a wrinkled hand on Cassandra's shoulder and Cassandra smiled gratefully at her. Mrs

Sween's presence eased the loneliness surrounding Cassandra like the netting covering the portraits of her parents to protect them from the beetles. It didn't banish it completely. Only during the brief moment in Richard's arms aboard his ship had the isolation swathing her seemed to lift. The feeling had been fleeting, like his comfort and his shallow love.

'Shall I take the little one to have her lunch?' Mrs Sween offered, brushing a lavender flower off her apron.

'Yes, please.' Cassandra picked up Dinah and kissed her on one soft and chubby cheek, then handed her to Mrs Sween, who carried her off, promising her fresh butter and bread.

The voices of men calling to one another caught Cassandra's attention. She went to the window, passing the large dining table dominating the centre of the room. She paused to trail her fingers over the dull and dusty top of it. Of all the meals she remembered enjoying with her parents at this table, the last stood out as the most vivid. Her father had listened while she and her mother had made plans for the upcoming holiday balls and dinner parties marking the start of Cassandra's first season. They'd laughed and revelled in talk of dresses and dance lessons, blissfully unaware that three weeks later a hurricane would level Belle View's crops and force the creditors to call in her parents' debts, ruining them. A month later, the fever that often followed hurricanes had risen from the carcase-filled fields and riverbeds to claim her parents and the bright future they'd all imagined for Cassandra.

With a heavy heart, Cassandra walked to the window overlooking the back lawn. Green grass covered the slope of the land to the dock where two farmers loaded sacks of grain into the shallop tied there, the single-masted boat bobbing with the current. When she was a child, she used to watch the small boats coming and going from her bedroom window, waving to the farmers from the Shenandoah Valley who brought their crops down the James to sell at market or ship to England. Her father would greet the incoming vessels, collecting gossip and passing on information from the latest session of the House of Burgesses. He was gone, but this small hub of activity remained, although it was, like her old life here, only a shadow of what it had once been. Over the years, many people had offered to buy Belle View, but Uncle Walter had advised her not to sell, saying it would be a safe haven for her if she ever needed it. He'd never had the chance to see how right he'd been.

*But is he right about Richard?*

Cassandra left the dining room and walked down Belle View's long central hallway, barely sparing a glance for the dusty sitting room, office and library flanking either side of it. The paint on the walls of the main hall had once been a vibrant red, but it had dulled to a rusty colour. Like everything at Belle View it needed seeing to, but she couldn't spend money on paint when there were labourers to be paid. She passed the wide front door and the tall clock standing beside it, her mother's wedding gift from her parents. It chimed the half hour, the bells as clear today as they'd been when Cassandra was a child. They were the one thing age and the hurricane hadn't appeared to touch in the old home. She climbed the staircase to the second floor, her hand brushing over the rough banister in need of a polish before striding down the upstairs hallway to her bedroom.

Once inside, she locked the door. Her large, four-poster bed filled most of the room. A turned wooden chair sat between the opposite window and the fireplace covered with an embroidered screen. Even without an overabundance of fine furnishings, this room was simple and comfortable in a way that none of the rooms in any of Giles's houses had ever been.

It wasn't comfort she sought at present, but something more disturbing.

She knelt in front of the fireplace and worked loose a brick near the bottom. The hiding place had once held her childish treasures, but today it concealed a darker secret. She pulled out the pouch of money, disappointed by how much lighter it was. The coins wouldn't last much longer and, to her shame, she almost wished Richard would send the pistol if it meant another bag and the slight easing of her financial concerns.

*No amount of money is worth the misery he'd bring if he returned.* The misery he'd already visited on her by pretending to be dead and convincing

Uncle Walter to support his lie. She set the money aside and tugged out a letter tied with a ribbon and encompassing a number of folded, weathered and water-stained parchments.

A few days after Cassandra's arrival, Mrs Sween had given Cassandra Uncle Walter's travelling desk. Inside, beneath the mundane accounts and letters from friends had been the items Richard had sent him. They'd been sealed between the pages of a letter to her from Uncle Walter, one that had proved more unsettling than the illicit documents and the memories of Richard they'd conjured up.

She untied the ribbon and set aside the documents to read Uncle Walter's last letter again.

> *Dear Cassandra,*
> *By the time you read this I will be gone, but know that I loved you like a daughter and cherished you as if you were my own. However, for all the love I bore you I have also lied to you in the most grievous of ways.*
>
> *I'm sorry I cannot tell you this in person, so that I may beg for your forgiveness, and I hope once you read what I have to say you will find it in your heart to forgive me and to understand why I did it.*

'I'm the one who should have asked for your forgiveness. I never should have left you,' she whispered, and tears blurred the paper while she read his account of what had happened with Richard five

years ago. The effort it had taken for him to un-
burden himself was evident in every scraggly curl
and shaky line of each word. It broke her heart to
imagine him, ill with fever, struggling to confess
to her. If only he could have known she'd discover
it for herself, it might have saved him the pain and
effort. Yes, he'd lied to her about Richard, but in
the weeks that had passed since she'd first read his
letter, she'd come to forgive him. His one sin didn't
erase the years of love and his hard work on her behalf at Belle View.

She flicked the edge of the paper with a fingernail, wishing she'd never left him or Virginia. After
everything Uncle Walter had done for her, she hadn't
been there for him in his final illness, and it tore at
her. He'd deserved her love and thanks and care, and
she hadn't been able to offer it to him. It was another
of the many things Giles, the Chathams and even
Richard had stolen from her.

She continued to read, trying to hear Uncle Walter's voice in each word, to remember his face and
his smile, but all she could glean were a few snatches
of expressions. Her inability to clearly recall the man
who'd taken care of her after her parents' death stung
as much as the words of his letter. The tone of them
reminded her of the one she'd written to him shortly
after Dinah's birth when she'd admitted her mistake
in marrying Giles and had asked for his advice. He'd
never judged her for the failure of her marriage, but
had helped her as best he could. He might not be

here, but he was asking for her help now, not for himself, but for Richard.

> *I'm entrusting Richard's evidence to you. Please protect it and assist him as I have. Neither one of us has the right to ask this of you, not after the way we deceived you, but please understand it was all done with the best of intentions.*
>
> *I spent my life in Virginia fighting for those who'd been wronged by others. I could not allow Richard, a man who was once my apprentice and your fiancé, to be falsely accused and do nothing.*
>
> *I failed to help him see justice done, but perhaps you can find a way to succeed.*

She folded the letter, then picked up the shipping passes and other papers. The contents made no more sense to her today than they had the many times she'd perused them in the past few weeks. Beside her, the cold fireplace beckoned her to strike the tinder and set the lot of it on fire and be done with Richard. There was no reason she shouldn't.

*Except Uncle Walter asked me to help him.*

She tucked the papers inside the letter and returned them and the money to the space behind the mantel and replaced the loose brick. For Uncle Walter she would keep the papers safe until she could return them to Richard, but she would do no more. She'd damaged her already weak position in Williamsburg once by defending Richard. She wasn't about to risk everything to do it again. Belle View and Dinah's future were all that mattered now.

Richard pulled the collar of his light coat up higher around his face and hurried through the dark streets of Nassau. He'd put aside his mask, frock coat and breeches for the simple clothes of a first mate. In this pirate haven, everyone minded their own business and he could move unnoticed through the riff-raff without fear of discovery. As he approached the centre of town, evidence of the hurricane from ten years ago marked the buildings on either side of the road. Many rose into the sky, their stone structures devoid of roofs, their walls pocked with gaping holes. People moved in and out of the shadows and small alleys, their shuffling footsteps followed by the gravelly voices of whores trying to entice clients inside. Richard stepped over a filthy drunk sleeping against a wall, ignoring the sodden wretch and the faint inkling of disgust and shame the sight of him conjured up. All this filth was too familiar to him, like the currents of the James River that he and Vincent used to navigate as boys or the smell of the tobacco ripening in the fields of Sutherland Place.

He passed a group of men whispering on a corner, eyeing them as warily as they eyed him. He reached into his pocket and clutched the smooth butt of the duelling pistol, ready to use it if he must. It hadn't been out of his possession since Cas's ship had disappeared over the horizon, leaving nothing but empty, rolling sea between them, and the tortuous imprint of her supple body against his.

*Curse fate*, he muttered under his breath. Curse it for bringing them together and distracting him when his plans were on the verge of crashing down around him because Walter was gone. He needed a clear head, especially in the midst of all these thieves and cutthroats.

He turned down a narrow side street and followed the familiar route to the tavern at the end. The rank stench of stale beer and sweat greeted him when he stepped inside. He twisted his way through the tables of barely clad whores and drinking men, ducking a low beam and the rusty lantern hanging from it. He searched the rough and creased faces, most of whom avoided his direct stare, searching for the man he needed before spying him at a table near the back.

''Ello, Rose,' the slender man drawled, taking a puff of his long, clay pipe. The smoke swirled around his head and added to the hazy fog filling the room. The tart smell of tobacco was preferable to the tavern's less savoury odours.

Richard slid into the chair next to the man, keeping his back to the wall so no one could sneak up on him. 'What news, Martin?'

The man smiled, revealing yellow, crooked teeth. 'In no mood for pleasantries?'

Richard tossed two coins on the table. 'How's this for pleasantries?'

The man's greasy fingers slid out from beneath his stained coat and covered the coins.

'I enjoy your banter.' Martin let out a craggy laugh, the sound of it lost in the noise of the tavern. 'It seems your friend is trading with pirates again and bolder about it than before.'

'I knew Vincent wouldn't stay away for too long,' he said. Especially with Richard interrupting his legitimate business. 'Who's he working with this time?'

'Captain Dehesa of the *Casa de Oro*.'

'Vincent must be desperate. Captain Dehesa won't be easily controlled by a gentleman.' Richard sneered at the word *gentleman*. He'd long ago stopped thinking of Vincent in such civilised terms. 'At least Captain Stowe could be manipulated.'

'Probably why he got caught.'

'And murdered before he could appear before a judge and risk revealing his pact with Vincent.'

'That was Mr Adams's doing. Pirates know it. Made them leery of yer Mr Fitzwilliam.'

'Then why is Captain Dehesa trading with him?'

Martin sucked on the pipe, exhaling smoke when he answered, 'Maybe he likes a challenge.'

From what little Richard knew of the Spaniard, even this scant explanation seemed plausible. He was a pirate renowned for taking risks, for his cunning and his lethalness. 'When's the trade?'

'Next Wednesday night at Hog Island.'

Richard turned a large coin over in his hand and danced it along the tops of his knuckles. If Richard could reach Captain Dehesa and convince him to turn against Vincent for a handsome price, he might finally gain the evidence he needed to ruin his former friend.

'Thank you, Martin. Always a pleasure doing business with you.' Richard flipped the coin across the table, and Martin snatched it from the air.

'Which is why I'll tell you one more bit o' news for free—you being me best customer, I'd 'ate to lose you.'

Richard leaned across the table. 'Yes?'

'Captain Dehesa won't be alone. Two men was in here a while back, hired by the schooner your Mr Fitzwilliam paid to trade with Captain Dehesa. They was bragging a right great deal about how this would be the end of the Spaniard.'

'It's a trap.' Richard thumped the table. 'Vincent gets his silver in the trade with Captain Dehesa. The schooner accompanies the *Casa de Oro* out to sea, turns on Captain Dehesa and gets a ship full of cargo to trade with another unsuspecting pirate. I thought Captain Dehesa too shrewd to fall for such a trick.'

'He's overconfident.' He pointed the stem of his pipe at Richard. 'They're always the first to topple.'

Richard straightened, eager to get back aboard his ship. 'Thanks for the warning. Send word if you hear anything else.'

Martin saluted him with the pipe. 'Aye, aye, Captain.'

Richard slid out the door and wound his way through the maze of crumbling buildings leading down to the wharf, the almost full moon illuminating the island and the wide expanse of ocean beyond.

The silvery light glinted off the slick palm fronds fluttering in the tropical breeze. The rustling sound reminded him of the tranquillity of Sutherland Place, his family's plantation on the James River. For a moment, he could almost forget the ugliness around him and how much he missed the peace of the Virginia countryside. During his last year at home, he hadn't realised how fragile such peace could be. Not even after his mother's death when he was fourteen had he suspected how much a man could really lose. While Richard had courted Cas, revelling in her caresses and his plans for his life as a privateer, his father had hidden the weakness invading his lungs, as well as his debts.

Richard drew the collar of his coat tighter around him to ward off the unusual evening chill and the old memories scratching at him. He could see again the letter from Walter explaining how Sutherland Place had been sold because Richard's father had secretly mortgaged it to purchase the *Maiden's Veil*, hoping the prize money would pay the mounting bills. Richard had sent his father money, hoping to save the plantation from the auction block, but it had been too late.

It was the letter that had followed soon after that made Richard stop in the street, barely able to hear the drunk pirate propped up against a wall begging for money. If Walter hadn't told Richard's father the truth at the end, his father would've died still cursing his only son.

Richard brought his foot down hard on an empty

bottle of rum, shattering the glass beneath his boot. *What the hell have I done?*

If he hadn't insisted on going to sea, they all could have been happy at Sutherland Place or Belle View and he ignorant of Nassau and what it was like to kill a sailor in a fight. He would have had the care of the planting seasons, a wife and a family to rule his days instead of the icy demands of revenge.

He met the beggar's watery eyes set in a gaunt, unshaven face. This wretch, racked by the thirst for rum, was better off than Richard and his consuming desire for vengeance. Richard reached into his coat and pulled out a coin and dropped it in the man's cup.

'Bless you, sir,' the drunk offered in a raspy voice.

Richard said nothing, but continued down the hill towards the docks. He was beyond blessings, and, with nothing left but his need to ruin Vincent, beyond redemption.

*'Leave this life. Take the money you've made from it and go to the islands and establish yourself as a planter. Many have done it before...'* Cas's voice whispered in the distant crash of the surf against the shore.

He slid his hand into his pocket and traced the fine engraving on the pistol with his fingertips. In the weight of it, he could almost feel Cas's back against his palm, her eyes heavy with passion, her red lips parted in wanting. Seeing her again had brought back too many things he'd willed himself to forget and sometimes, in the middle of the night, with nothing but the rolling ship for company, thoughts of her drove him mad with a longing he could not satisfy. Many of her words to him had been harsh, but her kiss had revealed her continued desire for him, one Vincent and all Richard's mistakes hadn't killed. Instead of revelling in it, he'd taken advantage of her weakness to chain her to him with his nasty bargain, exposing her to scandal and danger and proving himself no better than the pirate she believed him to be.

*I am nothing more than a pirate.* He brought his foot down hard in a puddle as he stormed on. Cas was right, the Richard she'd loved wouldn't have wanted any part of this filthy existence while this Richard all but wallowed in it. *It doesn't always have to be this way.*

He slowed his steps as the ground levelled out near the wharf, the raucous laughter and off-key music of the town fading in the breeze behind him. Cas had believed in him when others hadn't and not given up on him until she'd thought he'd never return. He couldn't reward her loyalty by inflicting more fear or pain on her. She'd been selfless in her desire to protect her child and others on the *Winter Gale*. It was his turn to protect her, to let her go as he'd intended to do before his determination to hunt down Vincent had overrun him. He'd find a way to return the weapon and release her from the deal. Peace of mind would be his last gift to her. As for the papers, she could do with them what she wanted. If Walter had never been able to use them then they could be of little use to Richard.

He approached the wharf and the spider web of masts and rigging clogging the horizon above the docks. Across the sheltered bay, the rotting hulls of captured ships blighted the wide sand beach. He strode down the creaking and lopsided dock towards where the *Devil's Rose* groaned against its mooring. It was quiet around him with only the distant surf and the thump of his boots over the wooden planks to welcome him. Then, from out of the shadows ahead, a man raced at him. Richard jerked the pistol from his pocket.

'Who's there?' He aimed at the fast-moving figure, ready to fire.

'It's Mr Rush.' The first mate hurried out of the shadows of a brigantine and into the moonlight before Richard.

Richard breathed a sigh of relief and pocketed the pistol.

Mr Rush stopped in front of him, panting from his run. 'Mr Barlow went off with some doubloons and a blunderbuss while you were gone. Should I send men after him?'

'No. We're better off without him.' He didn't have time to deal with a deserter, especially one of Mr Barlow's ilk.

'Still ain't a good idea to leave a loose end lyin' about.'

Richard strode up the *Devil's Rose*°Δ gangplank, Mr Rush at his side, his warning rubbing at Richard. The crew lounged about the deck, laughing and playing dice together. They jumped to their feet and stood at attention when Richard passed. He raised his hand in absentminded acknowledgement, and their laughter and the clink of the dice resumed when he and Mr Rush had passed.

They stopped before the helm, and Richard slipped a pouch from his other pocket, the coins heavy against his palm and his conscience. He'd almost put a bullet through his friend because he'd thought him a threat. Now he was about to all but order another man's death for the same reason, but it had to be done. He couldn't allow a conniving cooper to place his crew in more jeopardy. He handed Mr Rush the bag. 'Send Mr Tibbs into town to purchase supplies and have him put it about that Mr Barlow is in possession of a great deal of prize money. Some opportunistic scum will take care of him for us. Tell Mr Tibbs to be back before the morning tide. We sail with it for Hog Island.'

Richard explained to Mr Rush everything Martin had told him.

The first mate massaged the coins through the leather. 'How do you know it ain't us and not the *Casa de Oro* Fitzwilliam's ship is waiting for? Maybe your lass told him who ya really are. Women yap as much as drunk pirates.'

Mr Rush was right. A woman scorned the way Cas had been might seek revenge. He almost expected it given how all his other old acquaintances had already betrayed him, but he couldn't imagine Cas being so devious. She might hate him, yet the passion in her kiss had told him she wouldn't ruin him, but these weren't things to discuss with Mr Rush. 'After all our years of attacking his ships, Vincent has probably already guessed it's me.' And he prayed it tortured him every time word of another lost cargo reached him. 'Now see to Mr Tibbs and preparing the ship.'

'Aye, sir.' Mr Rush called out the orders to the men, and the crew sprang to life.

Richard flipped through the maps until he reached the one with the North Carolina coast. Excitement gripped him the way it did whenever the lookout spied a Virginia Trading Company ship on the horizon. Almost everyone in Virginia had turned their backs on him when the lies about his activities had reached them. Their lack of faith in him hadn't burned as much as Vincent being the cause of it. The man who'd shared his tutor, spent days sailing with him on the James River in his shallop and grieved with him when Richard's mother had died of the fever—that man had sacrificed Richard to save his own hide. At Hog Island, Richard would get what he needed to finally bring Vincent down. Richard would make sure Vincent paid for stealing from him everything he'd ever loved, including a life with Cas.

## Chapter Four

The cream of Williamsburg society mingled beneath the oak trees and over the wide lawn sweeping down from the back of Butler Plantation, Vincent Fitzwilliam's stately home perched on the James River. Indentured servants in crisp white aprons and smart lace caps carried trays of mint water and rum punch among the sweating guests. Even in the heat, no one in Williamsburg was willing to break with fashion and change their style of dress to something better suited to the weather, not even Cassandra who stubbornly stuck to her silk mantua. Even if it meant perspiring through five chemises before nuncheon, she would dress like everyone else and play the part of a respectable Williamsburg widow for their benefit and hers.

At the bottom of the rise, the low sun sparkled off the quick-flowing surface of the James River, silhouetting the large wharf jutting out into the water. On the dock, men worked to load the two ships moored there with hogsheads of tobacco, barrels of spirits and other goods brought downriver to send to England.

Occasionally, the voices of the dock men calling to each other, or a ship's bell, carried up the lawn to mix with the plucking strings of the violin and harp played by two of Mr Fitzwilliam's slaves. The musicians sat in the shade of the two-storey Georgian-style brick house and off to one side of the massive porch dominating the back, delighting guests with light music reminiscent of the finest English country manor.

Cassandra frowned at their presence. The growing practice of Virginia planters purchasing slaves instead of taking on indentured servants or hiring men in need of work disgusted her. Neither her parents nor Uncle Walter had bought slaves for Belle View and neither would Cassandra. Free men would do the work and share in the profits, assuming there ever were any. Cassandra tried not to sigh. Rebuilding her life in Virginia already felt like an ominous task, especially since there always seemed to be someone or something waiting to knock her down a peg or two. Sometimes it was a stranger, but more often than not it was people she knew and had once loved. She wondered who it would be this time.

Her spirits sagged like the roses in the heat until the sound of laughter drew her attention back to the lawn. Dinah ran past with the young sons and daughters of other prominent landowners, all of them oblivious to the heat and the sweating nursemaids begging the children to come sit in the shade. Cassandra smiled to herself, remembering the many garden parties she'd attended and how she and the children of the other planters had played the same way until they'd grown too old to run around the lawn. The invitations had stopped coming after her parents' death had ruined her.

*They'll cease all together if Richard sends the pistol and the authorities discover me helping him.* Cassandra opened her fan and waved it in quick flicks over her chest, trying to cool the heat increased by worry. She cursed Richard and all the anxiety he was creating for her when she already had enough because of Belle View and society. Not that she should worry. After all, Richard said he wouldn't call on her unless absolutely necessary, or he could be killed long before he ever got the chance. A chill came over her, despite the heat.

'Did you hear the amount Lady Spotswood will spend to decorate the Governor's Palace for her masked ball?' Mrs Baker, the esteemed wife of a well-known burgess, remarked to Mrs Chilton, drawing Cassandra back to the conversation. Mrs Chilton and her family had been one of the first to shun poor orphaned Cassandra Lewis and one of the first to rush to accept the Dowager Lady Shepherd.

They all stood together under the fragrant magnolia tree in the centre of the lawn. The spreading branches offered shade, but not much relief from the oppressive heat. The ladies gathered off to one side discussing the new styles of dress, especially with Cassandra wearing her full-hipped gown enhanced by panniers. The fashion had yet to reach these shores, making her attire the subject of great interest among the younger ladies. A short distance away, Mr Baker, Mr Fitzwilliam and Mr Chilton engaged Lord Spotswood in a debate on politics.

'A woman of her rank and position is allowed to be a little extravagant, especially with the premiere residence of Virginia and the event of the season,' Mrs Chilton replied, more in awe of Lady Spotswood's title and place as the Governor of Virginia's wife than she was disapproving of the lady's preference for fine things. Mr and Mrs Chilton were prominent members of Virginia society, with Mr Chilton serving on the Governor's Council and Mrs Chilton the grand dame of Williamsburg society. She'd been more neglectful than disdainful of Cassandra after her parents' death, offering condolences before quietly fading out of Cassandra's life. Even now, standing in her black *robe à l'Anglaise* with its riot of brown and gold embroidery, she seemed indifferent to Cassandra being among them, as if Cassandra had never been gone.

'I suppose her duties do give her some leeway to be ostentatious. I'm sure it's something all ladies of rank do in England,' Mrs Baker grudgingly conceded, sweating in her well-tailored but outdated short, green embroidered velvet jacket and matching petticoat.

Miss Baker nodded along with her mother, her pink silk dress with the lace along the bodice a touch more à la mode. Having been recently introduced to society, she drank in the adult conversation, reminding Cassandra of herself at fourteen. Like the young lady, she'd believed this initiation into womanhood was part of the natural course of things and hadn't realised how easily it could be snatched away. Cassandra opened and closed her fan. It should be a triumph to be here, but it didn't feel like one. The sense she was chasing the same illusion of success she'd been running after when she'd married Giles ate at her.

'What do you say, Lady Shepherd, are all titled men and women in London expected to be extravagant, especially where balls are concerned?' Mrs Chilton asked.

Cassandra set aside her concerns, ready to perform. All this effort was for Dinah and she would do well to remember it. 'They are, but not every lady is inclined to follow the fashion.'

'Is it the fashion to spend time alone with a pirate captain on his ship?' Mrs Baker snidely asked. The tale of the attack on the *Winter Gale*, and Cassandra facing down the infamous pirate Captain, had spread the moment the ship had docked. It'd created something of a sensation and brought her a notoriety she'd used to further her goals. However, her time on the *Devil's Rose* had also been a part of the stories and, as Dr Abney had warned, some people looked askance at her because of it. Cassandra tightened her grip on her fan and forced herself to smile the way she used to whenever she'd encountered Giles's mistress at the theatre. Like his mistress's nasty rumours about her, she could do nothing more than face them with dignity. 'It is when the safety of one's person and the entire crew is at stake.'

'I hear Captain Rose is very handsome,' Miss Baker tittered before her mother could reply.

'The newspaper stories make him seem quite dashing,' Miss Chilton added, making the fake roses on her wide-brimmed hat bob with her giggles.

Only Miss Fitzwilliam, Mr Fitzwilliam's half-sister, showed no interest in the conversation. She fixed her dazzling blue eyes on everyone, scrutinising them with the sharpness of a hawk, saying nothing but listening to everything. The heat seemed not to bother her while she stood in her grey silk gown with black ribbons along the bodice.

'Lydia, remember yourself,' Mrs Chilton chided her daughter. 'A dashing pirate indeed. What's come over you?'

'An unwarranted influence, I imagine.' Mrs Baker regarded Cassandra as if it was her fault Miss Baker held romantic notions about pirates.

'From what I saw of Captain Rose, he is very handsome.' Cassandra winked at the two girls, sending them into a fit of giggles and making Mrs Baker scowl. She opened her fan, refusing to wilt beneath the woman's chastising looks. She might seek their acceptance, but she wouldn't allow any of them to cow her or they'd be relentless in their hounding. It was a hard lesson she'd learned in London.

'Will Captain Rose still be handsome when he's hanged, Lady Shepherd?' Mr Fitzwilliam enquired, the arrogance of his position marking his stride as he left the men to join the ladies, his bergamot cologne as sharp as the late afternoon sun.

Cassandra stiffened in disgust when he came to stand beside her. Since her arrival, the burgess had made no effort to hide his interest in her, much to the chagrin of the matchmaking-minded Mrs Baker and Mrs Chilton. Cassandra would be glad if Mr Fitzwilliam turned his attention to either of their daughters and ended his dogged pursuit of her.

'He'll only hang if he's caught and no one's caught him,' Cassandra challenged in a light voice. Her need of his influence couldn't endear him to her. Nothing ever could after what she'd learned about him from Richard.

'Yet.' A wicked grin split his face, but failed to lighten the muddy brown of his eyes. Of average height, his jaw angled down to a rounded chin and full enough lips. He was handsome in a soft manner a few years of fine living and plentiful food would quickly erode. He wore a grey frock coat with gold embroidery around each buttonhole. His waistcoat was faced in dark yellow with matching breeches above his white stockings and silver-buckled shoes. He held a gold-tipped walking stick in his hand. Its dark, polished wood matched his fashionable shoes and tricorn hat. In Virginia, his fine clothes marked him as one of the elite, but in London, he'd instantly be recognised as a colonial. 'With pirates, it's only a matter of time before the Royal Navy catches up to them.'

Cassandra adjusted the fan ribbon on her wrist,

worry for Richard unexpectedly overtaking her. Blackbeard hadn't been able to elude capture for ever. Neither could Richard. The prospect he might be lost to her for good raised her flesh beneath her pale pink gown, as did the thought of him requesting her help.

'I've received authority from the King to pardon any pirate who seeks the King's Grace,' Lord Spotswood interjected, entering the conversation along with the shade and drawing the other men with him. 'The Crown believes it's the best way to rid the seas of their scourge. Lady Shepherd, if you're ever in close proximity to one again, please tell him about it.'

'I'll make a point of it should the chance arise.' A strange hope she shouldn't even contemplate filled her. If she could find a way to send word to Richard about the pardon, he might accept it. It would put an end to his troubles and at least one of hers. As fast as the idea came to her she dismissed it. If the purpose of forgiving pirates was to bring them back into good society, then a decree must have been read out in every pirate stronghold from North Carolina to Barbados. Surely Richard had heard of it. His not having walked into Williamsburg to claim one told her he wasn't going to give up the thrill of the ocean for a bland life on land. 'Though I wonder, if able-bodied men were given employment on our plantations instead of being pushed out of work by the odious purchase of slaves, would there not be fewer pirates?'

The gentlemen coughed and muttered into their

punch glasses while their wives' cheeks went red beneath their powder.

'Lady Shepherd, allow me to show you the view of the river from the back porch,' Mr Fitzwilliam offered, further rooting her to her new life, one which could never include Robert. With the trappings of civilisation sliding around her like the humid air, it was best not to think of him. 'It's breathtaking.'

She didn't want to be alone with him, but she should take her leave before her tongue did an amount of damage neither her title nor her lands could undo. 'I'd be delighted.'

He escorted her out of the shade of the tree and the strength of the sun added to her irritation at having to endure his company. All Williamsburg revered him as a member of the Governor's Council and the House of Burgesses, and a prosperous merchant and landowner. She knew the truth about his illegal business dealings and the lives he'd ruined, but could say nothing. With no evidence, she was as powerless as Richard to make him pay for his crimes. Instead, she had to smile and endure him and keep Richard's secret along with her hate of the burgess locked inside her.

Mr Fitzwilliam led Cassandra up the steps to the long porch spanning the length of the house. Across the river, an endless expanse of tress covered the rolling landscape, broken here and there by a square field.

'Your house is well situated,' was the best compliment she could conjure up.

'So is yours. Belle View has one of the only docks close to the Chesapeake where the river is deep enough for large-draft ships to moor. If my dock had similar access, I could beat the Chesapeake Trading Company in services offered to farmers and traders. It would make the Virginia Trading Company far more lucrative than it already is.' Mr Fitzwilliam's Virginia accent was punctuated by a nasally twang so unlike the steady tones of Richard's voice. 'If you build a larger dock and a warehouse and improved the roads to the wharf, you could establish a fine shipping business at Belle View. It's better than wasting it on poor farmers hauling hogs up and down the river in leaking wherries.'

'Poor farmers need access to docks, too. It's the larger landowner's duty to help their smaller neighbours,' she repeated her father's words. 'I already allow some sizeable ships to moor there.'

She needed the fees the boats paid to help fund improvements to Belle View.

'Without a better dock and stricter control of the cargo coming in and out of it, it'll never prosper as it should.'

'Yes, I've considered it.' If the tobacco harvest was good for another few years, she could develop the Belle View wharf and perhaps establish a trade business like the one Mr Fitzwilliam suggested, the one her father had dreamed of years ago when they'd sat before the fire as a family. Cassandra missed the secure comfort, love and companionship of those days. Her present situation was too isolating and precarious to offer her any of those things now.

'What you need is someone with experience to handle your business matters. If we combine our resources, we could become the most powerful couple in Virginia.' He stared at the tops of her breasts above the line of powder-blue ribbons decorating the bodice of her dress, his lips curling up at the possibility of possessing both her land and her body. 'Think of the influence you could wield.'

She snapped open her fan and waved it over her chest to block his view, the breeze from it ruffling the ribbon tied beneath her chin to hold on her wide-brimmed hat. The secret Richard had told her burned on her tongue as did her hate for Mr Fitzwilliam. He'd ruined her chance of happiness with Richard and there were no insults she could throw at him. Now, he wanted her to become his wife, to barter social esteem for her body, just as she'd done with Giles. She'd die first. 'What influence will you have if Reverend Blair succeeds in having Lord Spotswood recalled?' she asked in all innocence, determined to keep the conversation away from matrimony, but the question was as biting as the many flies down by the river.

Vincent jerked the edge of his frock coat. 'Even if Lord Spotswood is replaced, as one of the largest landowners and the owner of the Virginia Trading Company, I'll have a place on any future Governor's Council.'

'Mama!' Dinah's happy squeal and the thump of her feet on the porch stairs interrupted them. Jane, drooping in her simple wool dress, staggered behind her.

Cassandra knelt down and threw her arms open to catch her little mite. She hugged her tight, but Dinah wriggled free, chatting in short, hurried sentences about the caterpillar she'd seen in the flower bed. Cassandra listened, ignoring the disapproving scowl Mr Fitzwilliam fixed on them.

'I think it's time for the child to return to the others,' he chastised.

Cassandra rose with Dinah's hand in hers and faced him. 'She will return when she and I deem her ready to do so.'

'Of course.' Mr Fitzwilliam smiled with feigned deference, his irritation at having his suggestion and authority rebuffed evident in his narrowed eyes.

Cassandra flexed her fingers over Dinah's hand, then gripped her tight once more. She shouldn't cross this influential man, but she wanted him to realise he could not order her about, especially where her child was concerned. Giles had done enough of that in London.

The sound of a man clearing his throat made them turn. Mr Adams, Mr Fitzwilliam's man of affairs, stood at the back door leading into a drawing room. Cassandra swallowed hard, uneasy at the way Mr Adams regarded her. She'd had few dealings with him, but there was something about his light eyes set behind a long nose and his wide, pockmarked cheeks on either side of his thin lips which gave him the appearance of an owl waiting to swoop down to kill a mouse.

'Mr Devlin and his son would like to see you in your office,' Mr Adams announced in a voice as cold as an English winter.

Mr Fitzwilliam glanced back and forth between Mr Adams and Cassandra. It was the first time Cassandra had seen the gentleman's confidence flag. 'I'm afraid I must speak with them. I'll return shortly.'

'Don't hurry because of me.' With any luck, she could slip away while he was occupied. She'd had her fill of humidity, society and unwanted marriage proposals for one day.

'What the hell are the Devlins doing here?' Vincent growled. He and Mr Adams marched into the high-ceilinged entry hall and past the curving staircase dominating the far end. 'There are enough damning rumours spreading about the Virginia Trading Company's debts. I don't need the Devlins here creating more and driving additional business to the Chesapeake Trading Company.'

Vincent strode into the study where Mr Devlin stood helping himself to the brandy. His large stomach forced the bottom of his white shirt to stick out from beneath his grey waistcoat. His son, Evander, lounged in a chair near the window as though the office were his. He was elegantly dressed in a tan frock coat and matching breeches. His dark hair, tied back in a queue, was neat and orderly where his father's grey hair was frizzy and messy. If the son weren't with his father, and a rapacious maker of loans with more money than taste, one might mistake the young man for a true gentleman.

'Good day to you, Mr Fitzwilliam.' The elder Mr Devlin raised his glass to Vincent, revealing a large circle of damp beneath his armpit. 'Do you have my money?'

'Keep your voice down. I have guests here—influential ones.' Vincent slid the double-pocket doors closed, leaving Mr Adams to keep away nosy people who might happen by.

'Then let's saddle up your horses and take a ride and discuss the matter if you're so concerned about your distinguished guests overhearing,' Mr Devlin mocked, then threw back the drink. Vincent tightened his grip on the door handles. It was well known Vincent had never mastered riding. He preferred the elegance of sailing or his fine coach to a hard saddle. It was one of the many insults his father used to hurl at him during his drunken rants. 'If I were you, I'd be more worried about the large amount of money you owe me rather than your fancy guests.'

'And you'll have it soon.' Vincent let go of the door and took hold of the front of his coat, struggling to remain calm. The notes of the violin and harp drifting in from the garden were more grating than soothing. 'I have two shipments departing tomorrow.'

'Assuming they reach their destination. Pirates seem to have an appetite for Virginia Trading Company cargo.' He threw his son a nudging look, then set down his glass.

'It seems they do,' the younger Mr Devlin concurred, a thin smile cracking the sharp planes of his impassive face.

Mr Devlin covetously examined the ornate candlesticks flanking the mantel above the cold fireplace. He plucked the delicate candle snuffer out from between them and turned it over in his thick hands. 'If you can't pay me in coins, you can always pay in goods.'

Vincent snatched the snuffer out of the man's hand and raised it, wanting to beat him to death with the slender rod. The force of his movement wiped the covetous glee from the tobacco planter's aged face and brought Evander ominously to his feet. Vincent lowered the snuffer and stepped back, regaining control over himself. 'You'll get your money.'

'I'd better, or all Virginia will know your company is near sunk.' Mr Devlin stepped around Vincent and made for the door, shoving one panel aside so hard it screeched on its rollers. 'You have one month to pay or I'll own this place.'

The hard fall of Mr Devlin's boots against the floorboards faded off down the hall. His son followed, his pace leisurely as if he'd already taken control of Butler Plantation.

Mr Adams stepped inside the office and closed the doors behind him.

'How dare he threaten me!' Vincent slapped the

snuffer against his palm. 'Have you made the arrangement concerning the other matter?'

'Yes. If all goes well, you'll be in possession of a great deal of Spanish silver by the end of the week.'

Mr Adams didn't offer any additional details, nor did Vincent ask, doing his best to keep his distance from this illegal trade. 'And Captain Rose?'

'He's proven an elusive man to find. His crew is incredibly loyal to him. Makes it difficult to turn anyone against him,' Mr Adams replied in a tone of near-respect.

'Then search harder. I won't have society gloating over my ruin while they swoop in like vultures to snatch up my property, land and influence.' Vincent wandered to the portraits of his parents flanking the window across from his desk. The other paintings in the house were covered with netting for the summer, including the portrait of his mother that he'd brought down from the attic after his father's death. Her pale skin shone beneath the netting shroud, but a smile didn't decorate her youthful face. Even in the first days of her marriage, she hadn't been happy.

*I'm failing you.*

The Virginia Trading Company had been her father's. She'd raised Vincent to take pride in what would some day be his and what he could make of it and himself. All the while his father had done everything he could to destroy it and her. Vincent had been at her side when, bruised and broken, she'd finally given up. His father hadn't cared enough to look her in the face in the end, too engrossed in drinking at the Raleigh Tavern and gambling away Vincent's future.

'You will not win, sir,' Vincent sneered at his father's portrait. It remained uncovered and the beetles could chew it to bits for all he cared. Vincent's father had taken the coward's way out, leaving Vincent to clean up the mess. He would trade with every pirate on the Spanish Main, or hire a mercenary fleet the size of the Armada to destroy Captain Rose before he'd allow him to steal his mother's legacy from him the way his father had almost done.

'Any progress with Lady Shepherd?' Mr Adams asked, the question like salt in an already festering wound.

'She declined, but they all do the first time.' He hated this courting game, but it had to be played. 'A beautiful lady with lucrative lands and powerful relations in London is everything I need to make a bid for Governor once Reverend Blair has Lord Spotswood recalled.' Despite Vincent's outward support of Lord Spotswood, he'd be glad to see the self-important Governor leave. Virginia needed a firmer ruling hand and he was determined it would be his own. He'd rise to the heights of success as his mother had always dreamed.

'And if Lady Shepherd doesn't accept you?'

'I'll make sure she's ruined.' He hurled the snuffer at the metal firescreen where it clanked against the iron and snapped in two.

A noise from the other side of the door drew their

attention. Vincent stormed across the room and shoved them open to find Arabella standing on the other side.

'Yes, Vincent?' Nothing about his half-sister's composure changed except the tight clasp of her hands in front of her. She didn't flee like her mother used to do, or pretend she hadn't been listening at the keyhole. Instead, she pinned him with a cool disdain he despised.

'Why aren't you with our guests or conversing with Lady Shepherd?'

'Lady Shepherd and her daughter left a few moments ago.'

Vincent balled his hands into fists at his side and settled the anger welling inside him. He couldn't risk anyone seeing his carefully cultivated façade slip or losing control the way his father used to. 'Then I want you to call on her tomorrow.'

'I can't call on a woman of *superior rank*. She must call on me first.'

'Then find a way to arrange it—now see to our guests.' He flicked his hand at her, grinning when she flinched before she spun on her heel and hurried away. If marrying her off didn't mean relinquishing control of the pittance of an inheritance she'd received from her mother, the money which he desperately needed in these trying times, he'd bind her to the most depraved man he could find. She deserved to suffer as much as her thieving mother had under his father's firm control. A wilful wife was no benefit to a man, as Lady Shepherd would soon discover.

* * *

Arabella didn't return to the party, but raced upstairs. Let Vincent see to his guests. She wouldn't be ordered about like some servant. Reaching the top, she paused to draw in a deep breath, forcing the shaking spreading through her to stop. He'd given her an order and she must obey. She turned over her hand and traced the snaking scar on her inner arm, the ragged reminder of the single time she'd tried to free herself, and her money, from Vincent's control.

She yanked the lace of her sleeve back down to cover the ugly thing and stared out the window at the men and women promenading over the lawn. The afternoon sun lengthened the shadows of the trees across the grass as Vincent strode to where Lord Spotswood stood by the well with a number of burgesses.

'Some day, Vincent, you'll regret what you did to me.' She'd make sure of it and then she'd never be under a man's control again.

# Chapter Five

Richard and his crew stood silent at their posts as the *Devil's Rose* drifted past the reedy banks of the shallow inlet. It'd taken a week of hard sailing against stiff winds to reach this place and now the air was still. The brackish scent of stagnant seawater, wet earth and rotting leaves filled the air. The smell took Richard back to his first days as a privateer when he and his crew used to hide in the inlets along the Chesapeake waiting for French or Dutch ships to appear. Like a dog on a hare they'd dart out to intercept them, claiming for England the prize. He'd been proud to be a seaman back then, serving the King and looking forward to his future with Cas. But that was before he'd lost everything.

*Curse Vincent.*

A white bird rose up from the tall marsh grass, its wings catching the light from the full moon hanging low in the sky. Richard frowned as it flew off. He'd prefer the dark of a new moon, and more space to manoeuvre, but he had no choice. Better to intercept the schooner and the *Casa de Oro* here than risk losing them in open water. The *Casa de Oro* was one of the fastest pirate ships in the Caribbean and the schooner's light weight made it quicker than the *Devil's Rose*.

At last, around a bend in the inlet, white sails came into view, shimmering in the moonlight like the bird's wings. The shallow-draft *Casa de Oro* sat high in the water with the schooner on her port side. What little activity Richard could see on both decks ceased at the appearance of the *Devil's Rose*.

'Hoist the white flag, Mr Rush,' Richard commanded.

Mr Rush signalled to a man and a white flag rose beneath the black one of the *Devil's Rose*. Mr Rush handed Richard a spyglass.

Richard watched the *Casa de Oro*, waiting for a response. Men scurried across the deck, preparing for a fight. On the quarterdeck, Richard caught the glint of Captain Dehesa's spyglass. Richard opened and closed his fingers on the warm brass of his and a bead of sweat slipped down his forehead and past his eye. He didn't wipe it away, not wanting to miss the signal, or the faint spark of cannon fuses being lit on the gun deck.

'Think it'll work?' Mr Rush asked.

'If not, be ready to heave to and fire.' Half of Richard's crew hid below, blunderbusses loaded, cannons at the ready in case things turned bad.

Behind the *Casa de Oro*, the schooner crew paused in the offloading of crates and sacks on to the pirate ship to watch the *Devil's Rose* ghost steadily closer. The *Casa de Oro* blocked whatever cannons they had, but not the weapons each sailor carried.

At last, a man waving a white flag appeared on the quarterdeck. Richard let out a long breath, then collapsed the spyglass. 'Bring us alongside the *Casa de Oro*, but tell the men below to stay ready. A white flag doesn't mean we're out of danger.'

Mr Rush relayed the orders to the crew. Richard stood along the port rail as the *Devil's Rose* came alongside the *Casa de Oro*'s starboard side.

Men of every nationality and size, their faces and arms crisscrossed with scars, watched Richard and his men from their stations. Sharp cutlasses and loaded blunderbusses hung from leather belts and stained sashes, ready for use. This was no privateer crew attached to a man who'd been wronged. These were hardened pirates dedicated to a captain who'd brought them riches and who'd earned enough respect to hold his leadership position for many years.

'Captain Rose asks permission to come aboard,' Richard called across, adjusting his mask over his eyes.

'Permission granted,' an elegant voice with a thick Spanish accent called out from the quarterdeck.

Richard's men laid the plank between the two ships.

'Be careful, sir,' Mr Rush whispered. 'I don't trust these dogs.'

'Neither do I.' Richard made his way across, drop-

ping down on to the *Casa de Oro*'s deck, the duelling pistol hanging at his side. The *Casa de Oro*'s
appearance offshore had struck terror in the hearts
of citizens in coastal towns across the Caribbean
for years. They deserved to be double-crossed and
it sickened Richard to ally himself with this scum,
but he needed their Captain's help. This crew would
be the death of Richard if he didn't succeed with
Captain Dehesa.

'*Buenas noches*, Captain Rose.' Captain Dehesa
approached with a stride regal enough to rival the
King of Spain. He wore plain black breeches paired
with a dark coat with gold embroidery along the
front. The lace of his sleeves and his shirt beneath
his chin glowed orange with the lanterns hanging
about the ship. A Cavalier hat sat at a rakish angle
over his straight, dark hair, emphasising his square
jaw. 'To what do I owe the honour of this visit?'

'I have business to discuss with you.' He pinned
the burly schooner Captain standing behind Captain Dehesa with a pointed look. The sweat on the
man's wide forehead was evident even in the weak
light. 'Alone.'

'Why?' Captain Dehesa challenged, his dark eyes
narrowing at Richard.

'I have an offer for you, one you'll find very interesting and profitable.'

Greed replaced Captain Dehesa's wary look and
he motioned for Richard to follow him. '*Por aqui,
Capitán.*'

He started for his cabin when the schooner Captain stepped forward, blocking his way.

'Captain Dehesa, we must be on our way. It isn't safe to remain anchored here,' the broad man insisted. Across the deck, his crew resumed unloading their goods into the *Casa de Oro*'s hold, though a number of men continued to watch. Anyone with an interest in coming closer was blocked by a line of Captain Dehesa's men positioned along the balustrade.

Captain Dehesa dropped his hand to the handle of the ornately engraved silver and wood flintlock pistol dangling from his hip. 'This is my ship, Captain Taylor. Don't think to command me.'

'Of course, Captain Dehesa.' Captain Taylor stepped aside to allow Dehesa and Richard to pass, but savage hate flashed in the schooner Captain's small eyes. Richard followed Captain Dehesa to his cabin, realising when the schooner finally turned on the *Casa de Oro*, the attack would be vicious and Captain Taylor would enjoy it.

'Speak quickly, Captain Rose,' Captain Dehesa urged, closing the door behind them. 'Captain Taylor is right. It's dangerous to tarry here. North Carolina might be friendly to pirates, but others sailing these waters are not.'

The Captain's quarters were smaller than his own on the *Devil's Rose,* but still refined. A few fine portraits in heavy, gilded frames graced the richly panelled walls, giving credence to the rumours that Captain Dehesa was no common seaman, but the disgraced son of a Spanish nobleman.

'I've come with a warning. Captain Taylor has instructions from Mr Fitzwilliam to attack you once you're out to sea. They'll kill you and reclaim the goods he exchanged for your silver.'

Captain Dehesa crossed his arms over his chest and rubbed his chin with his thumb and forefinger. 'Why have you come all the way here on such a lovely night to tell me this?'

'I want you to recognise the kind of man you're dealing with and to help me ruin him. I need whatever evidence you can provide of Mr Fitzwilliam trading with pirates and I'm willing to pay handsomely for it. He's murdered a good number of men, all the while robbing and thieving like any blackguard. I want him brought to justice.'

'How do I know you're not tired of preying on Virginia Trading Company ships and now wish to attack others, to rule the seas without competition from me?' He dropped his hand to hang beside his weapon. 'To give you evidence might be to put my own head in the noose.'

Richard tensed, his fingers achingly close to Cas's duelling pistol, but he didn't so much as allow them to twitch. If he was forced to kill Captain Dehesa, the Captain's men would slaughter him.

'I respect you too much to see you swing,' Richard lied. 'It's Mr Fitzwilliam I want to see dancing at the end of a rope.'

The sharp distrust in Captain Dehesa's eyes failed to ease. He wasn't going to help him, and Richard would be lucky to make it out of this cabin alive. Richard's small finger twitched near the pistol as the candle in the lantern overhead sputtered in its wax.

Then, a wide smile broke the severity of Captain Dehesa's face. 'You risked a great deal coming here, so I think you are telling the truth, but I must find out for myself. If you are right, I'll help to teach others who want to double-cross me a lesson. If you're wrong, pray to the Virgin for a quick death.'

Captain Dehesa threw open the cabin door and marched straight to Captain Taylor, making the schooner Captain's eyes widen in fear. Captain Taylor reached for his pistol, fumbling and dropping it before Captain Dehesa grabbed him by the throat and slammed him hard against the mainmast.

The sailors loading the schooner came to a halt.

'Captain Rose says you are to dispose of me once we are out to sea. *Es verdad?*'

Captain Taylor scratched at Dehesa's tight fingers. 'He's lying.'

Captain Dehesa slid Richard a warning glance, then turned back to Captain Taylor. 'He went to a lot of effort to speak with me. You, not so much. So I ask again, were you hired to betray and kill me?'

'No,' the man gasped, but Captain Dehesa's fingers tightened around his throat before he could say more.

The sailors from the schooner gathered at the balustrade and Richard closed his hand over his pistol handle in anticipation of them stepping in to help their Captain. None tried to break through the line of scoundrels facing them, but there was no saying how much more they'd allow Captain Taylor to endure before they attacked. Richard glanced at Mr Rush who watched from the *Devil's Rose*, waiting for Richard's signal to summon the men from below.

'I don't think you are telling the truth, but there is one way to discover it. Perhaps you've heard of the garrotte?' Captain Dehesa snapped his fingers, and one of his men came forward with a rough three-legged stool. He placed it within sight of Captain Taylor while a shirtless man with a long scar across his chest snapped tight a piece of rope between his rough fists. 'If you tell me the truth, I'll send you to your ship and you can go home. If not, I'll send you to rest with *los pescados*. I ask you one more time. Were you paid to turn against me?'

Captain Taylor's wide eyes shifted from the stool to the pirate with the rope to Captain Dehesa. Sweat covered his face and seeped through his white shirt. Finally, he nodded. 'Yes. Mr Adams ordered us to attack you once we were out to sea.'

Captain Dehesa let go of the man's neck. Captain Taylor crumpled to his knees, gasping for breath.

Captain Dehesa turned to Richard. 'What evidence can I give you to bring down this pig?'

'Any letters or papers you've received from him.'

He shook his head. 'Men approached me. There was nothing in writing.'

Richard silently cursed, but kept on course. 'Then

you can provide a sworn testimony about what you've seen and when.'

'This I cannot do. It would mean admitting my guilt and it could be used against me.'

'I need something.' He hadn't come all this way or risked so much for nothing.

'I'll have my men search Captain's Taylor's ship. There must be something there.' Captain Dehesa turned to the scarred pirate, about to give the order for the search, when a flash of movement over Captain Dehesa's shoulder caught Richard's eye. Captain Taylor was on his feet, pistol raised. Richard shoved Captain Dehesa out of the way as a flash from the gun lit up the ship and the boom sent marsh birds fluttering up from the surrounding reeds. Something slammed against Richard, knocking him to the deck, his shoulder on fire.

Captain Dehesa and a dozen of his men drew their weapons and fired. Captain Taylor dropped like a sandbag, dead.

A frenzy of activity erupted on the schooner as the Virginia Company sailors rushed at the pirates. The crack of gunfire joined the horrified screams of men and the clank of cutlasses. Richard struggled to rise, but a bolt of pain tore through him. He touched his shoulder and warm blood spread from the wound to stain his fingers.

Captain Dehesa knelt beside him. 'You saved my life, *Capitán* Rose. I'm in your debt. I'll help you bring down Señor Fitzwilliam, but now we fight and

you must return to your ship and see to your wound.'
He motioned to one of his men to help Richard to
his feet. 'I'll be near Cape Hatteras, preying on ships
from Charleston. Find me there when you're ready to
collect my testimony and I will gladly give it to you.'

*'Gracias,'* Richard muttered, the burning in his
shoulder making the deck sway more than the current.

*'De nada.'* Captain Dehesa raced off to join the
fight while his men helped Richard to the *Devil's
Rose.*

Mr Rush and Mr O'Malley hurried across the
plank to bring Richard back on board.

'Bring us around on the schooner's port side and
roll out the cannons,' Richard commanded the gun-
ner, pushing free of Mr Rush and staggering to the
forecastle.

'We must see to your wound,' Mr Rush insisted.
The sails snapped behind him and the wheels of the
cannons below deck creaked with their heavy loads.

'Not yet.' He yanked off his mask and leaned
hard against a barrel, working to catch his breath.
Through the haze of gunpowder, he noticed the
schooner pulling away. If she broke free, she'd be
out of the shoals and in the open ocean in minutes.
'We have to disable the schooner, give us a chance
to search her papers. There might be good evidence
on board. We can't allow her to escape.'

Richard pushed away from the wood, ready to
call out more orders when everything went black.

\* \* \*

Cassandra sat in the dining room of the Governor's Palace, the garnet necklace and matching earrings the Chathams had given her during her first month in London sparkling in the candlelight from the chandelier overhead. In front of her, the large rosewood table dominated the white panelled room and supported an elegant collection of silver servers and gold-rimmed plates. Footmen wearing white wigs and Lord Spotswood's livery moved among the finely attired guests refilling wineglasses and serving a selection of enticing dishes. If it weren't for the heat, which failed to ease with the setting sun, Cassandra might mistake this for any dining room in London.

Lady Spotswood held court at Cassandra's end of the table, a necklace of fine diamonds gracing her throat. With her square face and narrow eyes, and a *robe à l'Anglaise* of grey silk trimmed with white lace along the V of the bodice hugging her slender figure, she appeared every inch the Governor's wife. At the other end, Mr Fitzwilliam and a few burgesses sat with Lord Spotswood and Mr Preston, the owner of the Chesapeake Trading Company. The men discussed business with Lord Spotswood who listened with interest, his high forehead made higher by his tall wig. With his wide chest and stern, dark eyes, he proved as commanding in the dining room as in the House of Burgesses.

'Lady Shepherd, I understand you held regular salons in London,' Lady Spotswood entreated.

'I did.' Discussing art and music with learned men had offered her a brief respite from the pain of her life with Giles, but this happiness had cost her dearly. Nothing illicit had taken place at her petite dinners, but society, led by Giles and his mistress, had rushed to invent tales of entertained lovers for everyone to devour. The deepest cut had come when Lord and Lady Chatham had chosen to believe the gossip instead of her. They'd been kind to her when she'd first arrived in London, showering her with gifts and offering her a taste of the life she'd lost with the hurricane. She been so taken in by them, she hadn't noticed them manipulating her into meeting Giles and encouraging the engagement. They'd been too busy trying to forge an alliance with his family to exploit in the House of Lords to care about what their ambitions might cost Cassandra. Cassandra took up her wineglass, in need of a bracing sip. 'They were most educational.'

'Educational for you or the men you invited?' Mrs Baker sniggered.

Cassandra tightened her grip on the stem of the glass, not surprised to see the stories had reached this shore, but it made her wary. This was how it had started in London with the viciousness of society's comments increased by Giles's encouragement, until almost everyone, including the Chathams, had turned their backs on her, like some at this table had after her parents' deaths. Yet here she was among them again, still chasing after people who didn't really care about her to achieve something she wasn't even certain she wanted.

*Of course I want it, for Dinah.*

'It seems London gentlemen aren't the only ones enamoured of your charms.' Mrs Baker nodded down the table to where Mr Fitzwilliam stared at Cassandra. He avoided the women's scrutiny by returning his attention to the men.

'At least he doesn't fall for false gossip and stories.' Cassandra set down her wineglass, making the crystal clink against the polished wood, refusing to allow the woman's insults to defeat her. No one admired a weak person and she would garner their respect with strength if she could not win it with affinity.

'Having met you, it's impossible to believe any of the stories from London are true,' Lady Spotswood complimented, ever the refined and polite hostess. 'Knowing something of how London gossip works makes it even harder to give them credence.'

Cassandra breathed a touch easier, grateful for Lady Spotswood's support. With all the recent attacks on her and her husband by Reverend Blair and others, Lady Spotswood understood what it was like to be treated like a pariah and the value of kindness from others, especially those of superior rank.

Cassandra was about to say more when one of Mr Fitzwilliam's comments caught her attention.

'I hired a schooner at my own expense to hunt down the pirates off our coast, especially the *Devil's Rose.*' He slid a speaking glance to Mr Preston. 'Unlike some gentlemen, I don't wait for the Crown to protect my interests but see to them myself.'

'If the *Devil's Rose* attacked Chesapeake Trading Company ships with the frequency it does yours, I would, too,' Mr Preston snorted from beneath the long, black wig framing his sharp face and aquiline nose. Mr Fitzwilliam's boasting smile wilted about the corners.

'Has your ship been successful?' Cassandra asked, nervously fingering the thick lace along the edge of the half sleeve of her lavender silk gown with sprays of roses printed on it. It would be to her benefit if Richard was killed or his ship sank, then she might never have to deal with him and his awful bargain, but the image of Richard shot in a skirmish or disappearing beneath the waves pained her more than her memories of the deceit. Richard's real death would extinguish for ever the small spark of hope his being alive had kindled inside her. Like his memory had done in the long hours of her lonely marriage, his mere existence helped her believe that the troubles she thought too difficult to surmount, like an old love returning from the dead, were not so impossible to overcome after all.

'We haven't found those cutthroats yet, but I'm confident the fiend who attacked your ship will soon be brought to justice.' Mr Fitzwilliam raised his glass to Lord Spotswood. 'As our esteemed Governor was forced to act on his own to rid us of Blackbeard, I intend to do the same with these current villains.'

'My decision to end Blackbeard's scourge had

more to do with securing evidence against North Carolina's Governor than killing the pirate. Governor Eden's encouragement of these rogues has caused problems for years.' Lord Spotswood finished his wine and waved away a footman attempting to refill his goblet. 'If you catch these brigands, Mr Fitzwilliam, the King himself will congratulate you.'

Mr Fitzwilliam's chest swelled so much it nearly popped the buttons off his grey embroidered waistcoat.

'Especially if you find evidence of any other esteemed men colluding with them,' Lord Spotswood added. 'The King is eager to root out those who assist pirates in their disgusting trade and bring them to justice. If I wasn't fending off a recall—' he looked pointedly at Mr Preston, who didn't flinch from the silent and severe accusation '—I might pursue these criminals myself.'

Mr Fitzwilliam's puffed-out chest collapsed, his guilt obvious to Cassandra and anyone else who cared to look for it. If only she had evidence against Mr Fitzwilliam to give to Lord Spotswood, but nothing Richard had sent Uncle Walter over the years was strong enough to convict a man of Mr Fitzwilliam's standing. Now, Richard might be in danger from Mr Fitzwilliam's ship.

*I must find a way to warn him.* Cassandra picked up her wine and took a long sip. Richard's bargain already hung over her like a sword. She was a fool to even consider warning him. If anyone discovered her trying to send him a message, it would ruin her.

A footman approached Lord Spotswood and whispered in his ear.

'Lady Shepherd,' Lord Spotswood called down the table. 'Your daughter's nursemaid is here and says she must speak with you.'

'Then I'll see her at once.' Cassandra rose, a different worry guiding her actions. If Jane was here then there must be something wrong with Dinah. Her daughter had so far avoided the seasoning fevers those not native to Virginia usually caught in their first few months here, but it didn't mean she would never fall ill.

'I'll escort you.' Mr Fitzwilliam stood with the other gentleman and began to shift around his chair, but Cassandra stopped him with a wave of her hand.

'There's no need. I will handle this matter.' She didn't want the tiresome man hovering about while she saw to her affairs. Ever since the gathering at Butler Plantation, she'd avoided being alone with him and soliciting another unwanted proposal. She would continue to do so.

She left the dining room and passed through the hallway with its wide staircase and into the main hall, eager to reach Jane. The rich wood panelling stood in contrast to the white dining room and made the entry hall appear darker and more imposing than the moonlit night suggested. The rows of crossed swords and pistols hanging on the walls, and the sharp circle of muskets with bayonets meeting in the centre of the high ceiling, added to her unease. Jane stood beneath the weapons, pale with worry.

Cassandra hurried to her. 'Jane, is something wrong with Dinah?'

'No, my lady.' Jane peered around, then shifted closer, dropped her voice and held out a small bundle wrapped in an old red handkerchief. 'A man brought this to the house after you left.'

Cassandra took it and unwrapped it. The silver snub of the duelling pistol glinted in the candlelight. She flipped the handkerchief back over it and clasped the ominous message to her chest. Of all the times Richard could have chosen to send the pistol, while she was dining in the Governor's Palace was the worst. 'Where's the man who gave you this?'

'Waiting for you in the woods at Belle View.'

Good, he was not nearby. It gave her a chance to think and to decide. She fingered the weapon through the thin material, her future, Dinah's and maybe even Richard's hanging on what she chose to do next. She owed Richard no allegiance. She could hand the gun over to Lord Spotswood to deal with Richard as he might. It would end the threat hanging over her, but she couldn't do it. Mr Fitzwilliam had won so many battles against Richard and in many ways against her, too. She couldn't be the one to give him the final victory, nor could she forget Uncle Walter's plea for her to help Richard who'd sworn he'd only call on her if he truly needed her.

*Perhaps he's come for a pardon and for me?* Her excitement faded along with the laughter of the burgesses carrying out of the dining room. A pirate, no matter who he might have once been, wasn't likely to be so sentimental and she shouldn't be either. This was a deal and nothing more. He wanted something practical and it was up to her to either discover what it was or turn him in.

'Is everything well?' Mr Fitzwilliam entreated, striding into the hall, his presence making Cassandra's back stiffen.

'Call the carriage,' she whispered to Jane. 'We'll leave at once.'

She faced Mr Fitzwilliam, struggling to keep her mind free from the panic engulfing her. Now was no time to lose her wits. She had no idea what she would do once she was away from here, but she needed privacy to consider the matter and she couldn't do it under Mr Fitzwilliam's irritating scrutiny. Cassandra dropped her hand to hide the pistol behind the heavy folds of her skirt. She had no explanation for why her maid had brought her a weapon and she didn't intend to invent one. There were others lies that were more convincing. 'Dinah is ill and I must go to her.'

'Let the nurse see to her,' Mr Fitzwilliam said dismissively with a wave of his hand.

'I'm her mother and I'll attend her,' Cassandra said through clenched teeth. She'd had similar conversations with Giles before and she did not appreciate Mr Fitzwilliam's husband-like tone. 'Surely you understand.'

The slight frown tugging down the sides of his lips told her he didn't, but he thought better of pressing the point. 'Then allow me to come with you and be of some assistance.'

Curse the man and his persistence. 'No, I wouldn't want to distract you from the business of making progress with Mr Preston tonight.'

He tossed a glance at the dining room before fixing back on her, his self-interest prevailing over any concern for her or Dinah. 'Yes, you're right. Please allow me to call on you tomorrow and see how your daughter is fairing.'

'You mustn't. Her fever might be contagious,' she exclaimed before settling herself, not wanting him anywhere near her or her household but still she had to be polite. The false and meaningless pleasantries required by society demanded it. She was tired of it all.

'You're right.' He reached for her hand, and she proffered it, careful to keep the other with the pistol hidden in the folds of her wide-hipped skirt. His skin was cold despite the heat of the evening. She tolerated his touch even while wanting to rush to meet whoever waited for her at Belle View, but she was trapped again by necessary courtesies. 'I hope for the speedy recovery of your child and for you to remain safe.'

'Thank you.' She withdrew her hand, grateful for the jingling equipage of her small conveyance rolling to a stop out front. 'Please, give my excuses to Lord and Lady Spotswood.'

'Of course,' he vowed with a solicitousness tinged with annoyance.

Without another word, she hurried down the front steps of the palace, took the driver's hand and stepped inside the small coach. Jane sat beside her and within seconds the driver had them beyond the iron and brick walls of the Governor's Palace and down the wide Duke of Gloucester Street.

Cassandra tried to calm herself in preparation for whatever waited for her at Belle View, but her stomacher bit into her ribs and she couldn't draw in a proper breath. Richard had called for her, putting her in danger at a time when Mr Fitzwilliam was determined to root out pirates. If Mr Fitzwilliam's hired men had followed Richard's ship then they might have followed his crewman and they would catch her meeting with him. Heaven knew what would happen to her then. She fingered the garnet necklace, knowing exactly what would happen. Her jewels would be exchanged for a length of rope.

Fear and anger made her shake the way they had the morning Richard had ignored all her pleas to stay in Virginia and sailed away. He never should have placed her in this position. She dropped her hand to her lap and swallowed hard, the rock of the carriage more annoying than soothing. She needed to pace, to move, but she could only sit and watch out the window as the white clapboard houses with lights burning in the windows came and went. The spire of Bruton Parish Church towered dark and ominous over them and the graveyard beside it at the turn to the road leading out of town.

Very soon, the lights of Williamsburg faded away, and Cassandra clasped the pistol close, the situation far more perilous and vexing than when she'd traversed this road two hours ago. She still had no idea what she would do once she reached Belle View.

## Chapter Six

A long hour passed during the coach ride through the dark Virginia countryside. Jane sat across from Cassandra, as pale as she'd been aboard the *Winter Gale*. Unlike then, Cassandra could offer her no reassuring words because she still had no idea what she would do. She should protect her family like she had with the pirates, turn the man and the pistol over to the authorities and be done with them, but her heart made this choice as difficult as any other. Richard had called for her and in his request was Uncle Walter's, and her own weakness to be wanted once again. Cassandra opened the handkerchief and slid her hand along the smooth barrel of the pistol. The metal was warm from where she'd held it, her heat echoing Richard's from mere hours ago. She wondered what he'd thought about while he'd prepared to send it. More than likely it was only his selfish need for supplies or the papers that had prompted him to call for her.

She covered the metal and stared out the car-

riage window. The dense forests of Virginia pine
and hickory lining the country road made the darkness even thicker and concealed any trace of the
houses and farms situated up the long lanes snaking off the main road. She raised her hand, once
again considered rapping on the roof and ordering
the driver to turn around so she could give Lord
Spotswood the pistol, but she didn't do it. If she
returned to the Governor's Palace, she would have
to admit to lying about Dinah and explain why she
hadn't brought this evidence forward sooner. Lord
Spotswood might arrest her for withholding such
valuable information and she would find herself in
deeper trouble than she was now. Nor could she betray Uncle Walter's last wish for her to help Richard
in so blatant a fashion.

*Uncle Walter, why did you ask such an awful thing
of me?* If he hadn't, she could have ignored the man
waiting for her and he might go away, never to trouble her again. Or he or Richard might seek revenge.
She'd seen the levels Giles had stooped to in order
to destroy her when he believed he'd been duped
into thinking her a wealthy colonial heiress by the
Chathams. Richard might do the same if she didn't
honour his request.

*No, he wouldn't be that cruel.*

Uncle Walter would never have continued to help
him if Richard had been so heartless, yet Richard
had held her to this bargain, even when he'd known
the danger it placed her in. He'd attacked ships and
frightened innocent people all the while stealing

goods. He was no longer the Richard she'd loved, but no matter how many times she told herself this, she still couldn't believe it. Beneath the weapons and the mask, the Richard she'd once cherished was still there. It'd been there in the sweep of his hand along her cheek when he'd comforted her and in his kiss—or had even that been another of his many deceptions?

*What am I going to do?*

The answer came to her at last when the coach made the turn for Belle View and the sight of the tobacco fields in the moonlight made her realise she couldn't sacrifice Belle View or Dinah's future for an illusion. She would retrieve the papers from the fireplace and give them to the pirate, sending him back to his Captain with a few choice words and a command to never trouble her again. The documents would serve Richard better in his possession than tucked away in a hole in the wall. There was nothing she could do for Richard. She was no solicitor or woman of influence, simply a dowager baroness trying to rebuild her home and her reputation. Giving him the papers would, in a small way, honour Uncle Walter's wish and, along with returning the pistol to its case, sever her ties to Richard for good. He was gone, maybe not dead, but dead to her, and she must accept it. If he wanted to come home, he could find his own way. It wasn't up to her to wait for him or to save him.

The plan should have heartened her, but instead it seemed as dreary as the shadowed tobacco-drying house on the edge of the field. She was tired of saying goodbye to people: her parents, her uncle and now Richard for the second time.

The full moon, beginning to wane, hung near its apex, making the straight, packed-dirt road almost white and revealing the staid outline of Belle View. The closer they drew, the more the silvery light shone on the grey-slate roof of the house, casting the brick front of it into deep shadow. The darkness hid the dust dulling the red bricks, the overgrown ivy and the peeling trim work.

The carriage slowed when it approached the top of the circular drive, and Cassandra clutched the pistol tight in her hands and sat up, ready to face whatever was to come. 'Where's the man waiting?'

'In the trees to the left of the dock,' Jane answered.

The driver pulled the horse to a stop in front of the wide front door. The rows of upper and lower windows along the front of it glittered with the moonlight, the rooms behind them dark except for Dinah's. Mrs Sween slept with Dinah tonight, the lamp burning low for protection against nightmares. Hopefully, the housekeeper wasn't awake. It would make sneaking off to meet Richard's man easier.

The driver handed them out of the coach and they hurried up the stone steps and into the narrow main hall. Moonlight streamed in through the windows, as Cassandra crept up the stairs to her room, Jane following behind her. She stopped at her door and pulled Jane close. 'Go to Dinah and stay with her tonight. Tell everyone I'm not feeling well and I've gone to bed and that I'm not to be disturbed for any reason. I'll see what the man wants and return as soon as I can.'

'But what if the man waiting for you means you harm?'

Jane was right. Cassandra had no idea who she was really going to meet. She wanted to believe it was someone sent by Richard, but it might be a ruse from his crew. Perhaps they'd followed the weasel's advice and overthrown Richard and now wished to extort money from her. After all, threatening a woman was safer than taking a ship. They could ask for all they wanted. She didn't have a spare farthing to give them.

'I'll take the pistol with me, but be sure to tell no one where I've gone.' If something happened to Cassandra, it might be hours before anyone went searching for her. She was as alone and vulnerable tonight as she'd been in London. 'If I'm not back by morning, then send someone to find me.'

'Yes, my lady.'

Jane dipped a curtsy, then made for Dinah's room, leaving Cassandra to fetch the papers hidden in the fireplace. She didn't change, wanting this business to be over with quickly and not intending to be gone for long. With the folded documents tucked into her bodice, she cracked the bedroom door and listened for any sign of activity in the upstairs hall. Jane's soft voice talking to Mrs Sween in Dinah's room drifted through the quiet, and Cassandra slipped out of her room and silently down the stairs.

She hurried into the dining room and opened the pistol box and loaded her pistol with one shot. It wouldn't do much if there were a gang of men waiting for her, but it was the best she had. She slipped the weapon and the handkerchief into the shallow pocket of her dress and made for the door set in the wood panelling next to the dining room.

The musty scent of damp earth mingling with garlic, lavender and other herbs drifted up from the darkness of the cellar. A passage led from there to the kitchen outbuilding in the garden. She crept down the stairs, closing the door behind her and fighting back her fears over what she might encounter. Rats were nothing to worry about compared to pirates. Running her fingers along the wall, she traced her way across the short passage, losing the comforting guide when it opened up into the post-supported cellar. Feeling for each rough wood beam, she stumbled forward from one to the next in a straight line until she was across the room. Searching along the dank walls with her hands, she found the door and pulled it open, freezing when it squeaked. She waited to see if anyone had heard the noise, but no footsteps sounded on the floorboards above her.

The passage was cold and lined in brick and she moved fast down it towards a faint glimmering at the far end. Following the stairs up, she entered the white kitchen, relieved to be free of the tunnel. She hurried over the stone floor, past the large wood table in the centre and the wide hearth where the embers glowed warm, reflecting in the copper pot hanging over them.

She flung open the door on the far side, making sure to close it behind her before she bolted across the kitchen garden to the line of trees along the perimeter of the lawn. The dry grass crunched beneath her slippers as she followed the cedars and pine trees down the curve of the land leading to the river. She kept close to the shadows of the trees instead of making herself visible in the moonlight on the main lawn. If anyone happened to look out from the house, she didn't want them to notice her. Thankfully, no boats were tied to the wharf and no one was about.

The lapping of the James River against the piers grew louder and she paused, searching for any sign of the man waiting for her. Then the snap of twigs sounded from somewhere in the trees up ahead and she froze. She watched as a lone figure emerged from the dark foliage and made his way towards her. She took out the pistol and pointed it at him, her breath catching while she waited to see if he was alone or if a group of ruffians would rush to finish what Mr Barlow had been denied on the *Winter Gale*. The man moved quietly and steadily up the short rise, then passed through a shaft of moonlight that revealed his weathered features and the Monmouth cap.

'Lady Shepherd, it's a pleasure to see ya again.' Mr Rush stopped before her and slid the cap from his head in deference, clasping it tight between his gnarled hands. 'I see you received my message.'

'I did and now you can send one back to your Captain.' She tugged the documents out of her bodice and tossed them at Mr Rush. They hit his chest hard, and he stepped back, clutching them against his stained shirt. 'There's the evidence you've been sending to my uncle. I kept it safe, as Richard asked. Since I have the pistol back, and you have the papers, our bargain is over.'

'You won't help us?'

'I won't continue to place my daughter and my household in danger because of him and you can go back to Richard and tell him that.'

'You must help him.' Mr Rush threw out his hands in desperation. 'He needs you. He's been shot.'

Cassandra slowly lowered the pistol, her throat constricting. Uncle Walter's voice as he'd sat beside her in the sitting room of his Williamsburg house five years ago, his hand covering hers while he'd told her of Richard's passing, whispered in the rustle of the leaves overhead.

'Is he—?' She couldn't say the word.

'No, milady, but he's badly wounded. No telling how he'll be come morning.' Mr Rush stepped closer, concern and worry softening the deep lines of his face. 'You hold all the cards, milady, like he did once. Will you show him the same kindness he showed you and help him?'

Cassandra touched the garnets at her neck, her determination to shove Richard away for good wavering. Richard was in grave trouble and, of all the people he could have turned to for aid, he'd chosen her. It shouldn't matter, but it did. What he needed of her might cost her everything, but he wasn't asking for papers or illicit information to aid in his revenge, simply for her comfort and concern. He was the only man she'd ever loved and who'd loved her in return. Perhaps a small part of him still cared for her, and through it she might convince him to accept the King's Grace and help him escape the awful life foisted on him as she'd longed for someone in London to help her escape hers. It wasn't her place to reform a rogue or to take him in, but she couldn't turn him away, not when there was a chance she could save him. For all the danger he'd put her through, for all the misery she'd invited upon herself by coming here, she wanted the chance to know him again as the man she'd once loved and not a pirate. 'Yes, I'll help.'

'Thank you, milady.' He set the Monmouth cap over his hair, relief easing his shoulders. 'He's down by the shore. Come along. We can't be lingering here waiting for someone to see us.'

He set off into the trees, and she followed him, returning the pistol to her pocket. The breeze coming off the river carried the musty odour of wet vegetation and mud. Leaves crunched beneath their feet, and the croak of toads added to the night sounds as they picked their way through the forest.

Cassandra held up her skirt, but the thick, damp leaves mired her satin slippers while sharp branches pulled at her heavy skirt, making each step difficult. It wasn't the difficulty of the journey making her thoughts race, but what she might find when they reached Richard and what she would do. She wasn't a surgeon and it was too dangerous to call Dr Abney. She'd have to see to him herself and hope her ministrations were enough.

'Not much further, milady,' Mr Rush reassured her, reaching out once again to steady her after she'd stumbled over a fallen log.

'I'll go as far as needed.' Faster if she could, but the dress wouldn't allow it.

Soon the trees began to thin and Cassandra could see the river a short distance away, rippling with the moonlight. She could only just make out the quick current moving the islands of reeds out in the water. Ahead of her, Mr Rush stopped and cocked his head to one side to listen.

'What is it?' Cassandra asked, coming up beside him, straining to see the water and if someone in a passing wherry had spied them.

From somewhere up ahead an owl hooted and, to Cassandra's shock, Mr Rush hooted in reply.

At the first mate's signal, men stepped out of the shadows, one of them carrying a lantern with the wick trimmed so low, it emitted the faintest of amber glows. In its dim light, Cassandra met the men's hard, suspicious eyes, searching for Richard's familiar blue ones and his strong, wide build, but he wasn't among them. She slipped her hand into the pocket of her dress and pressed her thumb to the pistol hammer, but didn't cock it, wishing she hadn't come here alone. It could still be a trick and, if she screamed, no one in the house would hear her.

'Hell.' A deep voice slipped out of the dark shadow at the base of a tree, the sound of it raising the hairs on the back of Cassandra's neck. Richard pulled himself up into the faint glow of the lantern, swaying when he rose. His heavy, ragged breathing and unsteady stance surprised her more than the arrival of the pistol. 'Is this your idea of help? I need a surgeon, not a woman.'

Her eagerness to see him faded beneath his terse words, but some of her worry eased. If he was well enough to snap at her and his men, then maybe his wound wasn't so bad.

'I can leave if you like.' She gathered up her skirts to go.

'Please, milady, he needs your help.' Mr Rush grabbed the lantern, held it up beside Richard and pulled back his frock coat. The light revealed what the shadows and wool hid. Cassandra gasped at the dark blood saturating the white shirt of his left shoulder.

'Douse that damn light before you give us away.' Richard shoved the lantern aside. The effort taxed what remained of his strength, and he sagged against the tree. Two men helped him down on to the moss and propped him up against the rough bark. Cassandra wanted to rush to him, but she didn't move. She refused to reveal her feelings or fears to Richard or weaken him in the eyes of his men by simpering over him like some nursemaid.

Instead, Cassandra knelt beside Richard with the same self-possession she'd exhibited during teas with

Lady Spotswood, hiding her alarm at his weakness. 'Bring the lantern closer, Mr Rush.'

The first mate obeyed, kneeling on Richard's other side and holding up the light. She reached out to move Richard's coat and better see the wound when Richard grabbed her wrist.

'Don't touch it. I wouldn't want a lady to stain her dress.'

Her heart skipped at the press of his fingers against the inside of her wrist. She ignored it and his curt remark, more concerned about his hot skin than his harsh words. She hoped it was the exertion of trying to stand and not fever heating him. 'Has the ship's surgeon seen you?'

'The surgeon is dead. Shot in the mêlée with the *Casa de Oro.* Another one of my good men, lost.' He let go of her hand and the air, despite the humidity, seemed cold without his flesh against hers.

'Two men aboard the *Devil's Rose* are sick with the fever,' Mr Rush explained. 'It's no place for a man weak with a wound to recover. It's why we came to you. We need you to care for him until he's well enough to return.'

'I'm well enough now,' Richard barked.

'So, I see,' Cassandra murmured. There was no missing the sweat drenching his brow and glistening in the lamplight. They were asking her to take Richard in and nurse him until he recovered, or— she didn't want to think of the alternative. Housing a pirate was infinitely more dangerous than handing him supplies or secret papers and sending him off, but if she didn't find a way to care for him, he would surely die. He might still, but she would do all she could to make sure he lived.

A brisk breeze rattled the leaves above her while she racked her mind to think of some plan, some place she could take him to care for him. Discretion and secrecy were absolutely essential, but with labourers and their families and other workers occupying the houses and outbuildings of Belle View, it might be difficult to find. And then it came to her. 'I can't take you to the main house, but the overseer is gone and his cabin is empty. It's set some way away from the other buildings and rarely visited by anyone. You can hide there until you're well enough to return to your ship.'

'I don't need your help,' Richard growled.

She leaned in so close their faces were inches apart. Sweat and the acrid scent of gunpowder filled the air between them, reminding her of the way he'd smelled when he'd pressed his lips to hers on the *Devil's Rose*. It was his hard eyes fixed on her that stopped her from leaning forward and tasting him again. 'You have two choices. You may refuse my help and I'll leave and consider my part of the bargain fulfilled. Then you can lie here and bleed to death or wait for putrefaction to set in. I suspect there's little you can do for your crew as a stubborn ghost.'

The anger in his eyes softened to resignation tinged with the strain of pain. He leaned his head back against the tree and closed his eyes with a sigh. 'And the second option?'

'Accept my help and perhaps survive and return to your crew and a life above ground.'

He opened his eyes and took in his men standing around them. Then he fixed on her. A little of the humour he'd employed with her aboard the *Devil's Rose* drew up one corner of the grimace tightening his lips. 'You're a strong-willed woman. I like strong-willed women.'

'And I like men who are alive.'

He frowned and shifted his shoulders, grimacing with the pain. She waited, wondering if he'd agree to the terms of her bargain. She would not beg him to stay for he was not hers to command.

At last, he nodded. 'I accept your help.'

'Good.' She stood and shook the mud and leaves off her skirt. 'Mr Rush, help him up. The rest of you stay behind. I can't chance you all being seen.'

'Never thought there'd come a day when I needed help walking,' Richard complained while Mr Rush and Mr O'Malley helped him to his feet, bracing him between them.

'As a pirate, I'm sure you've been carried out of several taverns.' Cassandra grinned, trying to lighten the mood, but his challenging gaze caught hers.

'At one time you thought of me as more than a pirate.'

'I might again if we can get you to the cabin and you live. Now come along, before someone spies us here.'

'The rest of you, return to the ship,' Richard ordered, leaning hard on Mr Rush and Mr O'Malley.

No one objected to the order and the sailors faded into the shadows of the trees as they started off towards the river. The loyalty he inspired in his gruff crew impressed her. From what she'd heard of pirates they normally turned on one another in a moment's notice. Yet these men were willing to risk danger to see to Richard's safety. It spoke to the good still in him, although she wondered how safe he truly was. 'Hurry, we must go before someone sees us.'

*Assuming they haven't already.*

Cassandra started off in the direction of the over-seer's cabin, and Richard and his men followed behind her. Once or twice she paused, struggling to remember the way or because she thought she'd heard a branch snap and feared someone was walking through the trees up ahead. Each time she paused, the men behind her went silent, listening like her to the woods around them for any sign they'd been discovered. They saw no one about, and she was eager to reach the privacy of the cabin, but they moved at a turtle's pace. The thick underbrush hampered their progress as did Richard's wounds. Each time Richard groaned in pain after being jostled, Cassandra fought the desire to rush back to him, take his face in her hands and reassure herself he was fine. She shouldn't care if he survived or not. He hadn't cared enough to tell her he was still alive, or to find a way for them to be together. He'd chosen this wound and the possibility of death over a life with her, but it was impossible for her not to care.

They reached a clearing in the trees where the

overseer's cabin stood dark and lonely, the moon glinting off the dirty windows. This place was a good distance from the main house and away from the path the farmers usually travelled to get to the fields from their homes near the river. A thick copse of trees surrounded it, offering privacy the buildings closer to the fields lacked.

'No one should disturb you here,' Cassandra whispered, then led them across the grass. *At least I hope not.* It was a touch closer to the carpenter's house and barn than she cared for, but neither the driver, her groom nor the carpenter were men accustomed to taking walks through the woods, or cutting through here to reach the main road into Williamsburg and the Raleigh Tavern. Work at Belle View kept them too busy to allow such idle occupation. She prayed they did not decide to change their regular habits. There was enough risk in housing a pirate without someone happening on Richard and informing the authorities. She'd be arrested and Dinah taken from her. If they were separated, there were no relatives to look after her daughter, no one to see to her future the way Uncle Walter had tried to see to hers.

Panic made her stop and turn to tell the men to go back, to leave her and take Richard with them, but the words died on her lips. Richard hung between Mr Rush and Mr O'Malley, his breath rattling in his lungs. He'd come to her at his most vulnerable, just as she'd faced him on the *Winter Gale*, asking for a mercy neither he nor his crew had any reason to extend to her or anyone else on board. If she sent him away, he might die and this time it would be her fault.

She led the men up on to the rickety porch, holding her breath when she turned the latch, then letting it out when the door opened with ease. Stale, musty air wafted out of the cabin, and moonlight cut through the windows, illuminating the narrow bed against the wall, the cold hearth and the simple wood chairs and rough table.

'Lay him on the bed,' she ordered and pulled the near-threadbare curtains closed over the panes. Feeling along the rough wood mantel, she found a candle and the tinderbox. Striking the flint, she sparked the tinder into life, lit the candle and set it in the brass holder. Dancing light filled the room, emphasising the sparseness of the furnishings. Mr Rush and Mr O'Malley helped Richard to sit on the edge of the bed, and it creaked under his weight.

'You two had better return to the others,' Richard commanded, determined to remain the Captain even while he struggled to sit upright.

'Aye, sir. Take this to protect yourself and this for what you need.' Mr Rush laid a blunderbuss on the small table beside the bed and placed two pieces of eight next to it. 'We'll be at Knott Island.'

'I'll send the signal when it's time for you to come for me.'

Cassandra didn't ask where Knott Island was or how Richard intended to signal his crew when he was well. She also didn't ask how she'd send the crew word if Richard died. It was a possibility she didn't wish to consider.

Mr Rush and Mr O'Malley made for the door. Mr O'Malley stepped out into the night, but Mr Rush hesitated on the threshold, scratching at his hair beneath the wool cap. 'Thank you, milady.'

'Don't thank me yet.'

Grim faced, he closed the door behind him. His footsteps banged over the wooden porch and then there was nothing except the hiss and sputter of the wick in the tallow and the cicadas in the grass.

Cassandra faced Richard, as afraid of being alone with him as of the deep stain matting the wool of his coat. Pain drew sharp the line of his mouth while exhaustion darkened the circles beneath his eyes. 'I must see to the wound.'

'What does a baroness know about wounds?' Richard snapped like a sick dog hiding under a porch and resisting all attempts to help it.

She rifled through the rickety cupboard, searching for supplies, trying to pretend his surliness didn't sting. 'My mother used to take me with her to treat the indentured servants. She didn't believe in sheltering me from reality.'

'How fortunate for me.' He shrugged out of his frock coat, groaning in pain with each movement.

Inside the cupboard she found an old bottle of rum, a wooden bowl and nothing else. She didn't dare light a fire to boil water, afraid the smoke rising out of the forest would catch someone's attention. The strong spirit would have to do. It was a pity the overseer hadn't left food behind—some pickled pork or even dried beans. With nothing here, she'd have to sneak food out of the kitchen without Mrs Sween noticing. Gathering up the bowl and rum, she decided not to worry about it until the time came. There was enough to concern her already.

She approached the bed and set the rum, bowl and candle on the table beside it. The light revealed the sickening wet of the blood on his shirt. It didn't pour out of the wound and was dark with age instead of fresh red, giving her some hope. With his youth and strength, surely he could survive this, but she remembered the indentured servants her mother used to treat and how once in a while the smallest of cuts would turn putrid and the man would die. Richard had a hole in his shoulder, and she didn't know what it would do to him.

She tugged the handkerchief that had hidden the pistol out of her pocket and laid it beside the rum. Worry would get her nowhere and there was work to do.

She knelt down and, wrapping her hand lightly behind his calf, raised his foot.

He dropped his heel with a thud against the floor. 'I can remove my boots.'

'With one good arm, I doubt you can.' She reached for him again, and this time he didn't pull away. The solid muscles of his calf flexed beneath her hand while she drew off first one boot, then the other and set them aside. 'I need to take off your shirt so I can properly dress the wound.'

'The bullet went straight through.'

'Good, then I won't have to try to extract it.' She grasped the sides of the shirt at his waist, the motion bringing her face so close to his she need only shift forward to taste something of what they'd known before the world had turned ugly. Beneath her hands, his chest rose and fell in deep breaths to match hers. Sliding the shirt free of his breeches, the musky scent of him took her back five years to the Belle View barn and the sweet smell of hay that used to surround them when they'd made love. Then she'd eagerly traced the line of his neck with her tongue, his skin tart like temptation and lighter than it was now. They'd been free and young, with nothing in the world except each other and their belief in a future together. Her heart ached for everything they'd lost.

She lifted up the shirt, uncovering inch by inch the tanned lines of his torso. He raised his good arm and she removed the stained linen, following the curve of his bicep and fist over his head and across his tightened muscles. He sucked in a fast breath when she brushed the top of his collarbone.

'I'm sorry, I'm trying not to hurt you.'

'It didn't hurt.' His face stiffened with a different pain she instinctively understood.

Doing her best not to touch his wound, or any part of him, she slid the shirt down over his injured arm. When the linen was at last free, his shoulders sagged with a fatigue to weigh down the heartiest of men. His weakness frightened her, reminding her of how fast the fever had taken her parents and how it could still sweep Richard off. If death was his fate, then nothing she did tonight would stop it, but she still had to try. She sat down next to him. 'I need to clean the wound.'

'Leave it be.' A bead of sweat slid down his temple and his skin turned slightly grey beneath the tan.

'No. Mother always said if filth can spoil the milk in the dairy house, then it can't be good for a man.'

He closed his eyes and let out a long breath. 'Do what you must. I trust you.'

She wasn't sure she trusted herself. With shaking hands she took up the rum. The glass bottle was cold against the perspiration of her palm. She poured some on to the handkerchief, allowing the excess to drip into the wood bowl. Moving close to him, she pressed the handkerchief to his shoulder and made small circles over his bare skin. The red and jagged wound stood out in horrid contrast to the smooth planes of his torso. She worked slowly, distracted by his occasional wince and the heaviness of his body beneath her hand. She fought to focus on her work, rising up to lean over him and clean the wound at the back, conscious of the dampness of his hair freed from its queue hanging down over his sturdy neck.

He stared straight ahead while she wiped away the red, the muscles beneath his eyes tightening whenever she came close to the injury. He didn't make a sound, his stoicism easing her worry over hurting him. After many tense minutes, the skin was clean, and she was glad to see the wound wasn't red or hot with inflammation and, to her relief, no new blood seeped out.

She set the dirty handkerchief and rum aside, re-alising she had no cloth to use to bandage him except the bed sheets. She didn't want to destroy those and deny Richard their small comfort. Rising, she lifted her petticoat from off the cotton-covered panniers.

'What are you doing?' Richard gaped at her, his surprise so different from five years ago when she'd slipped her plain dress from her shoulders, revealing everything to him.

'I need material for bandages. It's all I have.' She undid the buttons and tapes of the panniers and shimmied out of them. She let go of the skirt and it dropped down past her stockings to pool around her feet, longer without its support. Tearing the seams, she freed the light covering from the wicker frame, the rip of fabric harsh in the quiet of the cabin.

When at last she had a good number of strips, she sat on the bed beside him, her hips so close to his the silk brushed against them as his skin had done years ago in the barn. She pressed a wad of cloth against the wound, making him flinch, but he didn't jerk away. She began to wrap another strip around the wad to hold it in place.

'I'm surprised you came.' His breath brushed over her shoulders exposed by her dress.

'So am I.' She wound the strips of cloth under his arm, adding a wad to the wound at the back.

'Why did you come?'

She met his eyes, afraid to tell him the truth.

'Uncle Walter asked me to help you, in a letter before he died.'

If he was disappointed in her answer, he didn't show it. 'He was a good man.'

'Yes, he was.' The heat of his cheek so close to hers nearly made her fumble the delicate fabric while she tied the ends.

'This isn't work for a lady,' he said in a low voice, mistaking her agitation.

'This isn't a life for a gentleman's son.'

'It is the only one left to me.'

She met his eyes, the lack of hope in his words as disturbing as the wound. Even during the worst moments in London, her past had helped her imagine a better future while his made him believe it was bleak. If she could help him out of the darkness she would, but she didn't know how, or even if she should.

'Rest. You need your strength.' With the tips of her fingers she lightly pushed him down. He didn't resist, but settled back against the rough pillow and closed his eyes. 'I'll stay until you're asleep.'

'I don't deserve your care.' He slipped his hand in hers, clasping it tight over his bare waist, his skin damp with sweat and sleep already creeping over him.

'You don't have to deserve it, just accept it.' She held his hand while she watched his wide chest rise and fall with each breath until the rhythm of it grew longer and steady.

In the distance, an owl hooted, reminding her of the late hour, but she didn't rise. Every time they parted, the world came crashing down around them. She'd seen him off at Yorktown only to lose him. He'd sailed away from the *Winter Gale* to return to her bleeding. If she left him now, she might come back tomorrow morning to find him bathed in sweat and on the verge of death. If she stayed then maybe he would never slip away from her again.

The raspy sound of his heavy breathing filled the still air and the single candle on the bedside table flickered in the room, making the shadows dance. With her free hand, she lightly traced the hard line of his jaw, the stubble chafing her skin. He hadn't come to her because they'd made a bargain but because, deep down, under the hardness of his life and his heart, he still cared for her. It was there in the strength of his fingers around hers, even in his sleep. She couldn't love him again, not when he might abandon her at any moment to return to his ship, leaving her to fend for herself. Or he might die like her parents and Uncle Walter. Still, she could not ignore how much it meant to her to be near him and how much his wounds, all of them, frightened her. She wanted to help him heal, but for the moment she could do no more than hold his hand through this trial. He might not live until morning, but at this moment they were together and nothing could come between them.

Throbbing pain dragged Richard out of a deep sleep. In the semi-darkness, his senses sought out the familiar creak and groan of the ship's timbers and the rocking of the current. There was nothing in the quiet except the faint sound of someone breathing. Then, the events of the night before came rushing back to him: the fight with the schooner, Dehesa, the gunshot wound and Cas's appearance. He moved to feel his shoulder to see the damage done by the bullet, but his right hand felt trapped and heavy. He looked down to see Cas sleeping soundly beside him, clutching his hand. She lay with her cheek against his chest, her body tucked inside the curve of his good arm, lost in a rest too deep for a woman with so much to lose by his presence. Tendrils of her dark blond hair, freed from their pins, draped her cheek and brushed his bare chest. He slid his hand over the curve of her fingers where her other hand rested on his stomach, sickened by the sight of her skin stained a faint pink with his blood.

*You deserve so much better than this, Cas.*

He covered her hand with his and lay back against the pillows, fending off the restless sleep trying to steal over him. He could hear the curses on his breath when he'd seen her approach with Mr Rush in the woods and the disbelief that she was standing before him. He forced his eyes open to stare at the ceiling, still amazed she'd honoured the bargain. Unlike his crew, whose allegiance he'd won by sweating beside them and sharing their hardships and dangers, he'd done nothing to earn Cas's loyalty, but she'd come to him, not because Walter had asked her to but because she still had faith in him.

*She's wrong to, they all are.* He'd tricked her and

his crew into believing that the vengeance driving him on was a desire to see wrongs made right. It wasn't. It was a reflection of the ugliness inside him, the one that had grown deeper with each passing year he spent at sea.

He closed his eyes, but her sweet scent and the memory of her white skin brushing over his while she'd tended to him tortured him with everything he'd sacrificed to have his way. *I never should have left her.*

Dreams of her in Walter's house taking his hand and leading him into the garden filled his fitful sleep before they faded into the howling laugh of Vincent. Richard jerked awake, the force of his regret as startling as his pounding heart. He tried to calm himself, but it continued to plague him like the searing pain in his shoulder. When he'd left Yorktown, he'd naively believed he could have everything he wanted— a career as a privateer, Cas's love and Belle View. He had nothing now. He'd promised his crew a new life once they'd cleared their names, but there wouldn't be one for him.

She mumbled something in her sleep and shifted against him. He tensed, waiting for her to wake and leave, but she settled back into her slumber, her long eyelashes dark against her cheeks, her lips red and full even in the pale light. Bitterness and exhaustion dragged at him, adding to the torment in his shoulder and his heart.

*It doesn't matter, none of it does.* He tightened his grip on Cas's hand, struggling against the voices and memories pummelling him to hear her breathing and to feel her beside him. As pain gave way to sleep, the tortuous images began to fade, replaced by dreams of the two of them on the back porch at Belle View, the sun glinting off the grass and the river blinding in its brightness, the peace he experienced in her presence stronger than any revenge.

## Chapter Seven

The constant twitter of birds pulled Cassandra from a deep sleep. She opened her eyes to focus on the brass candleholder in front of her, studying the cold black wick set in the tallow candle. For a moment, she thought herself back in London, but the heavy air sitting thick on her sweat-covered body quickly brought her back to Virginia, as did the rum bottle and crumpled handkerchief on the bedside table.

*Richard!*

She sat up, relieved to see him smiling at her, the memories that had teased her last night no less potent in the coming dawn.

'Good morning, Lady Shepherd.' The circles beneath his eyes hadn't faded, but the ashy tint of his skin was gone. Around them, the grey light of dawn softened the coarseness of the stone fireplace and the rough board walls of the cabin.

'It's better now, but far from good.' She pressed her hand to his forehead, grateful to find it cool, but it didn't ease the anxiety tightening the muscles of her back. She hadn't intended to stay all night or to wake up and endure the embarrassment of him having discovered her beside him.

'I've ruined your dress.' He motioned to the dark mud matting the hem.

'A ruined dress is the least of my worries this morning.'

'I'll be sure to send you a finer one after I leave, maybe something meant for a princess of Spain,' he teased.

'Assuming you do leave.' She perched on the edge of the bed, trying not to be drawn in by his wry humour, but after the strains of last night it was hard. 'You may still expire and then I'll have to bury you under the roses in the garden.'

He curled one of the ribbons on her bodice around his finger. 'To be under a rose is very fine thing.'

'This is no time for teasing.' She lightly batted his hand away, trying to suppress a smile, but he clasped her hand in his and brought it to his mouth.

'I'm very serious. Thank you for everything you've done for me.' He pressed his lips to the back of her hand, his breath hot and moist against her skin.

She closed her eyes and curled her fingers, touching the tips to the solid line of his jaw, and willed herself not to settle back down beside him and forget everything in his arms. The risks facing her here were capable of hurting her and those she cared for far more than any of Giles's schemes. She opened her eyes and slid her hand out from beneath his. 'I'll check the wound, then I must get home before the sun is up and everyone rises.'

He let her go, and a small part of her was disappointed. 'Will you be able to return unseen?'

'I'll go through the kitchen outbuilding and the passage beneath the house. No one should see me. Except for Mrs Sween, there aren't any house servants any more, which is good because I'm too tired to think of a story clever enough to fool anyone.'

She shifted on the bed and began to undo the knot of his bandage, trying to ignore how close her hands were to his skin or the intensity with which he watched her. She held her breath as she gently pulled the cotton away, afraid of what she might find. If the wound was red and hot with inflammation, then there was nothing she could do except pray it didn't kill him. To her relief, his injury appeared better with no redness, so she removed the soiled wads.

'Do you remember the time Mrs Sween caught us sneaking up from the cellar after we'd eaten her apple pie in the kitchen?' he asked.

Cassandra smiled despite herself, having forgotten about their afternoon in the kitchen, spoons in hand, devouring the freshly baked treat like two ragamuffins who'd been deprived of food. 'How she berated us. And then when we tried to bake one to replace it…'

'We burned the bottom black.'

'And almost set the kitchen on fire doing it.'

'I've heard sailors use more genteel language than

she did that afternoon.' He smiled for the first time since she'd seen him at sea, all Richard with no trace of Captain Rose.

'I never realised she knew so many Scottish curses.' She wadded more strips of clean cotton and set them in place. 'Neither did the farrier who tramped through her kitchen last week, dirtying her newly cleaned floor. I fear Dinah will repeat one of her more vivid sayings some time soon.'

He reached up and stroked her cheek with the back of his fingers. 'It's good to see you smile.'

'I could say the same about you.'

He lowered his hand and rested it behind his head, but his smile and the rare humour gracing him didn't fade. 'Perhaps I should get shot more often if it brings us this much joy.'

'I think there are less lethal ways to find laughter.' Except, she'd found it for the first time in years with him. Even in the midst of their current troubles he'd lightened her spirit and she his, but it was his body distracting her at present. She laid a hand on his shoulder and gently urged him up so she could wrap a strip of cloth around him and secure the wads. Her fingertips burned from the heat of his taut skin, almost making her fumble the cotton before she let go of him. While she tied the knot in front, his chest rose and fell with quick breaths to match hers.

She sat back, the angles of his face increased by the dawn light becoming brighter behind the thin curtains. Outside, the birdsong grew louder, insisting she go.

'I'll return as soon as I can and bring food and fresh bandages.' Assuming he was still here— although in his current weakened state, she doubted he'd get far. It was a slim comfort. 'Try to get more sleep.'

'I won't stay here any longer than necessary.'

'You'll stay until you are well.' She stood and made for the door. 'I'll be back soon.'

Cas slipped out of the cabin and into the thick mist covering the countryside, taking her charm, comfort and laughter with her. Richard lay back against the pillows, lighter in spirit than he should be for a man with a hole in his shoulder. There was laughter aboard the *Devil's Rose*, a great deal of it when they were sailing on a steady wind in gentle water, but there wasn't the tenderness he experienced in Cas's care or the delight he found in her smile.

Richard reached over, fighting against his dizziness to pick up one of the thin strips of cotton she'd torn from her panniers. He drew it through his fingers, the fine fabric as soft as her touch. It pleased him to think he could still make her smile, even in the midst of troubles. It had allowed him to forget everything for a few precious moments, including the fool he was making of himself over her. His men would howl with laughter if they could see him, but they were at Knott Island and he was here with the fading impression of Cas's fingers against his skin and the delicate notes of her laugh enchanting him, offering him a taste of the peace he'd experienced only in his dreams.

*That's all they are, dreams. This is reality.* He needed to heal and leave, both for her safety and his. There was work to be done, plans to be made and Vincent to ruin. He closed his eyes, recalling charts and courses to Cape Hatteras to clear his mind of her until he fell asleep, the fabric still clutched in his hand.

'Richard!' Cassandra cried, struggling through the thick fog in the forest to find the cabin. The trail was gone, so overgrown with vines and weeds she could barely see more than a few feet in front of her. Mud clung to her shoes and weighed down the hem of her dress, making each step like marching through a bog. 'Richard!'

'My lady.' A voice pierced the mist. 'My lady.'

Cassandra wrenched herself from the tight hold of the nightmare and sat up, blinking against the noon sun pouring in through her Belle View bedroom window. Her body protested the interruption of sleep and exhaustion dragged at her limbs. Across the room, her muddy dress lay rumpled on the floor near the wardrobe where she'd dropped it before climbing into bed. Her return to Belle View had been easier than she'd expected except for the moment she'd narrowly avoided running into Mrs Sween in the hallway before the housekeeper had gone down the passage to the kitchen.

Jane stood beside her, scared like a mouse. 'Lady

Shepherd, Mr Fitzwilliam is downstairs waiting to see you. Should I say you aren't feeling well after tending to Dinah all night and send him away?'

Heaven smite the man. She didn't need the worry of him adding to those already pressing on her. She was tempted to send Jane downstairs with the excuse, but putting him off might only encourage the man to call again. He was irritatingly persistent where she was concerned. She needed to make sure he went away for longer than a day or two. Cassandra flipped back the covers and swung her legs out of bed. 'I'll go downstairs and see him. Help me prepare.'

At the nightstand, she splashed water over her face to clear the last of the sleep from her eyes. Jane approached with the simple peach-silk gown she'd selected from the wardrobe.

'No, I'll greet him *en déshabillé*. It's more fitting for a woman who's been worrying over her child.' It would also keep him from asking her to join him for a walk or some other impromptu outing.

Jane returned the peach dress to the wardrobe and removed the voluminous pale blue robe lined with yellow. She fluffed out the garment, then held it up for Cassandra to slide her arms into it.

'Where's Dinah?' Cassandra tucked her feet into her satin slippers, then sat at her dressing table.

'Taking her nap.' Jane pinned Cassandra's hair beneath a simple lace cap.

'Good. Keep her in her room. I don't want Mr Fitzwilliam to see her well.' Cassandra reached up to pinch some colour in her cheeks, then stopped. The more wan she appeared, the more likely he was to leave quickly and without a great deal of questions.

Cassandra swept from the room and downstairs, slowing her pace when she reached the bottom. Despite the agitation crawling through her, she must appear to Mr Fitzwilliam like a tired mother, not a nervous cat. The closer she came to the drawing room, the harder it was to control her agitation and her regrets. If she hadn't been so eager to court his influence, he might not have taken such an interest in her and been so troublesome.

'Lady Shepherd, is everything all right? You don't look well,' Mr Fitzwilliam exclaimed the moment she entered the sitting room. He tucked his tricorn under his arm, then waved for her to sit down on the faded sofa in front of the window, as overly solicitous with her today as he'd been last night, the sentiment ringing as false as a cracked bell.

She remained standing, intent on making it clear this would be a short call. 'It was a very trying night. Dinah is still sick.'

'Is it serious?' He clutched his chest like a frightened old woman and took a step back, ready to bolt from the house and save himself.

'It might be the ague,' she lied, hoping the potential danger hastened his departure. 'Perhaps it's best if you leave. I wouldn't want you to fall ill.'

'And what of you?' He took her hand, pressing his clammy palm against hers. 'We can't have you sick or fatiguing yourself over some harmless child-hood illness.'

Cassandra snatched her hand back, wanting to slap him for his disregard for Dinah's life. 'She has not been seasoned like the rest of us so I can hardly call the ague harmless. It could kill her.'

'We can't have that now, can we?' He lowered his head, trying to appear humble, but Cassandra caught the hope in his eyes and it disgusted her. Whatever designs he had on her, her no longer having a child certainly appealed to him. 'I apologise for sounding flippant, only you've both become so much a part of Williamsburg, I sometimes forget you've only been here a short time.'

She offered him a terse nod, neither withholding her forgiveness nor accepting his weak apology. Influence or not, she wouldn't stand this man a moment longer or allow him to believe he held too much sway over her and her choices. 'If you'll excuse me, I must return to my daughter.'

'I'm sure you are a great comfort to her.' He tapped the hat down over his short wig and made a move to leave, then stopped. He pressed the tip of his walking stick into the floor, resting his hands on the silver handle. 'Before I go, you should know that my schooner encountered the *Devil's Rose*. The pirates killed the Captain and a number of the crew, but most managed to escape.'

Cassandra's pulse thudded in her ears, but she forced herself to show no alarm or concern about his remark. 'I'm glad to hear your expedition was successful.'

'Captain Rose was wounded in the fray, but he escaped.' He fixed cold eyes on hers, as if taking the measure of her response.

'Really?' she asked in as light a voice as she could muster through the whirl of fear whipping at her. She wished Richard had sunk the schooner, then news of its activities wouldn't have reached Mr Fitzwilliam so quickly, or brought him here to regard her as if he knew she was hiding Richard on her property.

*Impossible, he can't suspect anything.* Or can he? She'd been Richard's fiancée and then she'd been alone with him, the man everyone believed was Captain Rose, on the *Devil's Rose*. If Mr Fitzwilliam suspected they might be the same man, she might be the one to confirm it. It further tightened her chest and made it difficult to keep her nerves steady.

Then Mr Fitzwilliam's scrutinising look shifted into his usual sycophantic smile, but it didn't ease the tension building inside Cassandra. It made it worse. 'Don't worry, my lady, either Captain Rose will die of his wounds or I'll find him and bring him to justice. Good day.'

Cassandra sagged against the doorjamb once the bang of his boots on the front steps faded outside. Overhead, the quick stomp of Dinah's feet across the nursery floor made the chandelier in the roundel in the sitting-room ceiling bounce on its chain. She'd ignored danger to indulge her whim to be with

Richard last night, but she could no longer ignore the risks facing her. Richard shouldn't be here and she shouldn't be helping him. If Mr Fitzwilliam discovered it, she suspected he wouldn't send her to jail, but use his knowledge to trap her in the same marital prison she'd endured with Giles before his death had freed her. There was only one way to remove the threat to both her and Richard. If Richard survived, he must seek the King's Grace.

Vincent tapped his foot against the floorboards in time to the rock of the coach carrying them down the long and rutted drive.

'The house is falling down around her and she has the audacity to hustle me out like a common pedlar all the while lying to me about her brat. Something kept her awake last night and I'll bet my teeth it wasn't the child.' Vincent had caught sight of the healthy-looking girl on the stairs, before the Scottish housekeeper had hustled her away.

'You think she's taken a lover?' Mr Adams asked.

'If she has, I want you to find out who it is. The secret most dangerous to a lady is the one a gentleman discovers and only threatens to reveal. If she won't marry me willingly, I'll force her to the church. I won't lose the opportunity to gain more influence in London or to expand my docks.'

With the deadline for repaying Mr Devlin fast approaching, the loss of the pirate's silver and the cargo from the schooner was a devastating blow. If he controlled Belle View, he could use a large amount of its land as collateral while keeping control of the wharf. He could raise the mooring prices and encourage more traffic. The main house could be rented out to a wealthy family, perhaps one new to Virginia, a second son of an English nobleman and his wife who could provide more connections to Parliament for Vincent to exploit. Lady Shepherd was very much mistaken if she thought she could put him off.

'I want to know if Captain Rose is dead, and the location of the *Casa de Oro*. Captain Dehesa can't be allowed to get away with this or it'll embolden others. I also want you to visit Mr Ross. I have another commission for him.'

By the time Vincent was through, Captain Rose would be dead and Lady Shepherd and Belle View would be his.

Faint footsteps on the front porch jerked Richard from a light sleep, sending a jolt of pain tearing through his left shoulder. He gritted his teeth until it passed, keeping an ear open for the sound outside again. This time it was the creak of the iron lock and the cautious turning of the door handle. He carefully reached over and took up the blunderbuss, cocked the hammer and pointed it at the door. He didn't blow out the candle flickering on the table beside him, not wanting to alert whoever was on the other side that he was awake. He should have put it out before he'd fallen asleep and maintained the illusion that the cabin was deserted. He hadn't planned on drifting off or sleeping after sunset, but the rum he'd drunk to ease the pain in his shoulder had made him sleepy.

The door finally swung open and Cassandra jerked to a halt in the doorway, her eyes flicking to the loaded weapon pointed at her. 'It's only me.'

The basket on her arm swung as she fought against a gust of wind to push the door closed. It made the light from the candle dance over the smooth planes of her brow and the fullness of her cheeks. She wore a plain, brown-cotton dress devoid of the fine embroidery, flourishes and the wide hips of her gown last night. Her hair was done up in a simple twist of pins and curls instead of an elaborate coiffure. She was more beautiful like this, reminding him of when she used to meet him in the fields for walks, her eyes wide and bright with anticipation for him.

Richard lowered the pistol, his heart racing. He'd become so accustomed to jumping at shadows, he'd nearly shot her. It sickened him to imagine it and he carefully set the weapon back on the table. 'I'm glad to see you.'

He'd spent the day holed up in this cabin with his thoughts, passing in and out of sleep and wicked dreams of her, his family and revenge. A sense of loss he hadn't experienced since the day he'd received Walter's letter informing him of his father's passing had gripped him during this last brief period of sleep and he'd awakened to the ringing loneliness of the sea.

'I'm sorry I didn't come earlier, but I couldn't get

away.' She set the basket down beside the candle, removed cold meat and cheese and set them on the table. 'A few farmers came to me to complain that the cows are in the fields and the fence needs to be mended so they don't eat the wheat. Once they were gone it was two captains from the dock wanting to barter flour and apples for the mooring fee. I would have refused them, but I'm in as much need of food as I am their coin.'

Richard smiled at her while she spoke in quick words, joy and pride in the daily work she did at Belle View evident beneath her complaints.

She stopped in her unpacking, one hand on her hip in feigned indignation, the old Cas from five years ago strong in the gesture. 'Do my concerns amuse you?'

'No, it's simply been a long time since I've thought of all the details necessary to running a plantation.'

'There's no end to them. I could amuse you for hours if you'd like.' She removed two apples and set them beside the plate. One rolled towards the edge and Richard caught it with his good hand.

'Please, I enjoy listening to it.'

'I had to wait until the house was asleep before I could even come here. As it is, I barely missed being seen by one of the field hands who was returning from Williamsburg. I didn't expect anyone to be out this late at night or to take the path close to here.'

'What time is it?' He bit into the apple, sighing at the fresh sweet taste of it.

'Past ten o'clock.' The thunder that had been

growing steadily louder for the last hour boomed over the cabin, announcing the coming storm.

She handed him a small loaf of bread from the basket. Richard's stomach growled at the earthy scent of it and he bit off a hunk, savouring the warm chewiness. 'I haven't enjoyed fresh bread in months. It's usually hard tack taken from Virginia Trading Company ships, hardly fit for rats much less men. Vincent doesn't waste money on supplies for his sailors. He thinks it's cheaper to replace a worn-out and scurvyriddled crew than to provide better food. He's always underestimated the importance of garnering the loyalty of those in his care.' It was a lesson Richard had grasped and why his men continued to follow him, even when he fell short.

'Speaking of Mr Fitzwilliam…' She took out a roll of bandages, fumbling with the tightly wound cloth with ill-concealed unease, and Richard paused in eating his meal. 'He knows about your encounter with the schooner and you being injured.'

The bread turned to dust on his mouth. 'How do you know?'

She lifted a bottle of wine from the basket and set it beside the food, flicking at a loose piece of cork with her fingernail. 'He came to see me this morning to tell me.'

The anger that had slammed into him the moment he'd learned of Vincent's betrayal struck him again. He tossed the bread on the table, the charm of this little scene gone. 'You know what kind of man Vincent is and what he's done and still you cavort with him?'

'I've done all I can to discourage his acquaintance, but my place in society here is tenuous and I can't have him undermining it. I have no choice but to be cordial and hide my disgust no matter what he says or asks of me.'

Richard gripped the coverlet, the rough cotton catching on the calluses of his palm. 'What has he asked of you?'

She trilled her fingers on the wine bottle and his stomach tightened, as reluctant to hear her answer as she was to give it. 'To marry him.'

Richard swung his feet off the bed and sat up. He focused on the blunderbuss on the side table as the room swam around him. He wondered when he'd have to use it to kill a soldier once she turned on him just like everyone had when he'd been accused of piracy. 'Tell me, how long until you send the Governor's men for me?'

She drew back at his harsh words. 'You accuse me of betraying you, after what I've risked to help you?'

'Yes, when you care so much for society's opinion you're willing to court it on Vincent's arm or in Lord Shepherd's bed,' he hissed through clenched teeth, surprised by the intensity of his jealousy. He shouldn't attack her. It wasn't her fault she'd continued to live after he'd pretended to die, but the anguish and rage of having lost her to another man, of Vincent courting her in the open while he remained confined to the shadows, tore at him.

'How dare you of all men judge me!' She stepped up hard on him, hands tight at her sides. 'Unlike you, who openly flaunts rules and laws, I have to live under them as best I can. If everyone turns on me because I insult Mr Fitzwilliam, I might not be able to sell my crops. Without an income I'll lose Belle View and there's nowhere left for me to go. Yes, I married Giles because I thought I could prove to everyone I wasn't the poor orphan they'd shunned, but a lady worthy of station and attention. But in every decision I've made to reach for more, I've been brought even lower than before. Sneer at me all you like, but I work for Belle View to give me and Dinah safety and security, and if I could do it without people like the Bakers and Mr Fitzwilliam, I would. But I need them for my survival more than I need you.'

A flash of lightning lit up the room, and regret shook Richard as hard as the thunder did the cabin walls. Like him, she'd been trapped by her choices and was doing her best to survive in the world as it had become. He respected her resolve and hated being the one forcing her to test it again and again. He longed to slip his hands along the sides of her delicate jaw and draw her mouth to his, to savour her with the same freedom he'd enjoyed when they were young and offer some comfort with his kiss. He couldn't because he was the cause of all her discomfort. 'I'm sorry, Cas.'

'Apologies aren't enough. As soon as you're well you can go. Mr Fitzwilliam knows you were wounded. It won't be long until he discovers you're here.'

She moved to leave, but he caught her hand. She

whirled around, as stunned as him by the meeting of their flesh. Outside, lightning flashed and thunder rolled across the sky before the rain began to pound on the cabin roof. 'Cassandra, wait.'

'Why? You accuse me of betraying you, but you're the one who abandoned me to run after your revenge.' Cassandra drew herself up with an impressive dignity he admired, but it couldn't hide the anguish marring her face. 'Do you know what it was like when Uncle Walter told me you were gone? I could barely rise from my bed to face each morning.'

'If there was a way I could undo it all I would, Cas, but there isn't.'

'Yes, there is.' She closed her eyes, and he expected her to pull out of his grasp and leave him and his betrayal behind as she had every right to do. She didn't, but opened her eyes and stood before him, the resilient, determined woman he should have appreciated and cherished more than his desire for adventure. 'Lord Spotswood is offering any man who asks for it the King's Grace. You could accept it, give up your pirate life and then we would both be safe.'

Cassandra held her breath while she waited for him to answer. The memory of him standing with her under the dogwood tree in Uncle Walter's Williamsburg garden, his hands on hers, anticipation thick between them while she waited for his marriage proposal, rushed back to her. Those words had changed her future as much as the ones he'd uttered a few months later about going to sea. How he answered her tonight could change everything again. The faint hope he'd summoned up in her with his kiss on the *Devil's Rose* welled in her again. If he sought the King's Grace, he might return to Williamsburg and they'd be free to court and fall in love again, and she'd finally have someone to help her at Belle View and ease all of her burdens.

Then his gaze slid away from hers as it had when they'd first met on the *Winter Gale*. Her heart dropped and she braced herself for the words she knew were going to come. 'I can't do that, Cas.'

'Why not?'

'Because of my men. I vowed to clear all our names in return for their loyalty. I can't abandon them to save myself.'

'If you all sought pardons, you could still see justice against Vincent done, except with the law *on* your side instead of against you. Surely you've earned enough from piracy to buy or establish a shipping company and, with your knowledge of the sea, you could destroy Vincent by taking his business.'

'It isn't only his business I have to cripple. It's him. I want his secrets exposed so everyone can see the real man behind the respectable façade, especially when he hangs.' The vengeance illuminating his eyes sent a chill tearing through her. 'I have to destroy Vincent completely.'

'Even if it means destroying yourself and me?'

'I never wanted you to be a part of this.' With his thumb, he caressed the delicate skin of her wrist, the subtle motion heady and distracting.

'Then why did you send me the pistol?'

'I didn't send it. Mr Rush did.' The fire in his eyes faded to resignation. 'If I'd known what he was up to, I wouldn't have allowed it. I'd intended to return it to you and release you from the bargain. Like all the other things I've sworn to do for you, I never got the chance.'

He let out a long breath of exhaustion, the impossibility of their situation weighing on him as heavily as it did her. He hadn't called on her as she'd believed and it stung her heart, but she didn't pull away. The rawness of his pain, and his willingness to have let her go despite his desire to ruin Vincent, and the way he continued to hold her hand, his fingertips gentle against her skin, revealed more than any summons ever could. He did care for her, deep enough to have almost sacrificed his papers for her safety. What might she be willing to sacrifice to have him at her side?

She turned her hand over in his, her fingertips pressing into the inside of his wrist. He'd been right to accuse her of wanting society too much because she did. If he returned, a pardon wouldn't erase his past and, if they courted, people would viciously whisper about them. It shamed her to be so petty, but having lived so long as an outcast and with Dinah's future to consider, she couldn't ignore the possibility of it happening again.

With her thumb, she traced an old scar on the back of his hand, her weaknesses not killing the encouraging words dancing on the tip of her tongue, eager to be spoken. It tore at her to see what his chosen life had done to him. Like Uncle Walter, she wanted to save him from ruin because she knew what it was like to be trapped by past decisions. Death had freed her from her mistake. The pardon could free him from his.

'You do have a chance,' she said at last.

He opened his eyes and looked at her as he had the day he'd told her the wedding would have to wait because he was going to sea. 'The pardon may seem like the perfect solution, but it isn't. I know Vincent's secret and the lengths he's already gone to in order to shield himself and his business from having it revealed. If I came back to Virginia, I'd spend every day watching and waiting for one of his men to slip a knife between my ribs during some dark night.'

'He wouldn't risk the gallows.'

'He's done far worse and you wouldn't be any safer with me pardoned than you are now. Our past guarantees he'll suspect you, too, and he'll do everything he can to ruin you the same way he ruined me. Like you, every decision I've made, even the innocent ones, have brought us to this impasse and there's no way out of it except through Vincent's demise. Like you, I have no choice but to do what I must to survive.'

She tightened her grip on him. 'No, I don't accept that, or the idea that everything we do and are will always be shaped by what we did in the past. Yes, we've made mistakes, but I'm tired of being haunted by them. I want to know that there's more to my future than misery, hardship and loneliness, and deep down, I think you do, too.'

Richard stiffened when she reached up and laid her hands on either side of his face, her touch delicate and at the same time potent with its intensity. It fuelled the fire rising inside him that had tortured him during the last month without her and in the hours of semi-sleep today when he'd dreamed she was lying beside him again. Richard's fingers tingled with the desire to trace the curve of her bare shoulder above her dress, but he kept them at his sides, afraid one touch might be his undoing. It wasn't right to dally with her heart after he'd made it clear he couldn't come home and yet she was the one touching him, urging him to defy his belief that his future held nothing because of his past and to give in to her beauty and the tranquillity of her presence.

It was difficult to resist and with each flutter of her pulse against his skin he felt himself weakening. Like him, she knew what it was to be deceived by the people closest to her and how it could ruin everything. He'd accused her of not honouring their love, but he was the one who'd lied about his death and left her to face the world without him or the hope of their life together. He was as bad as the others who'd abandoned her and he was about to do it again. He must.

He didn't step away and she remained before him, her skin warm against his, each long breath making her breasts rise and fall above her bodice, torturing him with her willingness to remain with him. He wanted her to hate him. It would make their separation easier and spare her from the anguish tearing at him. It wasn't hate illuminating her eyes, but the determination to make him fight for a different life than the bleak one dominating him, but it wasn't possible. The calm in her gentle touch was an illusion, like a water creature spied on the horizon, yet a part of him he'd thought long dead urged him to believe in it, to surrender to her and the possibility that there might be something more for him than revenge and the sea. 'I don't have a future. Can't you see that?'

'No, I can't and I don't believe it.' She drew his head down, touching her forehead to his, her breath teasing the sweaty skin in the V of his shirt. 'Neither do you.'

He raised his hands to her waist and pressed his fingers into the soft fabric covering her skin, the curve of her against him as alluring as her words. He thought he'd conquered the old desire for her, but the hesitant slide of her hands over his chest, the brush of her dress against his bare waist brought it all back. His life had begun when he'd first seen her, just as it had ended when he'd had to lie to her about his death. He thought he'd lost everything, but he hadn't. He wasn't dead and she was no longer an illusion to torture him with what could have been, but here in his arms and free.

'No, I don't.' He crushed her against his bare chest, claiming her mouth with all the passion denied to them during their long separation. There was danger in wanting her, the possibility she might make him forget all his lust for revenge, but lost in her caress, he didn't care.

He ran one hand through the curls gracing the back of her neck beneath her coiffure, revelling in the silken locks sliding over his skin. With his fingers, he swept the line of her shoulder, the feel of her firm skin beneath his like reaching back into his past and touching the man he'd once been and the woman he'd loved and lost. He buried his face in the curls escaping from the pins he drew out and dropped to the floor one by one, then laid a path of feathery kisses along the line of her neck, groaning at the soft moans his touch drew from her. With his good hand, he caressed the curve of her hips through her thin dress, unashamed to reveal his need for her when he claimed her mouth again.

Her delicious lips parted at the tender urging of his tongue, and her hand grasped his good arm, her rounded fingernails digging slightly into his flesh with restrained need. All his dreams had foundered, but at this moment he seized this one like he did every prize at sea. In her guiding kiss, he might finally find his way back to her and to himself.

Cassandra slid her hands under the dark hair along Richard's collar and around his neck, clinging to him the way she had the morning years ago in Yorktown when they'd said goodbye. It'd been too long since she'd been loved and wanted, and she revelled in the pleasure of Richard's arms around her, his mouth urgent in his demands, the heat of his body against hers. Tonight, she'd surrender to her yearnings instead of her fears and bloom as she hadn't for the last five years.

With her fingers, she traced the sharp line of his shoulders, careful to avoid his wound before she brushed the bronze skin of his chest. Breaking from his lips, she leaned down to sweep the hollow between his neck and chest with her tongue. He tasted of her youth and innocence. In Richard's arms, it was as if there was nothing separating the evenings in the barn from tonight, not years of despair, worry and hopelessness. She revelled in the heaviness of his hand caressing the curve of her hips through her dress. His need for her was potent in the length of his kiss when he claimed her mouth again and the firmness of him against her stomach. Eager to be closer to him, she took hold of the strings of her bodice and tugged them free of the eyelets. When the dress fell open, she cast her arms back to allow the cotton to fall free.

He watched with eyes as hot as the air while she shimmied out of the petticoat and let it drop around her feet. She undid the laces of her stays, sliding the ties free one by one until the creamy fabric dropped to the floor and she stood in front of him in nothing but her chemise. Catching it by the sides, she drew it up over her head and tossed it to the floor.

'Not even the ocean after a storm is as beautiful as you.' He raked her naked flesh with a hungry, wanting gaze and she didn't cover herself, the strength of his need increasing hers. Then he reached out and cupped one firm breast in his hand and circled the delicate tip with his thumb. She gasped when he leaned down and flicked the sensitive skin with his tongue. She wrapped her hands in his dark hair as he continued to tease her with his tongue, moving to her other breast and making circles around her nipple. He swept his fingers across her stomach before tasting her bare thighs above her plain stockings held up by thin blue ribbons. Under his caresses, her body continued to come alive, responsive and beautiful for the first time in ages. The memory of his body against hers had warmed so many cold nights in London, but Richard was here with her once more, as real as the storm engulfing the countryside.

With his fingers, he stroked the length of her thighs, working closer and closer in agonising circles to her centre. She arched her back in pleasure as he caressed her softness, driving her further beyond her senses and increasing her need to feel the full strength of him. He might be a pirate, but he was a man in charge of his destiny and she wanted to surrender to his heady allure. She held on tight to him, the silken pressure of his touch driving her to the edge of pleasure and she struggled to breathe, willing to follow him over the crest of this wave, but he withdrew.

Before she could protest, he wrapped his good arm around her waist and, pressing her hard against him, he swung them both around and to the bed.

She trembled as he slowly eased her down on to the mattress, the ropes beneath it creaking under their weight. They would be one again, as if they'd never been apart.

He supported himself with his good arm, his body covering hers like a fine coverlet. She traced the arch of his back and shoulders, careful to avoid his wound, not wanting to hurt him in the midst of their delight. Then he shifted off to one side to lie on his back and pulled her on top of him. She pressed her hands into his chest and sat up, smiling wickedly while she straddled him. Gone was the boy who'd first taken her innocence. Here was the man he'd become, powerful even in his illness, with a fierceness to steal her breath away. Sitting over him, she took in the contours of his chest and stomach to where his hips narrowed beneath the dark fabric of his breeches. She wanted nothing to come between them, not his past or hers or their uncertain future.

Sliding back over his legs, she undid the fall of his breeches and uncovered the sharp white line where his sun-darkened skin ended beneath the buckskin. She shimmied the sturdy fabric down over his hips, marvelling at the firmness of him, eager to join with him. She covered his body with hers while his wide hands caressed her back, following the line of it to her buttocks, his touch making her burn deeper for him.

'I've wanted you for so long,' she whispered in his ear, taking the lobe between her teeth.

'You have me tonight.'

She shifted back and settled over his solid manhood, her heart as filled as her body when he entered her. With his firmness inside her, his hand heavy on her waist, the disappointments and troubles they'd endured fell away. They were one, with nothing separating them.

He moved slowly at first, teasing her with long, lingering strokes until she thought she might faint from pleasure. She stretched out over him, his breath in her ear, his hands firm on her buttocks as they moved together, faster and faster until they cried out in pleasure together, a wave of ecstasy unlike any she'd ever experienced before spreading through her. She clung to him, drawing in deep and heavy breaths until quiet settled over them and the cabin.

She shifted to lie beside him as the faint tap of the rain on the roof replaced the pounding of her heart in her ears. In the semi-darkness, the world and all its demands were staved off, if only for tonight. She rose up on her elbow to study him. He ran his finger over the line of her chin, smiling at her not like a rogue, but like the man she adored.

'You're beautiful, Cas, you always have been.'

'Careful, you'll swell my head with your flattery.'

'Impossible, not even a title made you vain.'

She rested her head on his chest. 'My title has made me wise, more so than I ever wanted to be.'

He slipped his hands beneath her chin and turned her face to his. 'Had I known what kind of man Giles was, I would have risked the Royal Navy to sail up the Thames and killed him for making you miserable. I would have taken on all of London society as your champion until they saw the wonderful woman I see before me, the brave one who never allows anything to destroy her, but continues to struggle despite the actions of selfish and foolish men, including me.'

Tears filled her eyes. 'I never stopped loving you, Richard, not in London, not when you sailed away from the *Winter Gale*, not now.'

He tucked a strand of hair behind her ear and cupped her cheek with his palm, his eyes turning as stormy as the night. 'I fear the man you loved is gone.'

'No, he's still here.' She pressed a kiss to his lips, silencing further protests. He hadn't needed to speak the word for her to understand he still loved her as much as she did him. It offered a sense of hope she hadn't experienced since before England, and before Yorktown, the kind which had marked every evening in the barn when they'd lain together planning their future. The loneliness marring her life for so long was loosening its tight grip. Together, she and Richard would find a way to overcome his troubles and hers. She wouldn't allow him to push her away or to make her believe it wasn't possible for them to be together. It was, she only needed to find a way and she would. As his hands gripped her buttocks, the passion rising between them again, her confidence in their future increased. If the threat of Mr Fitzwilliam was what kept Richard a brigand, then she'd do all she could to make sure they were free of the odious man. If evidence was what Richard needed to ruin Vincent and pursue a pardon, then she would make sure he had it. He would stay here with her and they'd be happy. She wouldn't accept anything else.

The plink of rain slowed until the water dripping off the eaves of the porch was all that remained of the storm. Richard stared up at the rough timber ceiling, cradling Cas, who slept soundly beside him, her breath steady and light against his naked chest.

Her hand rested on his stomach, and he covered it with his, the solid metal of her wedding band beneath his fingertips a harsh reminder of everything he'd forgotten in her arms. It would be morning soon and she'd be forced to leave him for the world that governed her during the day, the one that no longer held any sway over him.

He stared at the rough wood of the ceiling timbers so much like those of his cabin aboard ship. She'd asked him to surrender to the bonds of civilisation, to give up his outlaw life aboard the *Devil's Rose* and walk with his head held high along the streets of Williamsburg, master of Belle View and a proper gentleman. It would mean meeting Vincent's smug smile and not putting a bullet between his eyes without risking the hangman's noose.

*I'm already facing it.* He'd sailed for years in search of his revenge and gained nothing for his efforts except more bitterness and the deaths of good men. Vincent still held his place in society while Richard remained a brigand. He'd thought this truth all there was left to him, until Cas had revealed another path tonight, one he'd never considered before.

Richard stroked the silken skin on Cas's thigh, the temptation of her as powerful as his desire for Vincent's downfall. The pardon would change everything, but it wasn't strong enough to change his past and who he'd become. He slid out from beside Cas, careful not to wake her, and trod quietly over the floor and stepped outside.

Rain dripped from the branches and a breeze rustled through the trees beyond the clearing. The flutter of the leaves and the croak of frogs reminded him of the hot nights when he used to lie awake at Sutherland Place trying to envision his future. It'd all seemed so clear then, but he struggled to see it tonight. He could return and his ill-gotten wealth might be enough to make most people overlook his former deeds, but there'd be some who would never forget. He knew a good measure of their pasts was no more sparkling than his, but Cas would care. She would flinch when he insulted men like Mr Baker and Mr Chilton or their wives, either by accident or by necessity. There might come a day when she wished she'd left him to the sea and married a more respectable and honest man, assuming they both survived long enough to develop any more regrets.

*No, she will stay beside me.* Their time apart hadn't wrecked her love for him and neither would the snide remarks of society, but Captain Rose might. The man gripped him as strongly as the peace Richard had experienced in Cas's arms, and he doubted if he could ever truly be free of him.

Richard stared up at the dark Virginia sky. The stars between the breaks in the cloud reminded him of the many difficult nights when he'd struggled to navigate at sea. Tonight, the struggle inside him smacked of the tense weeks five years ago when Richard Davenport had wrestled with the decision to become Captain Rose. He hadn't realised how murky a path his decision to become a pirate would drag him down, and he wondered how dark the road back might be. If he returned to Virginia, there would be no crew to support him this time, no men to rally to his cause or the nicety of manners and the law to ignore. It would only be him and Cas against the ruin inside him, the one he must find a way to conquer.

He leaned hard on the rough-hewn railing of the porch, the prospect of admitting the failure of his decision five years ago to Cas and his crew daunting. However, in humbling himself, he would leave behind the terrified widows at sea, the damaged ships and sailors, and any reason for Cas to live in fear of his presence. He could finally free his men from the danger haunting them and make this fight against Vincent what it truly was—a quarrel between old friends, one he'd win on land as he never had at sea.

Richard gripped the rough railing tight, looking forward to the fight. He was no longer the naive son of a planter, but a man who'd killed to achieve his goals and with a stash of money to rival Lord Spotswood's wealth. If Vincent could buy power, government officials and influence, then so could he. He'd seek out Lord Spotswood and obtain a pardon for himself and his crew and re-establish himself in Virginia. He'd use the law and the darkness he rued to wreck Vincent and secure his future with Cas. Then, when it was all over, with Cas's help, he'd find his way back to being Richard Davenport and lay Captain Rose to rest for good.

Mr Adams stepped into the dark and smoky Raleigh Tavern. He inhaled the stench of dirty men and stale beer, his past exploits coming back to him in the thick miasma. Raucous laughter carried in from the adjoining game room, punctuated by the knock of thrown dice and the cheers of winning men. It brought a rare smile to his pockmarked face. Give him a common thief over a gentleman any day. They were more honest, but not as lucrative. Mr Fitzwilliam had financial difficulties, but he never failed to pay him. The pompous burgess would regret it if he ever did.

Across the room, a thick man with his stomach straining his ink-stained waistcoat sat hunched over his tankard, doing his best to stay in the shadow of the lantern overhead. At a table near him sat a thinner man whose pointed chin and the continual dart of his attention around the room gave him the look of a weasel. He fixed on Mr Adams, swallowing hard before he dove back into his tankard.

Mr Adams ignored the weasel and strode over to join the rotund man.

'Good evening, Mr Ross.' Mr Adams laid his walking stick on the table in front of him, then he sat down across from the printer. 'Do you have it?'

'I do.' Mr Ross drew a piece of folded paper out of his coat pocket and laid it on the table. 'One forged deed to property, in Mr Fitzwilliam's name, done as well as I did those shipping passes.'

Mr Adams examined the deed. 'Very fine work. My employer will be most satisfied.' He withdrew a sack of money and tossed it on the table between them.

'I have something else of interest to your employer. See the skinny man there?' He cocked one finger at the weasel. 'Name's Mr Barlow. Came in here blathering about being cooper on the *Devil's Rose* and how what he knows might be of use to someone. I quieted him down with a couple of tankards and told him I'd send you to him once we were done. Can't have him mucking things up, now can we?'

'No, we can't. Thank you, Mr Ross, for being so conscientious where our employer's interests are concerned.' Mr Adams tucked the forged deed in the inner pocket of his coat, took up his walking stick and made for the weasel.

'Good evening, Mr Barlow. Mr Ross says you have information that might be of interest to me.' Mr Adams sat down across from the man, determined to pin him down before he scurried off and caused trouble.

'And who are you I should be tellin' it to?' the

weasel hissed, drawing his tankard closer as though the flimsy pewter would protect him.

'The servant of a man who'll pay for good information about Captain Rose.' He slipped two sovereigns from his coat pocket and held them up. This was the first crew member from the *Devil's Rose* that Mr Adams had ever met who'd turned on his Captain. Captain Rose was a man who inspired a great deal of loyalty, much to Mr Adams's consternation.

Mr Barlow snatched the coins away from him, smiling at the way they clinked together in his hand. 'The bastard. Thinks he's too high and mighty to share prizes like a captain should. Wears a mask so you can't see his face, but I saw him without it once.'

'What did he look like?'

'Tall with dark hair and blue eyes, and a scar on his left cheek, near his eye, one I hadn't seen before because it was hidden by the mask.'

Mr Adams leaned back in his chair and wrapped his hand around the head of his walking stick. 'I understand Captain Rose was injured recently. Do you know if he's alive or dead?'

'Can't say nothin' about that. Left the ship in Nassau, but I once heard the first mate tell the boatswain the owner of the Virginia Trading Company would hang if they ever found the right papers on one of his ships. He being here in Williamsburg, and such an upstanding gentleman, I thought he might like to know what's being said against him.'

'You were smart to come here. My carriage is just

outside. I'd like to convey you to my solicitor's office to get a sworn statement about Captain Rose's piracy and his identity.'

'And find myself dangling from the end of a rope? No, thank you.'

'My employer is a man of great influence who'll see to it you receive a pardon in exchange for your testimony. I assure you, it is quite safe and lucrative.' He held up another shiny sovereign. Mr Barlow reached for it, but Mr Adams yanked it back. 'You must come with me to reap the benefits of assisting us.'

Despite the greed illuminating the weasel's eyes, he lowered his thin brows in suspicion. Then, deciding to take the risk, he finished his tankard with a belch. 'All right.'

Mr Adams took up his walking stick and led Mr Barlow outside into the wet and humid night. They walked around to the back of the tavern, away from the faint glow of the blacksmith's forge to an empty field dotted with trees a short distance away. Mr Adams's black carriage stood beneath the gnarled branches of a spreading oak. Two men leaned against the black lacquered sides, tricorns pulled down low over their faces. They pushed up straight when Mr Adams approached with his companion.

'Have you told anyone else what you've told me?' Mr Adams swung his walking stick between them in time to his gait.

'No.' Mr Barlow danced around a large puddle. 'Didn't want anyone profiting from what I knows.'

'Good.' Mr Adams swung his walking stick and brought it down on Mr Barlow's head with a crack. The weasel slumped into the mud. The two men rushed over and caught him under the arms and dragged him into the carriage. Mr Adams stepped in behind them, closed the door and the carriage sped away, leaving not a shred of evidence in the still night.

## Chapter Eight

Cassandra stirred sugar into her lemon water with the delicate silver spoon. The clink of the metal on the crystal glass filled Mr Fitzwilliam's sumptuous Butler Place sitting room and drew tighter the anxiety already making her stomacher snug. She wore a yellow dress with silver embroidery along the bodice and white lace at the bust line. Flowers embroidered in the same silver thread decorated the skirt, the generous hips of which, supported by the panniers Jane had repaired, extended out over the small chair she perched on. She'd worn the dress, despite the heat, in the hope of appearing to Mr Fitzwilliam like any other fashionable lady, one who thought of little else except her *toilette* and the latest fashion, even if both were the furthest things from her mind today.

She'd left the cabin before Richard had risen this morning, making it easier to hide from him her plans for today and to keep him from trying to stop her.

She flicked a glance at the double doors off to her

left, which were slightly ajar, and what appeared to be an office just beyond them. She wasn't sure how she would slip in there without Mr Fitzwilliam noticing her or what she'd find if she managed it. She was silly to even consider sneaking in there, but after last night, the possibility that she could do something to bring Richard home urged her on. He still loved her, as much as she loved him, and she would be happy at last, with a companion to help her though her troubles. The past would lose its hold on her and she would claim a future with Richard.

Mr Fitzwilliam sat across the burled-rosewood tea table from her, his glass untouched, a lemon slice floating at the top. He had been solicitous enough since her arrival, but there was an edge to him today that added to hers, as if he were nervous about something. She wondered if he suspected her, then dismissed the idea. His opinion of ladies was too low and his imagination too blunted for him to consider what she was really up to by paying a call on him today.

'Am I to hope your unexpected visit is to give me an answer to my suit?' he asked.

Cassandra stopped stirring her lemon water and stared at the pips settling on the bottom of the crystal glass. She suddenly regretted her boldness for more reasons than the recklessness of trying to steal personal papers from an influential burgess on behalf of a notorious pirate. Not only was she about to become a thief, but she must irritate Mr Fitzwilliam by disappointing his ridiculous aspirations to be her

husband. If what she found wasn't enough to help
Richard, or if he still refused the pardon, making
an enemy of Mr Fitzwilliam would cost her dearly.
It went against everything she'd spent the last few
weeks trying to accomplish, but it had to be done.
She would not see Richard sail away from her again
and be left once more to fend off the difficulties of
life alone.

She set the lemon water down on the table between them and rested her hands in her lap, tilting
her head a touch to see him clearly from beneath the
curving brim of her wide hat. It would be a delicate
undertaking to refuse him without insulting him. The
most she could do was try to mitigate some of the
damage to both his ego and her position. She might
dislike him, but she needed access to him and his
house and more occasions to acquire evidence from
him if she was to help Richard. If she could convince
him that they could not marry because of a fault in
her and not him, it might satisfy his sizeable ego. 'I
thank you very much for your offer, Mr Fitzwilliam,
and I'm quite flattered by your proposal, but I'm still
in mourning for my late husband.'

She tilted her hand to display her wedding ring
and gazed on it with a tenderness to almost make her
choke. Giles might have done little for her in life except torment her, but she would use his death to her
advantage. He owed her at least this one small favour.

'And when you are finished mourning?' he asked
as if demanding from his groom when his horse

might be finished with its oats so he could get on with his morning ride.

'I don't know when that will be. Even when it is done, I don't think I will be inclined to marry. I don't ever want to endure the heartbreak of widowhood again.' She prayed she wouldn't be struck down for her lies. She'd enjoyed more happiness in her widowhood than she'd ever experienced with Giles.

'My offer isn't a matter of inclination, or sentiment, but a business proposal,' Mr Fitzwilliam clarified with a wave of his hand as though they were discussing the price of tobacco and not her entire future or the right to control her person and property. 'I'm sure you've discovered how difficult it is for an unattached woman to manage a place like Belle View. I'm offering you the protection of a husband, and to relieve you of the difficulties of running a large estate and everything it entails. Under my direction, it will be one of the most prosperous plantations in the colonies and you one of the most influential ladies.'

'While it is tempting to accept your kind offer to take care of me and increase my prestige…' she smiled sweetly at him, trying not to gag on her words or how he spoke as if their marriage was already decided. No wonder a man like him thought nothing of owning slaves. He believed he possessed some natural right to command and rule over others, including her '…as I said before, I have no intention of entering into a partnership of any sort at present.'

She offered a small shrug, more to shift the bead

of perspiration sliding down the centre of her back than to emphasise the solidity of her stance, at least where he was concerned. She'd gladly accompany Richard up the church aisle if they could find a way to keep him safely in Virginia. Assuming he accepted the pardon. She twisted the wedding band on her finger, hoping he hadn't taken advantage of her absence to return to his ship. *No, he isn't so deceitful.*

Mr Fitzwilliam sat back in his chair, a curl of disgust marring the thin line of his lips. 'So you're content to allow Belle View to moulder under bad management?'

She tightened her one hand so hard, her fingernails bit in to her palm while she kept everything else about her simpering and innocent. 'In time, I'll develop the dock myself.'

'You?' An unattractive red spread up his neck, hinting at her failure to rebuke him without creating too much ill will. 'What do you know about business?'

She sat up straighter, careful to keep her sweet smile despite wanting to rage at him for daring to judge her and her capabilities. 'My parents taught me how to manage Belle View.'

'Your parents ran it into the ground, just like your uncle.'

She dropped her smile, unwilling to play the empty-headed widow any longer and not caring how he regarded her in society. She would not tolerate his insults to sell a few hogsheads of tobacco and, if he spoke ill against her, she'd find another way to survive without his influence. 'You forget yourself, sir.'

'As do you, Lady Shepherd.' His unblinking eyes hardened like Giles's had when she'd refused to consent to the divorce and it made her stiffen with fear. This man was as unaccustomed to being refused as her late husband had been and he'd be just as vicious because of it. 'Think of your daughter and what will happen to her if you fail in your efforts to restore Belle View, which you will.'

'Don't you dare threaten me or Dinah.' She'd faced down her husband and all of London society to defend herself and Dinah. She wouldn't shrink from fighting this puffed-up colonial. Let him threaten her. She wouldn't crumple or cower beneath them any more than she had under Giles.

'It isn't a threat, but a reminder of your uncertain place in Virginia,' he hissed, and Cassandra caught the shadow of the man Richard had warned her about. Richard was right. Even if he came home, they wouldn't be safe until Mr Fitzwilliam was arrested. It added new urgency to her desire to find a way to slip through those double doors and see what was hidden behind them. How she would do it, she had no idea, for Mr Fitzwilliam wasn't about to leave her alone. With him looking at her like some fever-infested bit of swamp land, she doubted she'd ever be welcome in this house again.

He opened his mouth to say more when the sound of Mr Adams clearing his throat stopped him.

'Mr Devlin and his son are here to see you,' he announced from the doorway. Cassandra couldn't say how long he'd been there for he'd entered as quietly as an owl at night. 'They're in the library.'

Mr Fitzwilliam's anger shifted to near horror and the red in his cheeks drained away. He stood, his knee hitting the tea table and threatening to upend it, the crystal pitcher and glasses on top before he caught the edge and steadied it. 'If you'll excuse me, Lady Shepherd. I will return shortly.'

Cassandra, clasping her glass to keep it from spilling, wondered what about Mr Devlin's arrival troubled Mr Fitzwilliam more than Cassandra's refusal of his suit. Perhaps they were involved with his illegal trade and she should find a way to eavesdrop on their conversation, but with Mr Fitzwilliam gone, this might be her only chance to slip into his office.

'What the hell is he doing here?' Mr Fitzwilliam demanded as he marched out of the room, his words trailing him down the hall after Mr Adams.

She didn't hear his assistant's answer, but a moment later Mr Fitzwilliam's loud greeting to Mr Devlin, followed by the closing of the library door, told Cassandra it was safe to rise.

She hurried into the adjoining office, sliding the doors open wide enough for her and her dress to slip through and, if need be, for her to make a hasty retreat back to the sitting room. She crossed to the desk positioned a few feet away from the far wall. A portrait of a young man dressed in a much older fashion and with a severe expression hung near the window across from it, lacking the netting covering the other paintings. Cassandra ignored it and sifted through the correspondence, contracts, letters and ledgers arranged in neat stacks on top of the desk. With shaking hands, she searched for any evidence Richard could use against Mr Fitzwilliam. Nothing important or incendiary stood out, and she cursed the ridiculous idea. Of course Mr Fitzwilliam wouldn't leave anything incriminating lying about, but she couldn't give up. Her future, Richard's and even Dinah's depended on her finding something.

She tried the centre desk drawer, but it was locked. Then she noticed a piece of paper lying on the floor between the desk leg and the wall where it must have fallen. She plucked it up and read the handwritten letter from a Mr Powell, a gentleman in North Carolina concerning the receipt of a large quantity of Spanish silver in exchange for rum and other shipping supplies. Rum wasn't one of the commodities the Virginia Trading Company was known to deal in, but she knew from things she'd read how pirates had a special taste for the drink. It meant only one thing. This must have something to do with his illicit trades. It didn't seem like enough to help Richard, but it might be a start. Richard could find a way to speak to the gentleman from North Carolina and perhaps gather more evidence.

'Lady Shepherd, I didn't hear you arrive.' A lady's smooth voice cut through the quiet.

Cassandra dropped the paper and whirled around. She caught the edge of the desk with her hand to brace herself and her nerves. Miss Fitzwilliam stood in the doorway, regarding Cassandra with a face as blank as a Venetian mask. She was pretty but not stunning, although with a little more maturity she soon would be. Her cheeks held the fullness of her brother's, but her chin was narrower, her nose more defined and her hair much blonder and done up in large curls set tight to the back of her head. She wore a light blue silk brocade dress that highlighted her eyes. It was embroidered with roses and Cassandra marvelled at how, with such stiff fabric, the young lady had been able to sneak up on her.

Cassandra laced her fingers together in front of her, doing her best to regain her composure and offer no sign of guilt. 'Your brother and I were enjoying refreshments.'

Miss Fitzwilliam approached with the stealth of a cat in need of a bell, and Cassandra wondered if the young lady practised walking so as not to make a sound. 'I believe refreshments are served in the adjoining sitting room.'

'Your brother left me to attend to some business. I saw the portrait and wished to examine it.' Cassandra stepped around her and made for the staid painted face of the man hanging on the wall beside the window. He had Mr Fitzwilliam's nose and the same intense and haughty expression in his eyes she'd come to loathe in the man.

Miss Fitzwilliam didn't follow, but swept around the desk and picked up the paper Cassandra had dropped. She read it, then slid a sly glance at Cassandra. 'You have an interest in my brother's affairs?'

'He spoke to me of investing in his company,' she lied, wondering how soon it would be before Miss Fitzwilliam called for her brother to inform him she'd caught Cassandra rifling through his private papers. Cassandra had no plausible excuses to talk herself out of this muddle and cursed again her boldness. She should have known better than to come here and risk even more ruin by continuing to help Richard. 'I wanted to assure myself of its suitability.'

'By searching his private papers?'

'I've heard rumours about the company.'

'I don't doubt you have.' Miss Fitzwilliam laid the paper on the desk, then joined Cassandra before the portrait. 'This was my father. I'm sure you've heard the rumours about him, too.'

'I have.' It was the single truth she could offer the young lady. The elder Mr Fitzwilliam's suicide had been the talk of Williamsburg the summer it had happened.

'The stories are nothing compared to the truth. He was a cruel monster who delighted in threatening to cast out my mother and separate us if she didn't give in to every one of his drunken commands. She used to cry to me after he'd scream and slap her because his dinner was cold or some other trivial matter on the nights he was here. Thankfully, given his taste for dice and drinks, they were far less than they could have been. When he wasn't at the Raleigh Tavern squandering their money, she did all she could to protect me from his fists and his jeers, but she wasn't a strong woman and, in the end, he wore her down. I used to pray the drink would kill him and I was glad when my prayers were finally answered, I only wish they'd been in time to help my mother.' She brushed at her eye, and Cassandra felt for the girl. This was how it'd been with Giles. 'I'm sure you must think me wicked for saying such things.'

'Not at all. My husband used to threaten to take my daughter away from me and I privately rejoiced, too, when he took all his threats with him to the grave. Like you, I wish it could have happened sooner and spared my daughter and me a great deal of anguish.'

'With the exception of his temperance, my brother is no better than my father.' Miss Fitzwilliam's stoic masked slipped, and Cassandra saw the frightened young woman living beneath a stern father and now a heartless brother. It reminded her of herself in London and the lonely desperation that had nearly smothered her. She yearned to help Miss Fitzwilliam the way she'd longed for someone to help her.

Cassandra took Miss Fitzwilliam's hand and gave it a firm squeeze. 'If you ever need anything, please come to me. I understand what it is to be in your position and how isolated it can make you feel, but you must know you aren't alone. You have a friend who will assist you if you need it.'

Miss Fitzwilliam covered Cassandra's hand with hers, tears shimmering in the corners of her blue eyes. 'Thank you, Lady Shepherd. You have no idea how much that means to me.'

'Yes, I do.'

The thud of Mr Fitzwilliam's footsteps echoed in the sitting room behind them, forcing the women apart. Together they turned to face the door when he stormed into the room, each of them putting on a mask of innocence at his arrival.

'What are you two doing in here?' Mr Fitzwilliam demanded, his cheeks as red as when she'd refused to marry him. It made her realise how right she'd been to search in here. It was clear there were things in this room he was worried about others finding. 'This is my private office and you were not invited.'

As oppressive silence filled the room while Mr Fitzwilliam studied both ladies, reserving a more wicked scrutiny for his sister. Miss Fitzwilliam didn't back down under her brother's hard stare, and Cassandra wondered how many rows between brother and sister had come from her refusing to be cowed by him. Mr Fitzwilliam had been livid when Cassandra had refused him, so she could well imagine how enraged his sister's defiance could make him, enough perhaps to lash out at her. She admired the girl's pluck for she'd done the same with Giles in the beginning. Over time, he'd worn her down. She hoped Miss Fitzwilliam would escape before her brother broke her spirit.

Cassandra faced the burgess, bracing herself for Mr Fitzwilliam's accusations and a possible outburst, but it was Miss Fitzwilliam who spoke first. 'I was showing Lady Shepherd Father's portrait. She saw it through the door and was curious.'

'I thought it in the style of Sir Peter Lely, King

Charles's court painter,' Cassandra added, thankful for the art instruction she'd received during all her salons in England. 'Is it?'

Mr Fitzwilliam glanced back and forth between them, seeming to waver between anger at having caught them in his office and pride in the painting. 'The portraits are by Sir Peter. My father had them painted when he and my mother were in England in the early days of their marriage in order to secure business for the Virginia Trading Company.'

'They are magnificent,' Cassandra complimented, eager to bolster his ego and distract him from any hint of the real reason why she was standing here. 'Do you have any other works by the masters?'

'Yes, the landscapes in the sitting room and the dining room.'

'May I see them?' Cassandra prodded, in no hurry to resume any conversation about marriage, but ready to escape the palpable tension between brother and sister. 'I've enjoyed so little fine art since returning home. It is one of the few things I miss about England.'

'Another time, perhaps. Unfortunately I must end our visit today to attend to other matters,' Mr Fitzwilliam answered tersely.

'Of course.' She was as eager to get away as he was to see her leave.

'Lady Shepherd, Miss Fitzwilliam will see you out. Good day.' He didn't reach for her hand, but bowed stiffly, then turned on one heel and left, much to Cassandra's relief.

Cassandra returned with Miss Fitzwilliam to the sitting room to gather up her fan and reticule, then walked with Miss Fitzwilliam to the front door and down the steps to her carriage. 'I appreciate your assistance with your brother.'

'It was my pleasure.' The light of conspiracy danced in her round eyes. 'I only hope you found what you were searching for.'

'I didn't, but I still thank you for your help and my offer remains.'

'Thank you. I may need your assistance sooner than either of us expects.' She nodded to the young man leaning against a wagon parked near the corner of the house. Behind him, men loaded crates and sacks of items brought out from inside. Given the metallic clink when the sacks were thrown in the wagon, Cassandra guessed they were filled with household goods and not the cargo off one of the ships moored at the dock. Perhaps it was more goods for another raid against pirates, another attempt to catch Richard.

'Who is he?' Cassandra asked, having never been introduced to the young man. He wore a dark blue frock coat with no embroidery, the stark white shirt beneath sharpening the angle of his chin and setting him apart from the burly and coarsely clad workmen. A tricorn shaded his light eyes, but there was no hiding his appreciative smirk, one reserved for Miss Fitzwilliam, not Cassandra.

'Mr Evander Devlin. He and his father have a large holding downriver, but they make more money with loans to other planters than they do growing tobacco.'

Suddenly, the activity between the house and the wagons made sense.

*Mr Fitzwilliam is in debt and his sister knows it.* Cassandra wondered who else suspected his financial troubles. It meant all Richard's strikes against the Virginia Trading Company were working. If he did come home, he could establish a rival company and ruin Vincent's business and him.

Mr Devlin straightened and touched his hat to Miss Fitzwilliam. She frowned at the gesture.

'Good day, Lady Shepherd.' Miss Fitzwilliam strode back into the house.

The driver opened the carriage door, and Cassandra paused to nod at Mr Devlin. He swept off his hat and offered her a regal bow in return. She climbed into the coach, wishing she could enjoy whatever hold the young man and his father had over Mr Fitzwilliam so she could use it to her and Richard's advantage.

The conveyance rocked into motion, and Cassandra tapped her fan against her palm. The visit hadn't garnered what she'd hoped, but at least she'd come away with a few small things to help Richard, a name in North Carolina and proof Mr Fitzwilliam was in debt.

'The vase isn't Vincent's to give you. It's mine.' Arabella clutched the full sides of her skirt and marched down the front steps and up to Mr Devlin.

Mr Devlin pushed his long, lean body off the side of the wagon where he'd been lounging and motioned for his man to hand him the silver, shell-shaped vase supported by four dolphins. The man did as instructed, then went back inside to collect more of Vincent's things. 'It's worth a great deal and will help keep the roof over your head and pretty dresses on your very enticing figure.'

His gaze covered the length of her, drawing up one corner of his rakish lips. He was a foot taller than her, his hair beneath his tricorn as deep a brown as the silt from the river. It emphasised the steel-grey eyes above his stately nose.

Arabella dropped the sides of her gown and scowled at the wretched and intriguing man. 'I'll sleep in a field in rags, surrounded by my things, before I part with so much as a soup spoon to help Vincent. That vase is the only thing of my mother's I have left. Vincent and my father sold off the rest.'

She'd been fascinated by the silver animals as a child, and her mother used to make up stories about them when she'd put Arabella to bed. Those happy days seemed like a lifetime ago. Losing her mother had been one of the most lonely and difficult times in Arabella's life. It'd been made worse by her father's callous treatment of her mother's effects and her memory.

Mr Devlin's eyes softened beneath the shadow of his tricorn. He reached into his coat and withdrew a pocket watch, clicked open the gold case and held it up to her. 'My mother gave me this before she died. It belonged to her father.'

'It's beautiful.' With its finely engraved swirls and the mother-of-pearl face, it was an elegant piece.

He pressed the case closed and tucked the watch back into his coat, then held out the vase to her. 'I apologise for the mistake. I suggest you keep this hidden.'

She took it, stunned at his understanding. In the past, she'd paid him little heed. Today his languid air and intense expression entranced her, along with his kindness. She hadn't expected it. 'Vincent is going to lose everything, isn't he?'

'Most likely.'

She gripped the vase against her chest. 'Then it appears I might soon be sleeping out of doors.'

'Surrounded by your things.'

Her lips twitched with a suppressed smile. 'You'll warn me before it happens so I might prepare?'

'I'll do better. I'll offer you a way to protect yourself and your assets.' He took off his hat, his sharp eyes piercing her. 'But it comes at a price a spirited lady like you may not wish to pay.'

She traced one dolphin head with her finger, interested and terrified by his words. 'What is it?'

'What are you doing here?' Lord Spotswood gripped the arms of his chair where he sat behind his desk in his office in the Governor's Palace. With the last of the daylight disappearing from the sky, darkness began to descend over the formal garden outside and made the lamp on the Governor's desk burn brighter.

'I've come to ask for the King's Grace.' Richard stepped out of the deep shadow between the tall secretary and the wall where he'd been hiding, waiting for the Governor to arrive. His hands dangled at his sides, away from his blunderbuss, but close enough to seize it if he needed it. Outside the office door, the heavy footsteps of the guard passed before fading off towards the back of the palace.

'Whom do I have the pleasure of entertaining tonight?' Lord Spotswood asked, resting one hand on the hilt of his sword. It wasn't an idle threat. The man who'd fought at the Battle of Blenheim and led an expedition up the Rappahannock River was no dandy, but a skilled soldier capable of defending himself.

Richard flicked a glance at the window, judging the distance between it and him. It'd taken more energy than he'd anticipated to ride here on the horse borrowed from Cassandra's stable and then to sneak unseen over the wall at the far end of the garden, past the formally laid-out planting beds and topiaries lining the gravel walks leading up to the palace, and in through the open sash to wait for the Governor. Richard hoped the man was as honourable as he remembered and he wouldn't be forced to make a dash. He wasn't sure he possessed enough strength to outpace the guards if the Governor summoned them. He was taking a chance by being here and with what he was about to reveal.

Richard reached up and removed the mask. 'Richard Davenport.'

Lord Spotswood's dark eyebrows shot up before his expression settled into one of more curiosity than surprise. 'Back from the dead.'

'Better dead at sea than hanging from a gibbet.'

Lord Spotswood nodded his agreement, then motioned to the chair before his desk. 'Please, sit down. My condolences on your father. He was a good man.'

'Thank you.' Richard perched on the edge of the silk-covered seat, unwilling to relax. Nothing had been signed or agreed upon and he might still find himself hurrying through the garden and over the wall to safety.

'You appear as if you almost joined him.' Lord Spotswood nodded to the hole in Richard's coat and the wool dark and stiff with blood.

'A pirate's life isn't an easy one. It's why I want to be through with it.'

'I see.' Lord Spotswood opened the top drawer of his desk and removed a leather folio. 'His Majesty believes the best way to deal with pirates is to make honest men of them. It's certainly cheaper than funding Royal Navy ships to root them out.' He placed the folio on the blotter in front of him and removed a piece of parchment. In the lamplight, Richard could see the red-wax seal of King George affixed to the bottom. 'For whom do you seek the pardon?'

'For Captain Richard Davenport and the crew of the *Maiden's Veil*.'

Lord Spotswood took up his quill, flipped back

the lid on the ornate silver inkstand adorning his desk, dipped the nib and filled in the blank spaces on the document. When he was done, he fixed Richard with a pointed look. 'No other names for the pardon?'

Richard shifted in his chair, uneasy at the tone of the question. It appeared he hadn't guarded his secret as closely as he'd believed, but he still hesitated. It was one thing for people to suspect he was Captain Rose, it was another to confirm it and to the most powerful man in the colonies. He'd kept his real identity separate from Captain Rose's for so long, he almost couldn't utter the words to the official before him. If he wanted to leave this life, he had no choice but to put the man to rest. He didn't want his alias left afoul of the law where someone like Vincent might use it against him or his men. 'Captain Rose, of the *Devil's Rose*, and his crew.'

Lord Spotswood laid down his quill and laced his fingers in front of him on the desk. 'So the scant few rumours I've heard are true. You are the same man.'

'It was the only option left to me after Vincent Fitzwilliam betrayed me. He was shipping cargo under false flags, and when I discovered it, he accused me of piracy to save himself. I and my men were innocent.'

Lord Spotswood tapped the desk with his finger. 'You aren't so innocent any more, are you?'

Richard bent his toes in his boots, ready to bolt for the window. 'I will be once you sign the pardon.'

'Yes, you will be.' He picked up the pen and

scratched the nib over the vellum. 'Tell me more about Mr Fitzwilliam.'

'He used forged Dutch passes during the war to avoid the embargo and continues to employ them to secure shipping business unhindered by politics. He also trades with pirates to fund his failing company. I received this...' he tapped his shoulder '...in North Carolina while interrupting one of his illicit dealings.'

Lord Spotswood looked up at him from under his brow. 'Or perhaps you were participating in the activities and were stuck by an errant bullet.'

The suspicions darkening Lord Spotswood's eyes gave Richard a glimpse of how others might view him when he returned, but he didn't allow it to dissuade him. He didn't care about society the way Cas did, only about seeing justice for him and his men done, and finding another way to destroy Vincent. 'I had nothing to do with the trade. I was there to try to collect evidence against Vincent, as I've always done. I would have found it, too, if the schooner's Captain hadn't attacked.'

'Hmm.' Lord Spotswood didn't challenge Richard's proclamation, but clearly didn't believe it either. Given Lord Spotswood's hatred of pirates, Richard imagined, even with a pardon, he'd never have the man's—or society's—full trust. He would bear the prejudice for Cas and the chance to come home and strike at Vincent in the very place he lived and thrived. He'd also make sure a generous donation to some cause of Lord Spotswood's or any other influential man's would help make the sight of Richard among good people more palatable.

'You make some serious accusations against an esteemed man.' Lord Spotswood dipped the nib in the inkwell, tapping off the excess against the metal before returning it to the pardon. 'I suppose you have evidence of his dealings from the other ships of his you've captured?'

Richard dug at a nick in the chair's arm with his fingernail. 'A few passes which I believe are forged, but little more.'

'I see.' Lord Spotswood signed his name to the document, then took up a stick of wax and melted it over the candle.

Five years seemed to vanish with each drop of red on the vellum and the day he hadn't dared to imagine sat mere inches before him. While Lord Spotswood pressed his seal into the wax, Richard ran his thumb over the smooth end of his sword hilt. The pardon didn't remove the threat of Vincent striking at Cas and Richard, but Richard would no longer fear the law. Instead, he'd use it to find a way to make Vincent pay for his crimes. His men would enjoy their share of the wealth they'd collected over the years, and Richard would at last fulfil his promise to them to see their names cleared. This wasn't how he'd imagined this ending, but it was better than leading them to the gallows or the bottom of the ocean.

Lord Spotswood dusted the vellum, then held it up and blew off the excess.

Richard raised his hand to accept the document,

but Lord Spotswood set it on the desk and rested his elbows on either side of it like a lion guarding its prey. Richard's stomach tightened at the pause.

'This isn't the first time I've heard rumours of the Virginia Trading Company dealing with pirates,' Lord Spotswood explained. 'Usually the stories come from less credible sources who succumb to fatal accidents or jail fever before they can be of any use to my quest to root out illegal trading. I also have strong reason to believe, despite Mr Fitzwilliam's outward support for me, he covets my position and is far more involved in the recall effort than anyone realises.'

'He doesn't have the money or the influence in London to achieve it.' The thought of Vincent obtaining the governorship worried Richard. Vincent could wield the powers of the office against anyone, for any reason, including Richard and Cas. He might find a way to drive them from Virginia, or worse. He couldn't become Governor.

'I agree, but I'd rather see him convicted than risk him gaining support either here or in Parliament. His interests are not Virginia's interests and I won't see the lawlessness of North Carolina take root here.'

'Then why not seek more solid evidence against him?'

Lord Spotswood sat back in his chair and laced his fingers over his stomach. The pardon rested tantalisingly in front of him. 'My position at present is a precarious one. With Reverend Blair leading the recall effort against me, if I accuse a burgess like Mr

Fitzwilliam of criminal acts without evidence, it will weaken my position at a most inopportune time.'

'What does this have to do with my pardon?'

'I've granted Captain Richard Davenport and Captain Rose the King's Grace. However, the crew of the *Maiden's Veil* and the *Devil's Rose* will not obtain it until I receive irrefutable proof that the Virginia Trading Company is trading with pirates. Bring me enough proof of Mr Fitzwilliam's illegal dealings to convict him and I'll pardon your men.'

Richard gripped the arms of the chair. 'I can't leave my men outlaws, or abandon them after their years of faithful service to me.'

Lord Spotswood held out his hands in a helpless gesture. 'Then return to them and find the evidence I need.'

'If I defy the terms of the pardon, I'll be a wanted man again and anyone who helps me will be breaking the law.'

Lord Spotswood shrugged without sympathy. 'You and your cohorts in Virginia, whoever they may be, will be in no more danger than when you crept in here. Besides, you're a clever man, having avoided capture all these years. I'm sure you'll find a way to meet my demands.'

'And if I ignore your demands and appeal to the Governor of North Carolina for a pardon for me and my crew, which he is sure to grant, then what?' Lord Spotswood wasn't the only official capable of extending the King's Grace.

Lord Spotswood didn't flinch at the threat. 'Then

I will accuse you of breaking into this very palace and threatening me, of returning to a life outside the law and see to it you're hunted down. You will not escape this, or your past, Mr Davenport.'

Richard rose, indignity burning in his chest. 'You're forcing me to continue in a life of piracy.' *And away from Cas.*

Lord Spotswood stood and tugged the edges of his rust-coloured coat taut against his solid chest. 'I don't like pirates, Mr Davenport, of any ilk. They're an affront to men who earn an honest living, and it galls me to give them pardons, but as the King's minister in Virginia, I must. However, it doesn't mean you won't pay for your crimes, either by obtaining proof of Mr Fitzwilliam's treachery or through the Admiralty court.'

Richard opened and closed his hands, struggling to keep his rage against fate, Vincent, the Governor and himself under control. He'd been a fool to think he could simply leave this life with a pardon when it held him as tight as the grappling hooks securing a captured ship. In five years he'd collected little more than circumstantial evidence against Vincent. He wasn't likely to obtain something more damning now, unless he could find Captain Dehesa. It would mean returning to sea for hell knew how many more months or years. It would mean facing Cas and telling her he was leaving her, again.

Vincent stood over his desk, sifting through his papers, but nothing appeared out of order or missing.

While his back was turned, the women had been in here doing heaven knew what.

*Looking at the portrait.* He didn't believe the excuse for a moment. *The entitled whore. What was she really doing in here?*

Vincent rose and went to the window, ignoring how bare the mantel appeared without its candlesticks. The silver would only delay the Devlins. After the loss of the schooner's merchandise and the Spanish silver, he wasn't sure how he'd repay them.

'Sir,' Mr Adams entreated from behind him. 'My man has returned from Belle View. One of the field hands saw Lady Shepherd returning from the direction of the empty overseer's cabin early yesterday morning. My men investigated and although no one was there, they found traces of a rendezvous. Food, drink, rumpled sheets.'

Vincent glared at the portrait of his father. 'I won't be made a fool of by that whore. Find her lover and get rid of him.'

'I think there's more to it.'

Vincent turned to Mr Adams. 'What do you mean?'

'My man found bloody bandages, as if whoever was with her had been wounded. Then, last night, a crewman from the *Devil's Rose* approached me.'

'Impossible. No sailor ever leaves the *Devil's Rose.*'

'This one did and he's seen the Captain without his mask. Richard Davenport is Captain Rose, he has the scar you described to me, and Captain Rose was recently wounded. Now, Lady Shepherd attends to a bloodied man on her property, in secret. She was alone with Captain Rose on board his ship and, at one time, Richard Davenport's fiancé.'

Vincent ran one shaking hand through his hair, dislodging a few strands from his queue. 'So it's true. My old friend is the cause of all my present troubles.'

He turned to the window to watch the James River flowing dark and steady past Butler Plantation. The hours Vincent had spent sailing with Richard, and at Sutherland Place, had been Vincent's refuge from the strife at home. He'd envied his friend's happiness, especially his loving father. It'd been a bitter day when the schooner Captain had informed him that Richard had discovered his secret. He hadn't wanted to destroy his friend, but he'd known Richard's honesty wouldn't allow him to look the other way, and the last five years had proven him right. Richard could have disappeared, but instead he'd done all he could to steal the thing he knew Vincent cared about the most. He would not succeed.

'I want you to find him and bring him to me, alive. I want him to see he hasn't won and to watch his precious Lady Shepherd and all her lands become mine, for she will be or she will face the gallows for harbouring a pirate.'

## Chapter Nine

'Where have you been?' Cas rushed to Richard when he entered the cabin. She took his hand and pressed it against the softness of her chest and the yellow silk of her stomacher. Her fingers trembled where they clutched his, her fear as genuine as the small strand of pearls encircling her delicate wrist. 'I thought you'd left me and gone back to the *Devil's Rose.*'

'No.' *Not yet.* He stretched out his fingers to caress the top of one supple breast, making her sigh with a tenderness to gut him. She believed in his goodness when no one else did. Lord Spotswood was correct. Richard had committed many sins and now he must pay for them. He gently slid his hand out from under hers and sagged down on the rough coverlet, weary from hours on a horse to Williamsburg and back, not to mention his throbbing shoulder. Lord Spotswood's conditions, and what he now needed to tell Cassandra, sat heavy on his conscience.

'What's wrong?' She stood over him, the red of

her petticoat bright beneath the embroidered flowers of her yellow overskirt and bodice. She was beautiful, innocent, and he was unworthy to tarnish her with the filth of his life.

'You'll despise me when I tell you.'

'Then wait, and let's be together, like we used to be.' She leaned down to touch her lips to his. Heaven lingered in the taste of her, a paradise he'd only ever allowed himself to imagine during the darkest nights aboard ship. He wrapped his arms around her waist and held her against him, desperate to cling to her for ever, but he couldn't. All he could do was savour her for this brief time, and carry the memory of it with him back out to sea. It would comfort him through the hard and lonely days to come, the ones hovering before him like a storm on the horizon. He hoped this precious memory did the same for her. It was all he could give her before he left.

The warmth of her against him dispelled the pain in his shoulder and made his senses drunk on the taste of her. Gently, she slipped her hands around his neck, caressing the skin beneath his hair with a light touch before working her way over the sharp line of his shoulders to his chest and untying the laces of his shirt. When it opened, she slid her fingers over the bronze skin of his chest, her touch achingly light. With a groan, he pushed her back slightly, then buried his face in the rose-scented mass of her curls. She tilted her head, allowing him to trace the long line of her neck with his mouth. With his good hand, he caressed her back before grabbing her buttocks and pulling her closer. Gathering up the full fabric of her skirt, he worked his way under the folds to caress her bare leg. She sucked in her breath at the hot touch of him against her smooth thighs.

She ran her hands over the curve of his chest and across his flat stomach to the fall of his breeches. With deft fingers, she undid the buttons, freeing him from their confines. Letting go of her skirt, he pulled the long laces of her stomacher loose, freeing her from the voluminous dress before tugging his shirt over his head and dropping it to mingle with her brocade gown. He removed his breeches while she undid the panniers and padding until there was nothing but her chemise. When he rose from removing his breeches, he slipped the cotton off her shoulders, allowing it to fall and pool at her feet. It left them both naked and vulnerable with one another and yet he was hiding a secret, one that would destroy everything between them. He almost stopped them from going on, but she stepped up to him, her breasts brushing his chest as she rose up on her toes, her arms encircling his neck, and kissed him. She'd asked him for this last token of himself, and he would give it to her. It would be a much lonelier life for them both after this night, but for the moment they had one another and this brief time together.

Wrapping his arm around her waist, he guided her to the bed and covered her with his body. He slipped between her thighs, revelling in her soft moans of pleasure as he moved within her, deeper and deeper until he thought he would drown in the pleasure of her being. She ran her fingers over the taut muscles of his back as he clasped her to him, not letting her go, keeping her within the circle of his arms, knowing the passing hour would soon force him from her and this time it would be for good. In their coming together last night he'd made her a silent promise and he was about to go back on his word once more. He'd hurt her too many times to expect forgiveness when he returned, assuming he ever did. All he could do was lose himself further into her until their passion crested and he cried out in both release and regret.

They lay together in silence, the cicadas filling the night with their endless music while he held her close, enjoying the faint sweep of her fingertips across his back, the stretching silence telling him she worried about their future the same way he did. At last, he shifted down beside her and pulled her close.

'Where did you go today?' she asked.

He could no longer hold back the truth or reality. 'I went to see Lord Spotswood to ask for the King's Grace.'

She sat up, the hope filling her wide eyes increasing his torment. 'You received a pardon?'

He reached for his coat on the floor and slipped the useless document from the pocket and handed it to her. 'I did. My men didn't.'

She tilted the pardon to read it by the dim light of the candle on the bedside table, a crease of confusion marring the smooth skin of her brow. 'Why would Lord Spotswood do such a thing?'

'He wants me to procure solid evidence of Vincent colluding with pirates so he doesn't have to.' He explained the task Lord Spotswood had assigned him, conscious of the pain just behind her eyes. 'It's his way of punishing me even when the law says he can't because I sought the pardon.'

'What will you do?'

He stood up and tugged on his breeches. 'I have to find Captain Dehesa and secure his testimony against Vincent. It's the best evidence I can secure.'

She opened her fingers and the paper fluttered to the floor. 'You're going back to sea?'

'I have no choice. Until I fulfil my end of the bargain, my men are still wanted. I can't leave them at risk while I walk free. It would be a betrayal of the faith they've placed in me these last five years.'

'And if this Captain Dehesa's sworn testimony isn't enough, then what will you do?'

He turned to face her where she knelt on the bed, her long hair falling in thick ringlets over her shoulder to cover breasts as tantalising as any prize ship. He didn't want to leave her, or break her heart, but if he didn't do it now, he never would. 'Continue on as I have before until I gather what I need.'

'It will mean violating the terms of the pardon and becoming a wanted man again.'

'It's a chance I have to take.' He turned his back on her to gather up his frock coat and pull it on, wincing at the pain in his shoulder and his heart. All his newfound plans to be with Cas and destroy Vincent were coming apart, just like every other plan he'd ever made for his life.

'No, you don't. You can stay and gather evidence here. The sea can't be the only place where Vincent has made deals or spoken to people.'

'None of whom are likely to tell me with the threat of retribution from Vincent hanging over them.' He pulled on his boots with angry jerks. 'Assuming I can even find those people.'

'I know who one of them is.' She tugged up the sheet to cover her beautiful body. 'A man in North Carolina named Mr Powell who Vincent has been corresponding with, and I'm sure it has to do with his illicit trades. I also discovered that Vincent is deeply in debt to the Devlins. It means your efforts to weaken his company are working and he's close to ruin. If you stay here, you could talk to Mr Powell, and perhaps the Devlins, and drive home the final blow.'

He faced her, stunned by her news. 'How did you find out all this?'

A red flush spread across her cheeks and she twisted the corner of the sheet around one finger. 'I went to Butler Plantation today to see if I could find evidence to help you and I did.'

He clasped her upper arms, sickened by the chance she'd taken for him. 'You're not to jeopardise yourself for me, do you understand? If he'd discovered what you were doing, he could've killed you, or worse.'

'I can't sit idly by while you risk your life to obtain proof. I can't watch you hang when you fail to find what you need.' She reached out and took his hand, covering it with both of hers and trapping him in her sweet grip. 'I didn't nurse your wounds to see you die of jail fever or worse.'

'I didn't set you back on the *Winter Gale* to watch you throw your life away for me.' He pulled his hand out from between hers.

She didn't reach for him again or protest more about why he should stay and how she might help him. Instead, she stared up at him as everything he told her and what it meant to them and her dreams of their future descended over her. The pain making her eyes shimmer with tears made him curse fate for bringing them together, for revealing he was alive and allowing her to hope for their future before he yanked it away. He reached out and stroked her cheek with the backs of his fingers. She didn't melt into his touch like she had before, but remained rigid. In her stiffness, he could sense the anger boiling inside her, the one tearing at him, too. 'I would stay with you if I could, Cas.'

She jerked away from him. 'I'm not sure you would, not when I see you rushing back to your ship like Giles used to rush back to his whore.'

'I'm nothing like him.' He rose and stuffed the blunderbuss into the inner pocket of his frock coat.

'You're exactly like him, except all he cared about was pleasure. All you care about is revenge.' She snatched up her chemise and pulled it over her head, then tugged on her panniers and the dress. 'I wonder if it was Lord Spotswood who ordered you to prove

Vincent guilty or if it was your own desire to see him ruined that drove you to make this deal.'

'I care about my men too much to save myself at their expense. I promised them freedom and I will damn well deliver it.' He banged his fist on the table, almost making the candle topple out of its brass holder before he caught and righted it.

'And once again, your promise to me to be my husband and stand beside me through everything means nothing.' She did up the stomacher, her fingers trembling so hard she could barely slip the laces through the eyelets. He reached out to assist her, but she knocked his hands away, then yanked the laces so tight they scraped over the eyelets. 'Don't try to help me, not when you've never been there for me before or cared what happens to me.'

'I do care, I always have.'

'Talk of affection from a pirate,' she snorted. 'You'll ruin your fearsome reputation with such idle chatter.'

The disgust in her eyes made him want to crush her to him and bring back the fiery passion of only a few moments before, but it was too late. He hadn't left, but already he'd placed too much distance between them, one she increased with her insults.

'Yes, I'm a pirate and, ever since our reunion on the *Devil's Rose*, I've made no effort to hide what I am and who I've become, or to conceal how firm a grip this life has on me and how much it has changed me for the worse, but you refused to believe or accept it.'

'I do now. I hope you find your evidence, Richard, and I hope your vengeance brings you comfort. It's clear nothing else ever will.' She flung open the cabin door and ran out into the darkness, not even pausing to give him one last look before she left him alone.

He stepped on to the porch, catching the faint yellow of her dress made white by the moonlight before it and she vanished into the darkness of the trees. He opened his mouth to call her back, to hang on to her once-powerful belief that he could stay with her and somehow still defeat Vincent, but he remained silent. There was nothing he could say or do to heal the damage he'd wrought.

He went inside, took the pardon and the pieces of eight off the table and stuffed them in his coat pocket before hurrying out of the cabin, across the clearing and into the forest. Tramping down to the river, he found a small path along the shore and followed it, fighting against his exhaustion to move fast, eager to be away from his enemies and the ghost of the life he might have enjoyed with Cas. He paused and leaned against a tree, dragging in a deep breath to beat back the sharp pain in his shoulder and the failure engulfing him. She'd been in his arms and willing to defy Vincent and her eagerness for his and society's acceptance to help him. He'd won her and then he'd lost her again.

He banged one fist against the rough bark of the tree, scraping his skin. *Curse it all.*

He pushed off the tree and resumed his steady

pace, soon coming upon a skiff tied to a slanted and rickety wharf. Up through the trees sat an equally dilapidated cabin barely visible through the dense woods. Its curtained windows were dark, but a thin wisp of grey smoke drifted out of the chimney.

Richard trod quietly across the rotting wood dock to the vessel. He kept an ear out for its owner, but nothing except the croak of frogs, the lap of water and the continuous humming of the cicadas reached him. Richard lowered himself into the bobbing vessel. Despite the poor condition of the cabin, the wood and sails of the skiff were sound. Richard fished a single piece of eight from his inner coat pocket and left it on the dock. The money was worth three times what the vessel was and he hoped the owner would put it to good use.

He cast off from the dock and caught the current. When he was far enough away from the shore, he raised the yellowed sail and it filled with the breeze. Richard gripped the tack line with his good hand and used his weak one to work the rudder. Ignoring the pain in his shoulder, he guided the craft towards the Chesapeake Bay and the open sea, fleeing in the night in a stolen skiff like a criminal with Cas's curses ringing in his ears.

He tightened his grip on the tack line when the craft sailed around an all-too-familiar bend in the river and into sight of Sutherland Place. It stood on a hill overlooking the James River, the view of the windows along the brick façade exactly as he remembered. The windows burned with the light of numerous lamps and illuminated the many people gathered inside. The breeze being hard at his back dampened the sounds of the shore and the river grew quiet around him, but it didn't muffle the faint notes of a pianoforte being played inside, his mother's pianoforte, entertaining another woman's guests in another man's house. The property had been sold lock, stock and barrel to pay his father's debts, the ones he had acquired because of Richard.

*Damn it. This is not how it will be.* He was sick of loss, of not keeping his promises, sick of losing to Vincent time and time again and of being ruled by revenge and the darkness of Captain Rose. With each bob of the craft over a small swell or the slap of the water against the hull, his determination to finally end this hard and ruthless life increased. During the last two days, Cas had given him a taste of what he could have if he gave up the sea, and he wouldn't allow it to be ripped from him the way Sutherland Place and his youth and innocence had been torn from him. *I won't fail again.*

He'd follow the coast to Knott Island and rejoin the *Devil's Rose*. They'd prepare for their final voyage to rendezvous with Captain Dehesa off Cape Hatteras, then sail to North Carolina and find a solicitor willing to take his affidavit for a few pieces of silver. Once there, he'd find the Mr Powell Cas had spoken of. She'd risked her safety to gain him this information and he would use it, either purchasing the man's testimony or forcing it out of him. Resolve welled inside him to equal the one that had made him choose the alias of Captain Rose, but this time he would kill the pirate Captain for good. He was done with him and defeat. He would give Lord Spotswood what he demanded and then seize for himself the things he craved: Vincent's end, a life on land and Cas's heart.

Cassandra rushed down the path to Belle View, trying to outrun the pain strangling her. She paused beneath a thick tangle of trees, wanting to return to the cabin before Richard left and somehow convince him to stay, but she forced herself forward towards the house. He was leaving her again and nothing, not her kisses or her pleas, had moved him enough to make him change his mind. There was no reason to run after him and humiliate herself. For the second time, she'd seen something in a man that wasn't there.

*He didn't love me, he never did.* She should have guessed as much last night when he couldn't even bring himself to say the words after she'd laid bare her heart to him. She tugged at the tight laces of the stomacher, trying to loosen them and take a deep breath, to not collapse beneath the weight of disappointment. Everything she'd ever believed and thought she would find with him had been a lie. He hadn't loved her any more than Giles had, or, if he had, his affection had been little more than the whims of a young man and easily forgotten. She'd been naive to trust in his affection, duped by her desperate need for love and to recreate the family life at Belle View the fever had taken from her all those years ago. She'd swallowed Richard's lies about returning to her at Yorktown and had almost believed them today. He was never coming back. The sea was a better lover and one she could not outdo. She couldn't offer him the thrills and danger he must enjoy in piracy. All she could give him was the quiet and steady rhythm of a planter's life and the peace and comfort of being a husband and a father. At one time she'd thought him eager for these simple things, but his having gone to sea the first time should have told her he'd never wanted them or her.

She resumed the march up the rise to Belle View, her feet coming down hard on old twigs and snapping them. With each step, she tried to take hold of her pain, to shove it into the small place in the back of her mind where she'd kept all of her anguish over Giles, the Chathams' betrayal, Uncle Walter's death and the loss of her parents. No one knew Richard had been here, forcing her to mourn the loss of him and his love alone.

Alone.

It made her heart sink further. She'd been left to struggle against troubles by herself for so long and, for a moment in Richard's arms last night and today, she'd thought her solitude had at last come to an end. Instead, it had grown even deeper than before.

Up ahead, the trees began to thin and the red brick of Belle View came into sight. A few windows downstairs blazed with light. This late at night they should all be dark, but Dinah or Mrs Sween must be up, or perhaps they'd forgotten to douse the lamps. Cassandra sighed. If someone was up, it would mean more lies, more deceit, more hiding of her feelings, and she had no strength for it. She couldn't face Mrs Sween or Jane and not have everything come tumbling out. Hopefully, they would understand and not chide, scorn or blame her for her present misery and her hand in it. There was no one else she could turn to for comfort.

She wandered listlessly up the back lawn, the ivy and weeds choking the brick deepening the pain of Richard's leaving. She'd come here to rebuild her life and with it Belle View. For a short time, Richard had become a part of her plans, her future. He was once again her past, just like the prosperity of the plantation and her loving and safe childhood. Whatever happened now, she'd face it by herself, like nearly every calamity which had befallen her since Richard had first gone to sea.

When she drew near the house, the sound of a man and woman arguing inside made her stop. It sounded like Mrs Sween and a man's voice she faintly recognised, but couldn't place, but there was no mistaking the harsh tone of it. She quickened her pace, hoping it wasn't the overseer returning to collect past wages. It was strange to choose this late at night to confront her, but drinking at the Raleigh Tavern often turned sane men angry, especially those who felt they'd been wronged. He could demand all he liked, she had little to give him, but she would find something to soothe him and send him on his way.

She hurried up the porch steps and quietly entered the back sitting room.

Mr Fitzwilliam's raised voice from the entry hall made her freeze in the centre of the faded rug. 'Tell me where she is.'

'It's none of your business where she is,' Mrs Sween shot back. Cassandra crept up to the door and peered around it and into the main hallway to see the housekeeper planted in front of Mr Fitzwilliam, her thick fists on her ample hips, as determined as the burgess. 'She doesn't receive visitors this late at night.'

'Don't insult me with your flimsy regard for convention.' He reached out, ready to shove Mrs Sween aside when Cassandra stepped into the entry hall.

'What is the meaning of this intrusion?' Cassandra demanded in the same voice she'd used to halt the marauding pirates on the *Winter Gale*. It didn't stop Mr Fitzwilliam.

'I've been patient in my pursuit of you, but no more.' He stepped around Mrs Sween and marched to Cassandra. She raised herself up to face him, refusing to be cowed even when he leaned in close to her, his voice like the hiss of a copperhead snake beneath a bush. 'You've been hiding Richard Davenport.'

She stiffened with panic and forced herself not to move or react, afraid even the slightest twitch or flush might reveal her guilt. *How did he find out?* 'That's impossible. Richard Davenport is dead. It's cruel of you to come here this late at night for no other reason than to make up such stories.'

Over his shoulder she caught Mrs Sween straining to hear, but Mr Fitzwilliam kept his words menacingly low. 'Don't play me for a fool. Richard, or should I say Captain Rose, is very much alive thanks to your tender care.'

The sound of hard footsteps on the front steps echoed through the house. Mr Adams entered, more morose than usual, with two sallow and burly men flanking him.

'Did you find him?' Mr Fitzwilliam demanded.

'No, there was no one there when we reached the cabin. We searched the nearby woods, but found nothing.'

Cassandra would have sighed in relief if she dared, but she could do nothing to confirm Mr Fitzwilliam was right.

Mr Fitzwilliam whirled on her. 'Where is he?'

'Buried at sea as you and everyone else well know.'

'He's no more dead than you or I.' He curled up his lip, revealing one crooked tooth. 'Now tell me where he is or I'll see to it Lord Spotswood finds out about your treachery.'

'What will you tell him? You dreamed of seeing a ghost here at Belle View?' she mocked, despite the iciness creeping through her. Lord Spotswood knew Richard's secret. If Mr Fitzwilliam went to him with his accusations, the Governor would know they were true and might reveal it. If he was determined to bring down Mr Fitzwilliam for colluding with pirates, Lord Spotswood might convict her, too. She'd be ruined and Dinah taken from her, Belle View seized by the Crown leaving her daughter a pauper and an orphan. Heaven smite Richard and her for having been naive enough to care for him.

'Don't you dare talk back to me, you lying whore!' He raised his hand to strike her, and Cassandra cringed, waiting for the blow. Then Mr Fitzwilliam stopped, the red in his face fading a touch as he regained control. He lowered his hand and turned to his men. 'Find Richard. He must not escape again.'

Mr Adams gave a terse nod and headed back out into the night, followed by his henchmen.

Cassandra prayed Richard was far enough away to avoid danger, even if she wasn't. If they caught him, it would give proof to Mr Fitzwilliam's accusations. Something inside her made her doubt Richard would turn her in to protect himself, but his willingness to abandon her made her doubt her intuition. Richard had left her to face Mr Fitzwilliam, like her parents had left her to deal with Belle View and the Chathams to bear Giles. Despair made her knees weak, and she almost sank to the floor in desperation before she locked them tight. She'd never succumbed to wilting fear before. She wouldn't tonight. She must remain strong against this threat as she had all the others she'd ever faced.

'As for you...' Mr Fitzwilliam fixed on the crooked stomacher and the hastily tied skirt, her air of having hurriedly dressed all but giving her away '...don't think you've won.'

She raised her chin in defiance. 'I wasn't aware we were in battle.'

'Oh, we are, and I am the conqueror. I believe you are trespassing on my land.' He withdrew a document from his pocket, unfolded it and held it out to her. Horror gripped her. It was the deed to Belle View executed in Mr Fitzwilliam's name. 'Before your father died, he borrowed from mine a large sum of money, using Belle View as collateral. He didn't pay back the debt and I renegotiated the loan with your uncle for the same terms. He also failed to repay it before he died.'

'That's a lie. There was no agreement of any kind between my father and yours, or Uncle Walter, in their papers after they passed. Even if there was, the plantation is in my name, not his. Uncle Walter had no legal right to renew the debt without consulting me first and I never would have agreed to it.' She was grasping at straws, but she had to. The deed appeared real, but she still didn't believe it. Uncle Walter had urged her so many times not to sell Belle View. She couldn't believe he would have mortgaged it out from under her.

'How quaint, a woman attempting to argue the law with a burgess.' Mr Fitzwilliam lowered the deed and chuckled, making Cassandra want to slap the condescending smile off his face. 'Walter Lewis held the power of attorney to manage the estate and therefore the right to extend or enter into contracts. It isn't my fault he failed to mention it to you. You have since defaulted on the terms of the agreement and by right of law this plantation is mine.'

'This is a forgery. Show me the original agree-

ment between my father and yours, show me the renewed contract between you and Uncle Walter. Point
to where my father and uncle signed their names.
Explain to everyone the terms and why you waited
so long to claim what you say is yours.'

His superior smile vanished and the angry red
flush returned to his cheeks. He caught her by the
wrist and yanked her close, his hot breath nearly
suffocating her and his fingers making the pearls
bite into her skin. 'I'll provide it and any other documents necessary to take ownership of this land.
And what will you do about it? Who will you, a
London whore, appeal to in order to say it isn't legal?
No one will believe you and I'll make sure you,
your brat and every servant and farmer who works
this land are tossed off it. What will you do then?
Where will you go? How will you and your daughter survive?'

He let go of her, and she stumbled back, rubbing
her wrist where a circle of angry bruises began to
develop. Jane appeared at the top of the stairs, Dinah
clinging to her legs, both of them watching and listening, the fear on their faces as intense as it had
been on the *Winter Gale*. If Cassandra lost Belle
View, there was nowhere they could go, no one to
appeal to for help. The Chathams had turned their
backs on her, she had no inheritance, no income from
England and Richard was gone.

She didn't bother to refute his assertions because
he was right. With him holding a deed to Belle View,
and threatening to tell Lord Spotswood of his sus-

picions, the fight was as good as lost. A woman couldn't argue the law with a burgess and no court was likely to side with her against Mr Fitzwilliam even if she could raise enough money to hire a solicitor and challenge him. He had the deed and his respected word while she had nothing but accusation about forgeries she couldn't prove.

Her mother's clock chimed the quarter-hour, and Cassandra pressed her fingertips against the fine mahogany case. If Mr Fitzwilliam took Belle View, all connection to her past and all hope for Dinah's future would be lost. It wasn't only her and Dinah at risk, but the many other families who relied on Belle View for their livelihood.

For the first time, she understood Richard's dilemma and why he'd chosen his crew over her.

*If only Richard were still here*. But he wasn't. He never would be again.

Cassandra's heart sank. Everything she'd dreamed of finding in Virginia was being ripped away from her tonight.

'Whatever you may think of me, or despite what people may say, I'm not a cruel man. I don't wish to see a child starve, or her mother hang for abetting a pirate.' Mr Fitzwilliam folded the deed and tucked it into his pocket, the calm he normally displayed covering him once again, but the level tone of his words proved more frightening than his rage. 'Marry me and I'll ensure both you and your daughter are well taken care of and Belle View returned to its former glory.'

Cassandra worked to steady herself, unable to believe the lengths Mr Fitzwilliam had gone to in an effort to secure her hand, but she wasn't about to surrender herself or her freedom to this man. She'd seen the monster behind the gentlemanly façade and refused to allow it to govern her or her daughter's lives. 'If you have the deed, why do you need me to marry you?'

'You're a charming woman, Lady Shepherd, and you might have left London carrying the taint of scandal, but you still have the blood of aristocrats in your veins. Marriage to me will restore your respectability and, with your honour renewed, you'll encourage Lord and Lady Chatham, and whatever noble friends you still possess in England, to petition Parliament on my behalf and support my endeavour to become the next Governor of Virginia.'

The man was insane, willing to believe anything in his quest for power. 'I have no influence with the Chathams or anyone of note in London. I can be of no help to you, especially not as your wife. As you were so kind to point out, I left London a disgraced woman.'

'You'll have money once the Belle View dock is established as a prime shipping wharf. Money is all you need to make London forget your past and help us build our future as the most powerful couple in Virginia.'

'If you want Belle View, then take it. Make money off the dock and buy your own influence. It's more than anything you think I can offer you.' She would not marry him. She still had some of the money Richard had given her on the *Winter Gale*, jewellery and a few other things of value. She could sell them and it would keep her and Dinah and Jane until she could find work and another place to live, assuming she could. She possessed no real skills, nothing to offer anyone in exchange for the money she needed to live. Perhaps one of the Williamsburg ladies might hire her as a companion, assuming Mr Fitzwilliam didn't darken her name. If he did, she could go to another colony, somewhere where people didn't know or care who she was and find work there, but it would once again mean abandoning everything she'd ever cared for to face a grim and unknown future. Cassandra sagged down in a wooden chair beside her mother's tall clock, her courage and faith in herself and the future quickly fading.

'No, Lady Shepherd. Marriage is what I am offering you and the only option you have. If you refuse my hand tonight, I will bring charges against you for abetting a notorious pirate and see to it that you are convicted. I will have your daughter taken from you and placed with a family of my choosing to raise as they see fit. If you accept me, I will give your daughter a good life among prominent people and you will be the lady of the manor once more. You'll no longer have to worry about maintaining Belle View or struggling to keep it, and all those relying on it, afloat.'

She glanced past him to where Jane sat trying to soothe Dinah, who'd buried her face in the nurse's shoulder. They depended on her to protect them here as much as aboard the *Winter Gale* and she couldn't fail them, even if it meant placing herself in this man's control. Her mind searched for a way out of this, some other path to keep her from binding herself to Mr Fitzwilliam, but she could think of nothing.

'Well, Lady Shepherd?' Mr Fitzwilliam laid a heavy hand on her shoulder, and she shuddered. 'Will you marry me and see you and your daughter raised to the highest levels of society, to have respect and influence, or will you reject me and have you and your child thrown out of Belle View, the two of you separated for good?'

Just like Giles, Mr Fitzwilliam held all the power and, with a word to Lord Spotswood either about Richard or the deed, he could destroy her. She didn't want to marry him, but she couldn't allow Dinah to suffer at the hands of strangers, to be raised without love or neglected. At least in marriage, Cassandra would be here to shield her from Mr Fitzwilliam, to give her the care and concern she deserved and needed. Cassandra had fought a cruel husband to keep Dinah close and she'd endure another to protect her. She could do nothing for her if she was in prison or dead. 'Yes, I'll marry you.'

'I knew you'd see reason.' He ran his hand over her hair, and she winced, wanting to push him away, but she couldn't. Everything she did now must be to defend Dinah. She didn't trust Mr Fitzwilliam's assurances to be good to her. 'We'll make a formal announcement at Lady Spotswood's masked ball in two weeks. I want all of Virginia to know of our union and for my good name to prevent anyone from besmirching yours. Tomorrow, I'll call for you so we may obtain our marriage licence.'

He slid his clammy hand beneath hers and raised it to his lips, pressing his wet mouth against it, the nearness of him almost making her wretch. The fading impression of Richard's gentle touch and the pleasure they'd enjoyed in their brief time together would torture her now more than it had during all her lonely years with Giles. It added to the bitterness already consuming her, for Richard's affection had never been real and the comfort of it was gone. There would be nothing for her to hang on to in her marriage to Mr Fitzwilliam, to give her hope in the darkest moments except her love for Dinah and the need to keep her safe.

'I'll call for you in the morning.' Mr Fitzwilliam dropped her hand, offered her a low, sweeping bow that did nothing to hide his smirk of triumph, then strode from the house.

'You can't let him do this to you.' Mrs Sween rushed up to Cassandra once he was gone. 'There must be some other way.'

'If there is, we must find it before the wedding.' It was the only thing keeping her from sliding to the floor and weeping tears of desperation. Like Richard, she'd been ensnared by her decisions and his. There was nothing left to do but face the consequences, alone.

'And if we can't?' Mrs Sween pressed.

Cassandra shuddered, sickened at what she might have to endure every night if she couldn't find a way to break this betrothal without it costing her everything. She pushed herself up out of the chair, trying not to succumb to her fears. There must be some way out of this and she would find it. She had to. The alternative, like the idea that Richard never truly loved her, filled her with too much despair.

## Chapter Ten

Cassandra entered the ballroom of the Governor's Palace on Mr Fitzwilliam's arm. Even with the tall sashes open to let in the night air, the crush of gentlemen and ladies combined with the persistent Virginia heat made the room as suffocating as her gown. The last two weeks had consisted of nothing but one defeat after another with Mr Fitzwilliam. Every shred of evidence she'd demanded to see in regards to the deed he'd produced. She still wasn't convinced it was real, but she couldn't prove it was a forgery any more than Richard could prove Vincent was trading with pirates. She hadn't given up, but with the day of their wedding drawing steadily closer, her hope was quickly fading.

Cassandra moved to pass the two red-coated dragoons guarding the door and enter the room, but Mr Fitzwilliam made her pause on the threshold.

'Wait. I want people to really see us, to know we're here.'

The blue-walled ballroom with its white wainscoting was splendidly decorated with vines interwoven with flowers. A stringed quartet sat along the far wall playing their melodious tune. In the centre of the room, couples stood lined up across from one another, ready to turn and promenaded down the line for the latest *contredanse*, one that had been in England for some time, but which had only just reached Williamsburg. Among the dancers, and the many guests crowded together around the dance floor, women dressed as shepherdesses mingled with harlequins, but most of the revellers donned their own dresses with only a few alterations to hint at the medieval princess or the ancient kings they'd chosen to impersonate. Despite the masks and costumes, it was easy to recognise nearly half the guests. Mr Fitzwilliam all but flaunted his identity. He wore a fine suit of French blue with gold embroidery and a matching cape lined with fleur-de-lis to give the slightest appearance of a musketeer costume. A slender mask draped across his eyes, which glistened with a delight matched by his disgustingly wide smile.

Cassandra had taken some pains to conceal her identity with a larger half mask, ashamed to be seen with Mr Fitzwilliam despite the spreading news of their engagement. She wore her black-silk mourning dress trimmed in grey embroidery with a matching grey petticoat. It hadn't been out of the trunk since the week before she'd left England. Despite having inwardly revelled in Giles's passing, she'd done all expected of a widow in London, hoping to win back the Chathams' favour. It hadn't worked. They, like society, had refused to remember the dead man's sins and had accused Cassandra of making a mockery of mourning. If she'd possessed enough money for new clothes, she would have left the dress in England. Instead, she'd kept it, thinking it could be cut into an outfit for Dinah. She never imagined she'd wear it again. Thankfully, her white half mask hid the puffiness of her eyes from the long nights spent pacing the Belle View halls, worrying about the future and how to extricate herself from this before it was too late.

Mr Fitzwilliam patted her hand where it rested listlessly on his arm, his touch making her skin crawl. He grinned with satisfaction when a bustle of revellers paused in their conversations to offer their congratulations. Sickened by his conceit, she cursed her inability to tear off the mask of the burgess hiding the criminal and to expose the thieving wretch Mr Fitzwilliam really was to these people. She might despise Richard for having abandoned her, but she shared his desire to ruin Mr Fitzwilliam. For this reason, she prayed he did find Captain Dehesa or Mr Powell and could give Lord Spotswood the evidence he sought. It was a thin prospect to hang her salvation on, for she doubted Richard would succeed where he'd failed before, at least not in time to save her from marriage. Mr Fitzwilliam would retain his place in society, and Cassandra would be the one debased by him.

'Come along.' Mr Fitzwilliam guided her into the

crowd. Near the dance floor, more than one matron ducked behind her fan with a friend to whisper about them. Their daughters lit up the centre of the room with their own flashes of historic colour, oblivious to anything but the young gentlemen they danced with. In the last week, despite no formal announcement, Mr Fitzwilliam had done all he could to make it clear to everyone they were to marry, including securing the licence and setting the date. Tonight, he intended to inform anyone who hadn't heard or who hadn't chosen to believe the gossip.

Mr Preston, dressed in a dark green velvet frock coat with elaborate silver embroidery, white breeches and a white waistcoat, his identity poorly concealed by a handheld mask, frowned at their arrival. When they passed him, Mr Fitzwilliam bowed to him with a flourish, silently gloating about his impending acquisition of the Belle View wharf. Mr Preston lowered his mask, not relishing Mr Fitzwilliam enjoying the advantage of reviving the Virginia Trading Company and cutting into the Chesapeake Trading Company's growing business. Like Cassandra, he'd be glad to see the Virginia Trading Company sunk.

'There's Lord and Lady Spotswood. We must tell them our good news.' Mr Fitzwilliam led her across the room like a Roman general parading a conquered queen before his emperor.

The one victory she'd enjoyed over him this past week was Richard's escape. Despite an exhaustive search, Mr Adams and his men had never found him.

She couldn't imagine where he'd gone, but he wasn't here, helping her. He'd never been there when she'd truly needed him, not in London and not tonight. Regret made her steps heavy until Mr Fitzwilliam jerked at her, increasing their pace.

Miss Fitzwilliam trailed behind them, as sour in her appearance as she'd been in the carriage, seeming to rejoice in the forthcoming nuptials as much as Mr Preston. She was dressed as the devil, with a deep red gown trimmed in black lace. In her blonde hair, done in ringlets and tight curls, she'd pinned two small horns and a black-silk mask covered her blue eyes. Her costume, much like Cassandra on Mr Fitzwilliam's arm, raised a number of eyebrows and set many matrons to whispering behind their hands. There'd been a heated discussion between the siblings before they'd all set out with Mr Fitzwilliam demanding his sister change, but she'd held firm in her decision to wear her chosen costume. Cassandra had sided with Miss Fitzwilliam, insisting that devil costumes were all the fashion in England. With time to leave running short, he'd grudgingly given up and they'd set out. Miss Fitzwilliam appeared oblivious to the stir her costume caused and probably delighted in embarrassing her brother on the night of his great triumph.

Cassandra hoped the girl enjoyed the moment for she felt sure she would suffer for her insolence later. Cassandra probably would, too, but she'd enjoyed this small victory over Mr Fitzwilliam. It would be one of many acts of defiance against her husband-to-be. He might be gaining a wife, but she would not be a compliant one. Once she was installed at Butler Plantation, she would do all she could to help Miss Fitzwilliam and herself. She'd use the advantage of being there to better search his private papers. Maybe then she could at last secure evidence against him. It would send him to the gallows and free her and Dinah, assuming she could locate what she needed. She swallowed hard, her spirits flagging. He might not keep incriminating papers at Butler Plantation and she'd have to endure him for years.

Mr Fitzwilliam led her to where the Bakers stood beside a half pillar supporting an elaborate candelabra with tapers dripping wax on the wooden floor. When they stopped, Miss Fitzwilliam drifted off into the crush. Cassandra wished she had the girl's freedom to leave. Instead, she had to stay and dance for these people like a puppet.

'Good evening, Mr and Mrs Baker.' Mr Fitzwilliam bowed, then straightened. 'Have you heard our wonderful news?'

'Indeed we have. Congratulations to you both,' Mrs Baker offered with more respect than she'd shown at the Governor's Palace. Dressed in an older-style mantua of rich brown brocade stitched with ivory-coloured thread, she appeared as a medieval queen, while Miss Baker stood beside her, just as well dressed, but equally behind the fashion in her attempt to be a milkmaid.

'Thank you,' Cassandra flatly replied, and Mr Fitzwilliam stiffened beside her. He spoke with Mr

Baker while Cassandra offered curt answers to Mrs Baker's questions about their wedding plans. She no longer cared what the lady thought of her or her past. Social ostracism paled in comparison to the very real possibility of Mr Fitzwilliam becoming her lord and master.

When they were finished conversing, Mr Fitzwilliam drew her away, his fingers digging into her bare arm.

'Stop appearing as if you're at a funeral,' he hissed, the echoes of Giles's demands reverberating in every word.

She wrenched her arm free, but didn't flee. Unlike Richard, she had nowhere else to go. The bars of this new cage pressed in on her until she almost couldn't stand. She was about to plead illness and retreat to the ladies' retiring room when two men entering the ballroom caught her notice. One wore a black tricorn, the other a Cavalier hat set rakishly over his jet-coloured hair. Their faces were covered by full Venetian face masks of fine quality. The mysterious men cut dashing figures in their similar suits of black brocade with glinting silver swords hanging from their hips. They were difficult not to notice and more than one young lady turned to take them in, wondering at their identities. The more slender of the two men she didn't recognise, but the cut of the taller one's shoulders and the confident way he stood, hands on his hips, surveying the room, reminded her of Richard.

*He came back*. No, it was impossible. He'd violated the pardon by returning to piracy and would be arrested the moment he entered Williamsburg, especially if he was bold enough to appear at the Governor's Palace. Mr Fitzwilliam would see to it and there'd be no one to stop him. Richard couldn't have found anything against Mr Fitzwilliam so soon and, without it, Lord Spotswood would side with the burgess. Even if Richard had found something, once he surrendered his evidence to Lord Spotswood he'd most likely leave again. There was nothing holding him here, especially not Cassandra.

'What's wrong?' Mr Fitzwilliam demanded, following the line of her gaze to the door, but the men had moved on to blend in with the crowd and were no longer visible.

'Nothing.' She stepped up to one of the open windows overlooking the garden, unfolded her fan and began to wave it under her chin. Outside, tall torches burned along the gravel paths, illuminating the couples walking between the neatly clipped hedges, topiaries and square planting beds. 'Except it's too hot in here.'

'Bear it. We need to make a good showing tonight,' he ordered. 'Come, we must speak with the Governor.'

'Let her rest here a moment where it's cooler, Vincent,' Miss Fitzwilliam insisted, suddenly appearing at Cassandra's other side. 'She looks as if she's about to faint from the heat.'

'I am,' Cassandra insisted, waving her fan faster, sure there was more to Miss Fitzwilliam's intervention than mere manners, and she wanted to know what it was.

'I'll stay with her and we'll join you in a moment when she's recovered. After all, you don't want anyone to accuse you of mistreating your poor bride-to-be, do you? They'll think you're just like Father.' Miss Fitzwilliam raised her voice in defiance of her brother, drawing the attention of a number of people standing around them.

Mr Fitzwilliam frowned at her, but she smiled innocently at him. He studied the people watching the exchange. 'Of course not. I wouldn't want my love to be uncomfortable. I'll be with the Governor. Join me as soon as you can.'

He flung back his short cape and stormed off. Cassandra didn't watch him leave, but searched the guests for the men in the elaborate masks. It was difficult to see through the crowd, or to distinguish one white mask paired with a tricorn from another. It didn't matter. It wasn't Richard. He'd left and he was never coming back. Even if he did, he'd made it clear he didn't want her.

Miss Fitzwilliam linked her arm in Cassandra's and drew her nearer to the window. A weak breeze filtered in through the open sash, barely cooler than the air inside the crowded ballroom.

'We haven't had much of a chance to speak since your betrothal to my brother,' Miss Fitzwilliam whispered, glancing around them to make sure no one was listening. The music continued, along with the dance and most people's attention was there or on their own conversations. 'You mustn't marry Vincent. He's a monster, capable of terrible things.'

'He'll ruin me if I don't,' Cassandra choked, her chances of overcoming him fading. 'He'll see to it I'm jailed and my daughter taken from me.'

'How can he? What does he have against you? I know you wouldn't marry him if it wasn't something awful.'

'I can't tell you or it will ruin you along with me.'

Miss Fitzwilliam nodded and didn't press for more. 'Then you must ruin him first. You aren't married yet. There's still time.' Miss Fitzwilliam reached into the front of her bodice, withdrew a folded paper and pressed it into Cassandra's hand. 'I believe this is what you were looking for when you were in his office the other day.'

Cassandra took the paper and opened it to reveal a letter to Mr Adams with detailed accounts of the merchandise to be traded with pirates from the *Casa de Oro* and the amount of silver he'd receive in return. A bead of perspiration slid down Cassandra's back, and her heart beat so fast she was afraid she might faint. This was everything she'd been searching for in the office, exactly what Richard had scoured every ship he'd ever taken to find and, in the end, acquiring it had been as simple as this young woman handing it to her. Cassandra folded the paper back up and clutched it against her chest, afraid someone might see it or suspect the two of them were up to something. Mr Adams was here, but she had no idea where he was or if he'd placed spies around to watch her the way he'd watched the cabin and discovered that Richard had been there. 'Why are you giving this to me? If I show it to anyone, it'll ruin not only your brother but also you.'

'I hope it sees him hanged. I hate him.' Her eyes became as hard as cut sapphires behind her mask. 'I was in love with a young man, but Vincent forbade the marriage. He was too afraid of losing control of my small inheritance from my mother to let me go. Peter and I ran away one night, but Mr Adams found us before we could wed and dragged me back here.'

'And Peter?' Cassandra was almost afraid to ask.

Miss Fitzwilliam rubbed at a scar on her wrist, her voice thick with unshed tears. 'Mr Adams turned him over to a press gang. Three months later I received a letter from a ship's captain telling me Peter was dead.'

Cassandra took Miss Fitzwilliam's hands and squeezed them tight. 'I'm so sorry.'

Determination blotted out her sorrow. 'I won't let him do to you what my father did to my mother, or have him ruin your life like he's ruined mine.'

'What about you?'

'I've made a few arrangements without my brother's knowledge.' She glanced at the opposite side of the room near the entrance to the dining room where refreshments were set out on silver trays. Mr Devlin stood there with his father, both of them unencumbered by masks. Young Mr Devlin studied Miss Fitzwilliam with amusement while his father enjoyed a hearty slice of cold ham. 'Use the letter however you see fit. I don't care.'

'Thank you.' Cassandra tucked the letter into the bodice of her dress.

'Now, we must part. Mr Devlin isn't the only one interested in our conversation.' She nodded towards the pockmarked man leaning against the wall in the corner, arms crossed while he watched them from behind his thin mask. Like Mr Fitzwilliam, Mr Adams had done little to conceal his true identity.

Cassandra left Miss Fitzwilliam and wound her way through the crowd towards where Mr Fitzwilliam stood with Lord and Lady Spotswood. She gripped her fan tight to keep her hands from shaking. Tonight was the perfect opportunity to give Lord Spotswood the damning evidence and secure her freedom, but she wasn't certain how she would manage it with Mr Fitzwilliam here. She would have to find some way to slip away from him again and speak to Lord Spotswood in private.

She came to a halt, a new fear overtaking her. She pressed her hand against her bodice, slipping her thumb inside to flick the edge of the letter. If Mr Fitzwilliam was convicted and all his property confiscated by the Crown, she'd lose Belle View. She lowered her hand to smooth it over the creased lace of her gown. She'd have to find the deed and destroy it before she could reveal the evidence, or she could hold the letter over his head to end the engagement. Either way, she would make use of what she'd been given and ensure Mr Fitzwilliam could never threaten her or Dinah again.

She slid a glance to where Mr Adams stood watching her like an irritated chaperon. The letter would see the nasty man jailed, too, assuming either he or Mr Fitzwilliam didn't silence her first and leave Dinah an orphan. Forcing herself forward through the crowd, she attempted to appear calm. She'd find a way to use the letter. She had to.

Cassandra stopped to allow a group of knights and ladies to pass when someone bumped into her from behind and knocked her off balance. Two hands clasped her around the waist to steady her, their firmness making her drop her fan to swing by its ribbon on her wrist. She was about to turn around and chastise whoever it was who'd had the audacity to touch her so intimately when a rich, deep voice made her stop.

'Meet me at the far end of the garden,' Richard whispered in her ear, his lips so close to her skin, his breath brushed her neck. 'At the horse topiary next to the wall.'

Hope fluttered inside her despite every effort she made to squash it. He was here and he'd dared to approach her in a crowded ballroom where anyone, especially Mr Adams and his men, might recognise him and have him arrested. Maybe she'd been wrong about him. Maybe he did care for her. With him so near and his firm hands encircling her waist, she wanted to lean into him, to clutch his thighs and hold on to the solidity of him, to tell him everything that had happened since he'd left and trust in him to help her overcome it.

Before she could move or respond, the pressure about her waist lifted and a faint breeze ruffled the strings of her mask, making them caress her bare shoulders when he swept off as silently as he'd approached. All that remained was the subtle scent of the ocean and his musky sweat, and the shock of his unexpected appearance.

She wavered a bit on her feet before recovering herself enough to take up her fan again.

*Perhaps he had found his evidence.* He'd insisted he'd return once he did. If so, combined with what she held, he could meet Lord Spotswood's terms and at last be a free man, his crew pardoned and Vincent arrested. He would be able to come home and be hers once more.

The blunt hand of experience slapped her soaring hope to the ground. Richard hadn't returned because he loved her, but because he needed something from her, just like on the *Devil's Rose* and at the overseer's cabin. Once he had it, he'd find another excuse to rush back to the life he so cherished. She shouldn't trouble with him or dare to meet him outside. It risked her being arrested or having someone see her dallying in the shadows with a man who wasn't Mr Fitzwilliam. She detested her fiancé, but she didn't need rumours of her being a whore spreading about the countryside. She'd taken a chance for Richard once before and he hadn't cared enough about her to stay, leaving her to Mr Fitzwilliam's designs. He could rot in the garden waiting for her. She wouldn't help him again.

She started for Lord Spotswood and Mr Fitzwilliam, but she couldn't put aside her curiosity about Richard or why he was here. She stopped and tilted her head to adjust one earring and caught sight of Richard slipping out the door and into the garden. There, masked couples promenaded along the stone paths beneath the flicker of torchlights. He was quickly lost in the parade of people and the shadows beyond the torches.

*What if he has evidence against Mr Fitzwilliam? It could save me and Belle View.* Perhaps Richard needed her to facilitate a meeting between him and Lord Spotswood. If she didn't help him, and he was arrested before he could speak to Lord Spotswood, his evidence might disappear, leaving only hers to convict Mr Fitzwilliam. She wasn't certain hers was strong enough, but if they both presented something, Lord Spotswood would be forced to bring charges against Mr Fitzwilliam, ridding them of the evil man. It galled her to jeopardise her future and safety to help Richard again, but in doing so she might help herself.

She peered leisurely about the room to spy Mr Fitzwilliam and Lord Spotswood deep in conversation. Mr Adams continued to watch her with a suspicion to make her nervous. Had he noticed Richard? She doubted it for his features were well concealed behind his Venetian mask, but she had to remain wary. If he saw her slip outside he might follow her, catch her with Richard and see to it Richard was arrested.

Cassandra strolled to the door. Near it stood a young lady she didn't recognise dressed like a regal Egyptian queen. Cassandra complimented her on the fineness of her costume and enquired after the seamstress who'd created it. The vapid woman chatted about her attire and sang the praises of her Williamsburg modiste long enough to bore both Cassandra and Mr Adams, who at last turned his attention to his employer. Seeing the man lose interest in her, Cassandra bid the Egyptian queen a hasty goodbye and bolted through the open door and into the darkened garden.

From the shadow of the large horse topiary, Richard watched Cassandra make her way out of the palace and down the gravel path towards the garden wall at the far end. It'd taken her so long to come, he'd feared she wouldn't. He'd left her at Belle View, and it would serve him right if she turned her back on him tonight, but she hadn't, at least not yet.

The moon illuminated the walkway and the neatly trimmed shrubs while catching in the lighter grey lace decorating her black-silk gown. She was careful to smile and exchange pleasantries with the other couples strolling about the garden before she left the light of the torches to reach the darkness draping the back wall. Even with the stress of their coming meeting making her steps halting and unsure, she was radiant in a way the other ladies could never match.

When she came close enough, he reached out and took her arm and pulled her into the darkness behind the topiary. With her slim waist between his hands, her fingers tight on his forearms, he found her mouth. Her soft lips pressed to his were forbidden and familiar all at once. Anyone might stumble upon them here, but he didn't care. They were together.

She fell into his embrace and sighed beneath his gentle touch, her hands light on his chest, surrendering to her desire and his before she jerked out of his arms. 'How dare you leave me, then come back and take liberties!'

'Half the garden is alive with people taking liberties.' He smirked, her anger unable to dull his excitement. Even if nothing went as planned tonight, her caring enough to meet him offered more possibility of happiness and redemption than he deserved. He'd discarded his mask and hat off to one side, determined to face her without fear of discovery or recognition. Let someone notice him, he would no longer live in the shadows.

'If you're discovered, you'll be arrested,' she warned, 'and I will be ruined.'

'I'll gladly ruin you tonight if you'd like.' He slipped his hand behind her neck and bent down to place a soft kiss on her throat and brought his lips close to her delicate ear. 'I couldn't stay away from you.'

She stood stiffly, arms crossed, unwilling to show him mercy. 'Which surprises me since you're always so quick to leave.'

'Not this time, Cas. Captain Dehesa is with me.'

She lowered her arms to her sides. 'The man in the Cavalier hat.'

'He's going to accept the King's Grace, then give a sworn testament to his dealings with Vincent.'

'You trust a man like him to help you?'

'Dehesa may have a fearsome reputation, but he also has a sense of honour most pirates lack. I saved his life. He'll repay the debt.' The thought of the struggles of the last five years and his time as Captain Rose finally coming to an end lifted Richard's spirits as much as the sight of Cas standing before him. Except she didn't look on him with the same desire and love as at the cabin, but remained rigid with well-deserved indignation. He didn't care. She could threaten to shoot him again with her father's duelling pistols and he would still do all he could to win her back. Her willingness to defy convention and meet him here told him capturing her heart, like the pardon, was possible. 'I also found your Mr Powell and I carry an affidavit from him attesting to his dealing with Vincent through Mr Adams. The sworn testimony of two scoundrels is the best I could acquire and it will have to be enough. I won't run any more. I will come home a pardoned man and fight Vincent with the law on my side.'

'Your evidence will be enough, especially when you give Lord Spotswood this.' She slipped her fingers into the front of her bodice and removed a folded piece of paper tucked between her skin and the brocade and held it out to him.

He took it, the parchment still warm from the heat of her body, and opened it, tilting it towards the faint torchlight and struggling to read the scrawl. 'What is it?'

'A letter in Mr Fitzwilliam's hand detailing his trade with pirates and the silver he received for it.'

He gaped at her. It wasn't possible. 'How did you get this?'

'Miss Fitzwilliam gave it to me.' She explained Miss Fitzwilliam's role in obtaining it and the grudge the sister held against her brother, one powerful enough to crush him.

Richard studied the document before him. The one thing he'd never been able to find and Cas had secured it for him. 'You can't imagine what this means to me, what you mean to me.'

'You're right, I can't.'

Her grave words startled him, and he glanced up to find her studying him the same way she had when he'd revealed himself to her aboard the *Devil's Rose*—remembering the strength of their love, but not trusting it or him.

He tucked the paper in his frock-coat pocket and took Cassandra's hand. She didn't grip him back or surrender to his slight tug to draw her closer, but stayed firm, like one of the statues along the garden walk. He took her other hand and stood over her, ready to ask once more for her to share his life with him, unsure this time if she would accept. 'I was wrong to leave you, both times, and I was selfish in all my pursuits. I've never enjoyed peace like

I have when I'm with you and I was a fool to throw it away to run after something as fleeting as riches, glory and adventure. At one time, I thought there was nothing left for me but a life at sea, then you came to me. Even at my weakest and most wounded, in pain and worried about my men, with you beside me I could touch something of what I'd lost and picture a future I hadn't dared to imagine before. I refuse to allow it and you to slip away from me ever again.'

The mask covering her face made her green-brown eyes turn deeper in the shadows, but the whites sparkled in the low light of the garden with her tears. He reached behind her and untied the strings of the mask, uncovering her beautiful features. 'I love you, Cas. I never stopped loving you and I never will.'

The words he hadn't said to her in the cabin when she'd opened her heart to him curled around her as he pressed her into a deep embrace. A single tear slid down her full cheek, and he brushed it away with his thumb, his hand heavy and warm along the side of her face. The sounds of laughter and music stole over them and she wished she and Richard were like the other couples promenading in the light, their cares nothing beyond crops and dresses, their time together at its beautiful start instead of tainted by the journey. She longed to accept him, to have faith in the need in his voice and his touch, but with the scabbard of his sword and the hardness of the blunderbuss hidden beneath his coat reminding her of the man he really was, she was afraid to trust him again. 'You've left me twice. I can't believe you won't do it again.'

He tugged a piece of parchment out of his coat pocket and held it up to her. 'Is this enough proof for you?'

'What is this?'

'Open it and see.'

She stepped back enough to take the document, but he didn't let her go, keeping her within the protective circle of his arms. With quick flicks of her fingers she unfolded the paper, struggling to read it in the moonlight mixed with torch flame.

Shock made her gasp and she raised her face to his, as incredulous of this as he'd been of the paper she'd handed him. 'You sold the *Devil's Rose*.'

'To Mr Powell. It was the price I was willing to pay for his testimony and to come home to you.'

Cassandra opened her mouth to speak, but the words didn't come. He'd given up the *Devil's Rose* for her. It didn't seem possible. 'But your men? You said you wouldn't leave them to fend for themselves.'

'I haven't. They're aboard the *Casa de Oro*, safely moored in an inlet beyond Lord Spotswood's reach, waiting for me to send them word of their pardons. Once they have it, we will retrieve our wealth from Knott Island and start our lives over, they in the islands and I here with you, if you'll still have me.'

Cassandra rested her hands on his shoulders, the letter of transfer for the *Devil's Rose* crinkling beneath her palm. He was keeping his promise to return to her and severing his ties with Captain Rose for good. For a brief moment there was no palace or masks or giggling young ladies with their escorts, but only her and Richard, as it had been in Uncle Walter's garden. He was proposing to her for the second time, offering to struggle and work beside her to make Belle View prosperous again and to create for Dinah the happy family life Cassandra craved. There would be more children, siblings for Dinah to play with, to share the wonderful moments and to help her bear the sorrows, like Richard would do for Cassandra.

'Tell me you still love me, Cas,' he implored, his face tight in expectation of her answer. 'Tell me I still have your heart.'

'Yes, always.' She rose up on her toes and pressed her lips to his, sliding her arms around his neck and drawing him close. She didn't care who might pass by and see them—it didn't matter, nothing did except Richard's pledge to her and hers to him. They would be together, united against all challenges. He would be her husband, and she would never be alone again.

She lowered herself to her heels, breaking from his kiss, but refusing to let go of him. 'What will everyone say when I marry a pirate?' she teased, glancing up at him through her eyelashes while fingering his finely embroidered lapel.

'You'll be the talk of Williamsburg.' He bent down and nuzzled her neck with a muffled laugh. 'Are you sure you can endure more notoriety?'

'With you beside me I can endure anything, even a few rumours and some whispering, but I wonder if you can remember your manners.'

He leaned back in her arms and smiled, deepening the faint lines at the corners of his eyes. 'I'll do my best to be a respectable planter and, if that's not enough, I'll buy everyone's good graces. Either way, it doesn't matter. I have enough money for us to rebuild Belle View with or without anyone's approval.'

She stiffened in his arms. The threat of Mr Fitzwilliam had faded in Richard's embrace, but it came rushing back to her. 'I may not be able to keep Belle View to rebuild.'

She explained to him what had happened with Mr Fitzwilliam after he'd left, pacing in her agitation.

'The deed must be a forgery, like his Dutch passes,' he spat, the thirst for revenge filling his eyes once more.

'But we can't prove it. If he's convicted, everything will be confiscated by the Crown, even Belle View.'

He took her hand, as sincere as he'd been when he'd shown her the letter of transfer. 'I'll find a way to make sure it isn't. Once Vincent falls, anyone connected with him will tell what they know in an effort to save their own necks.'

She gripped his hand tight, still unsure. 'How can you be sure they won't flee instead?'

'Even if they do, the single advantage of having lived among lowlifes for so long is my unsavoury connections. I'll call on them to root out Vincent's agents if they try to escape, and prove the deed and the shipping pass that first convicted me are forgeries. I promise you, I will make everything right.'

For the first time since he'd left her in Yorktown, she was sure it was a promise he would keep. 'Then let's go to Lord Spotswood and finally end this.'

Richard picked up his mask and hat and put them back on. 'I'll go first. You follow soon after so as not to draw attention to either of us.'

'Be careful,' she called after him, retying her own mask across her eyes. He turned, offering her a small salute before heading up the path and into the palace.

Cassandra waited until he was inside the ballroom, then began the long walk back to the Governor's Palace, dread and worry accompanying her. Richard had his evidence, but it was still difficult to imagine this would all end well. Lord Spotswood might turn on Richard and condemn both him and her. Without his ship, the one he'd given up for her, he could not escape.

No, there would be no need for him to flee. The evidence was solid and Lord Spotswood was a man of his word. He would honour his bargain, the way she'd once honoured hers with Richard.

Ahead, Mr Fitzwilliam stood at the door to the ballroom, his face dark. Disgust drove out her worry as she approached him. This man would not force himself on her or command her life, but die at the end of a rope. She climbed the stairs and, ignoring his outstretched hand, strode past him into the lively ballroom.

'What were you doing out there?' he demanded, coming to her side.

'Taking in the cooler air.'

'You aren't to wander off alone like that. What will people say? I won't have you behaving here like you did in London.'

She ignored his lecture on decorum while across the room, Richard and Captain Dehesa stood with Lord Spotswood. The Governor rubbed his round chin while he read Mr Fitzwilliam's letter, the affidavit and then listened to Captain Dehesa speak.

She held her breath, waiting for Lord Spotswood's response, her attention darting from him to the two soldiers flanking either side of the ballroom door. Would Lord Spotswood believe Richard and the pirate Captain or turn on them and arrest them, allowing the true villain to escape from the law while condemning Richard to the gallows? Everything hinged on Lord Spotswood's decision and the moments seemed to stretch out while she waited for some sign or indication of which way he would decide.

Next to her, Mr Fitzwilliam continued to berate her about her behaviour, while on the dance floor the revellers completed their intricate turns and steps in time to the flowing music.

At last Lord Spotswood folded the paper and raised his hand. Cassandra held her breath, waiting for him to summon the guards, but he held it out for Richard to shake. Cassandra's knees almost gave out under the weight of her relief. He believed Richard and the evidence. They would be safe.

With a flick of his fingers, the governor waved over one of the guards. He whispered to the dragoon who nodded then hurried off, she felt sure, to gather others.

'Did you hear what I just said?' Mr Fitzwilliam raged in her ear.

'No, not one word of it,' she snapped, all the deference she'd been forced to pay to him for the last two weeks gone.

He noticed the change and snatched her by the arm, his fingernails digging into her skin. 'You'd better not have been enjoying more than the air. If you do anything to embarrass or disgrace me like you did Lord Shepherd, I'll make sure it's not you who suffers, but your daughter.'

She tugged the mask off her face, reserving for him the heaviest look of hate she could conjure. 'Whatever hold you think you have over me, it doesn't exist. You're about to be ruined and you're no longer in a position to harm me, my daughter or anyone else I love ever again.'

He let go of her, fear and surprise flittering across his face beneath his mask.

Mr Adams rushed up to him. 'We must leave at once. They're coming for us.'

He nodded to the soldiers filing into the room. The musicians stopped their playing and the dancers stumbled in their steps to stop and watch, everyone talking and wondering what was happening.

A red flush spread up Mr Fitzwilliam's neck as he realised he was at last found out. Her curled his hand into a fist and jabbed one warning finger at her. 'You bitch. You'll pay for this, I'll make certain of it.'

'Another time. We must go or we'll be hanged.' Mr Adams pulled him by the arm out the open door.

'Arrest Mr Fitzwilliam on charges of colluding with pirates,' Lord Spotswood ordered the dragoons, his command sending a wave of surprise rippling through the room.

'He left,' Cassandra cried, pushing her way through the throng to reach Richard and Lord Spotswood. 'They went through the garden.'

'Sergeant Grant, send men after him,' Lord Spotswood ordered the thick-necked soldier beside him. 'Mr Fitzwilliam can't sit a horse well enough to get far by the roads.'

'He can escape downriver by boat,' Richard reminded him.

'I'll dispatch men to Butler Plantation.'

'He won't go there.' Miss Fitzwilliam joined the group. 'There aren't any ships moored at the dock tonight.'

'But there's one at Belle View.' Fear hit Cassandra like lightning. 'Dinah! He said if I ever did anything against him he'd make her suffer.'

'I won't let him harm her.' Richard took her hand and pulled her towards the door.

'Take horses from my stables,' Lord Spotswood called after them. 'Sergeant Grant and his men will accompany you to Belle View.'

*'Voy contigo.'* Captain Dehesa tossed aside his mask and sprinted after Richard. 'We'll kill Mr Fitz-william like the dog he is.'

## Chapter Eleven

The uneasy stillness surrounding Belle View was more ominous than reassuring. Richard, Cassandra, Captain Dehesa and the six soldiers led by Sergeant Grant crept up the main drive, keeping to the shadows. They'd left the horses a quarter-mile back to hide their arrival. Despite their quick mounts, it had taken nearly an hour to get there by the rutted and dark roads. Cassandra hoped they weren't too late. The current on the river was fast and the water route much quicker.

'Do you think they're inside?' Sergeant Grant whispered while they watched the house, searching for signs of Mr Adams and Mr Fitzwilliam.

A woman's scream followed by a man's raised voice silenced the night sounds.

'They're in there! Hurry!' Richard ran up the drive to the house and slammed into the front door, but it was bolted shut.

'Break it down,' Cassandra ordered when Dinah's shriek split the air. She'd tear Belle View apart brick by brick to reach her daughter.

'You two, grab a log. The rest of you go around the back and make sure they don't slip out,' Sergeant Grant ordered, and four men hurried out of sight as they rounded the house. The two remaining soldiers picked up a thick log from a pile near the corner of the house. Holding it between them, they stood before the door and swung it into the wood. In one hit the weathered door broke open.

'Dinah!' Cassandra called, following the men inside. 'Dinah!'

'Mama!' Dinah answered from the back sitting room.

They raced down the hall and burst into the room to find Jane kneeling over Mrs Sween. The housekeeper lay unconscious on the floor, an angry gash above her left eyebrow. Dinah cowered in the corner behind a small ottoman, her face red with tears.

Cassandra rushed to her daughter and swept her into her arms. 'It's all right, my love. You're safe now.'

'Where are they?' Richard demanded of Jane.

'I don't know. They tried to take the child, but Mrs Sween wouldn't let them. The ugly one knocked her down. Then, when they heard the crash at the front door, they fled.'

One soldier picked up Mrs Sween and laid her on the sofa.

The thud of footsteps beneath the floorboards echoed through the room.

'They're trying to get out through the cellar passage to the kitchen,' Cassandra said to Richard, stroking Dinah's hair to soothe the child's frightened sobs. 'You remember where it is?'

'I do. This way.'

Richard sprinted out of the room, Captain Dehesa, Sergeant Grant and one soldier following close behind him. He rushed to the door set in the panel just off the dining room and pulled it open. The musty stench of old air and damp earth struck him. He moved cautiously down the sagging treads, blunderbuss raised, eyes adjusting to the faint light falling into the darkness from the chandelier in the hallway. Richard could see little except for the outline of support timbers, sacks of flour and the dust covering the old stone floor. Anyone hiding in the shadows below held the advantage.

They entered the narrow passage outside the storeroom, creeping steadily along. With their eyes still adjusting to the darkness, their senses were keen for any movement or sound alerting them to danger. There was nothing but the creak of floorboards overhead, the sifting of dust and faint voices. Richard continued on, step by cautious step, unwilling to relax his hard grip on his blunderbuss.

Then the flash of a pistol lit the room and Vincent's face. A deafening boom shook the cellar, and Sergeant Grant grunted and fell against the wall, a stain of dark red spreading out over the wool covering his upper arm. From overhead, the women exclaimed with alarm.

'Richard, are you all right?' Cas called out, her voice muffled by the floors and walls between them.

'I am, but Sergeant Grant is wounded.' Richard turned to the soldier. 'Help him up to the ladies.'

Richard lunged forward, struggling to see through the darkness to where the smoke hung in the air on the far side of the room. Captain Dehesa followed a short distance behind him.

'Stop,' Richard commanded. 'You're outnumbered.'

'No, I don't think so,' Vincent hissed, the whites of his eyes glinting in the faint light coming down the passage from the kitchen building, the scrape of metal making Richard's skin crawl as Vincent rammed the rod down the barrel of his pistol, packing his next shot. Richard levelled his blunderbuss at him, ready to drop the man when the floorboards behind Richard squeaked. He felt more than saw Mr Adams behind him.

'Goodbye, Captain Rose.'

Another flash and blast filled the room. Richard shuddered, expecting the familiar burn of the bullet through his flesh but there was nothing. Vincent fled down the passage.

Richard whirled around. Mr Adams swayed on his feet, blood trickling out of one side of his mouth. His eyes clouded with his fading life before he dropped to the floor. Captain Dehesa stood behind him, smoke drifting out of his finely engraved pistol.

'You saved my life, now I've saved yours.' Captain Dehesa grinned.

'We aren't through yet.'

Vincent's footsteps echoed up the stairs to the kitchen. Soon, he'd be free of the house and past where the soldiers waited for him. Richard could follow him down the passage, but in the narrow tunnel he'd be an easy target for Vincent's single bullet. 'Back upstairs before he gets away.'

They hurried up from the basement, meeting Cassandra in the hallway.

'I heard a second shot. What happened?'

'Mr Adams is dead, and Vincent is heading for the back and the river, but I won't let him get away.'

'No, we won't.' She held up the duelling pistols.

'Well done, my love.' He brushed her lips with a kiss before they rushed through the house and out to the lawn.

'Follow us—Vincent's gone through the kitchen,' Richard called to the soldiers waiting there and he, Cassandra and Captain Dehesa hurried around to the rear of the kitchen. Richard reloaded his blunderbuss while they ran, too many fights at sea making him quick to ram the powder and shot home.

They reached the back of the kitchen outbuilding to find the door open and the surrounding night still.

'Where did he go?' Captain Dehesa asked. The woods behind them were dark and difficult to see through.

Cas pointed one pistol at the wharf. 'There he is.'

Vincent, silhouetted by the reflection of the moon off the river, stood aboard the shallop moored to the dock, hoisting the sail and preparing to set off.

They ran towards the wharf, the soldiers following. They were halfway there when a burst of flame and a crack broke the stillness. Everyone ducked. The high-pitched whine of a bullet flew over them before shattering the bark of a nearby tree.

Richard, Cas and Captain Dehesa moved aside as the soldiers dropped to their knees and lowered their muskets.

'Ready. Aim. Fire,' the most senior man commanded.

A volley of musket balls hit the crates stacked on the dock, sending splinters of wood tearing through the sails and plunking into the water.

Mr Fitzwilliam cursed and grabbed his cheek, then struggled against the rocking shallop to fling off the line. The shallop began to drift away from the dock, caught by the current, the wind filling the sails.

'Reload,' one of the soldiers ordered.

'He'll be gone before you can fire again.' Richard flew down the rise, refusing to allow Vincent to get away. He wouldn't spend the rest of his life looking over his shoulder each time he walked down the street, waiting for someone to stab him, and he wouldn't worry about Cas every time he left her alone, afraid she might fall victim to Vincent's wrath. That was how a pirate lived and he was no longer that. He was a gentleman again. Everything would end here tonight. He would make sure Vincent was arrested and tried, then he would stand in the square at Williamsburg and watch him hang, surrounded by society who would at last see him for the villain he really was.

Richard raced down the hill and to the dock, stopping and firing his blunderbuss the moment he thought he was in range. The ball missed Vincent, sending up a splash of water behind the boat. A lantern hanging over the dock swung in the breeze. It cast its faint orange light over the scarred wood, highlighting the line of red blood on Vincent's cheek from where the splinter from the musket ball had hit him. He grinned at Richard from the drifting shallop.

'You missed again, as all your strikes against me have.'

'Not this time.' Anger filled Richard, blotting out all rational thought of the law and a proper hanging. 'I will have you and you will pay for the wrongs you've done.'

Vincent's grin turned to horror when Richard tossed away the spent weapon and thundered down the dock. The wood quivered beneath each fall of Richard's boots until he launched himself off the end, arching above the water to land in the stern of the shallop. The vessel pitched and rocked violently, knocking Vincent off balance, and Richard grabbed the side to steady himself.

'Richard!' Cassandra jerked to a stop at the edge of the dock. Captain Dehesa caught her by the waist and pulled her back before she could fall into the cool water. 'Take these!'

She tossed the duelling pistols to Richard. One

landed in the boat between him and Vincent. The other he caught before it was lost over the side. Vincent lunged at the weapon, taking it up and levelling it at Richard, who pointed his at his old friend.

'Surrender, Vincent,' Richard commanded, as he would any captain of a captured vessel at sea, Captain Rose descending over him. 'You're outnumbered and you can't escape.'

The wind died down, making the sail sag and the boat, caught in the current, began to drift back towards the bank. The soldiers gathered there beside Cassandra. The shallop was in range of their muskets, but if they fired, they'd hit Richard and Vincent.

'What do you think will happen after tonight?' Vincent sneered. 'Do you think Williamsburg society will welcome you back like some prodigal son? No matter what you do, you will always be a pirate, a thieving scum reviled by everyone.'

'It didn't have to be like this.' Richard kept his arm steady, aiming at Vincent and working to keep his balance as the shallop rocked with the current. 'You were my friend. You didn't have to turn on me. I would've helped you if you'd told me the Virginia Trading Company was in trouble. You never gave me the chance.'

'Yes, you were such a saint with your glorious ideas about serving your country and a father who'd sell his soul before seeing his precious son suffer as a mere solicitor. My father left me to twist in the wind while he escaped the problems he created by taking the coward's way out. He wasn't content to ruin his own life, but he tried to crush mine, too, after destroying my mother.'

'And you think ruining the lives of innocent men to save yourself isn't cowardly or makes you any better than him?'

'I did what I had to do to survive, just like you, Captain Rose. The Virginia Trading Company was my mother's legacy to me and I vowed to her that I would see it thrive again and not let my father fritter it away. I wasn't about to let it go, just as you couldn't let go of me. You could've disappeared to some remote port, reinvented yourself as a fat planter, but instead you wanted your revenge. Tell me, how many men have you killed in your crusade against me? How many passengers aboard ships have you terrorised? You want to condemn me, but you're no better than I am.'

'We're nothing alike.' Richard slid his finger along the curve of the trigger, ready to pull it and send a musket ball through Vincent's smug face.

'Aren't we? Look at the lengths you've gone to, the sad depths you've sunk to in order to chase me.'

'I did it to see you brought to justice and for innocent men to have their names cleared.'

'You did it for yourself and all for nothing because I won't hang. I know too many influential men and their secrets. I will best you in this matter as I did when you attacked my ship. When I walk free, and I will, you won't be able to chase me and your failure will haunt you for the rest of your life.'

Richard cocked the hammer of the pistol, his finger against the trigger shaking with the effort to hold it steady. Every wrong this man had ever done to him, all the venom that had urged him on through every hurricane and fight at sea and every wretched pirate town in the islands hardening his heart and demanding he act. 'Then I'll kill you now.'

'Richard, don't do it. He isn't worth it,' Cas pleaded from the dock, her voice as light as the calls of the night birds.

'I won't let him escape or be freed by corrupt men.'

'He won't be. He will face justice, but not like this.'

Richard curled his finger around the trigger, his eyes never leaving Vincent's. This was the moment he'd plotted for years and he would not let it slip away.

'Richard,' Cas urged. 'Don't throw everything away again because of him.'

The sweet tone of her words cut through the hate he'd carried for too long, the one urging Richard to pull the trigger. If he shot the man in cold blood, then he was no better than him and he never would be. Revenge had brought him here but he needn't carry it any further. He'd freed himself and his men tonight and put an end to Captain Rose. He wouldn't step outside the law again and lose himself to more years of futile searching and running, and being separated from Cas. She'd offered him a future; it was time to let go of the past and seize it, and her love.

Richard took his finger off the trigger and slowly

lowered the hammer. 'It's over, Vincent. You don't have the money to buy your way out of these charges, and the evidence I have against you will mean no man of standing in the colonies will risk his reputation to defend you. There's nowhere for you to go and nothing for you to do but face the charges, and you will. And then I'll watch you hang and never think of you again.'

The hopelessness of his situation began to dawn on Vincent's face and the scowl on his brow lengthened to a look of wretched defeat, but still he didn't lower the pistol or surrender. 'You think you've won, but you haven't. You think you've taken everything from me, righted some wrong, but you've failed. I'll see you suffer. You've stolen from me the one thing I cherished the most, my last connection to my mother, just like my father tried to do. I will see you suffer for it by taking away something you cherish.'

Vincent whipped his pistol around towards Cassandra. He thumbed back the hammer, the hesitation fatal as Richard pulled the trigger of his weapon. His shot slammed into Vincent's chest, jerking him around to face Richard as his gun fired. The bullet winged Richard's arm, slicing his coat and shirt and the skin beneath.

Red spread out from Vincent's chest to stain the blue brocade of his frock coat, and a strangled whisper escaped his lips before he dropped to his knees, his eyes meeting Richard's one last time before he pitched forward against the thwart board, dead.

Richard opened his fingers and the pistol dropped

to clatter against the wooden hull. He stared at his childhood friend, relief and regret flooding him. They'd spent many warm nights like this one sailing these waters together as boys, dreaming of the future. Neither of them could have imagined it ending like this.

'Richard?' Cassandra called out, her voice more beautiful than a safe port in a storm.

He took up the line and tossed it at the dock. The soldiers caught it and hauled the shallop back in.

'Are you all right?' Cassandra rushed to him as he climbed out of the boat. She shoved his frock coat off his arm to examine the wound in the dim lantern light.

'It's only a scratch.' He smiled, too enamoured of her to mind the pain.

'I hope you won't take such risks when we're married. I won't be made a widow again.' She slapped his broad chest, not as amused as him by the near miss.

'The most I'll risk is a missed dance step or two.' He pulled her back against his chest, and she melded into the curve of his body.

She rested her hand on his shoulders, her touch hesitant. 'It's really over, isn't it? The last five years, everything?'

Her disbelief matched his. He glanced past her to where the dragoons pulled Vincent's lifeless body out of the boat. His old friend and greatest enemy was dead and he could never threaten or come between them again. 'It is, all of it, and there's nothing to stop us from being together.'

'No, there isn't.'

He cupped her cheek with his hand, bringing his face so close to hers he could feel her breath on his neck. 'I love you, Cas.'

'I love you, too.'

He covered her lips with his.

At last, he was home.

## Epilogue

The candles burning in the candelabras of the Butler Plantation sitting room danced with a draught, making the light waver over the wainscoting on the walls and the thin and nervous reverend's solemn expression where he stood before the fireplace.

'I now pronounce you man and wife. You may kiss the bride,' the reverend said in a small voice hampered by meekness.

Arabella's tight grip on the bouquet of hastily picked roses from the garden cracked the stems. Evander Devlin turned to her. His dark brown hair was tied in a red ribbon at the nape of his neck and his black frock coat made his wide shoulders and towering height even more impressive. At one time she'd vowed never to fall under a man's control. Tonight she'd sold herself to this one to keep from losing everything.

'Ahem…' The reverend cleared his skinny throat. 'You may now kiss the bride.'

'Yes, I know.' Evander adjusted the tricorn under his arm, but did nothing else.

Arabella raised her chin to the man who was now her husband, refusing to reveal any hint of the nervousness twisting her insides. She'd made a deal with Mr Devlin and she'd see it through, all of it.

Mr Devlin studied her, more intrigued than besotted. He was lean but coiled tight, like a venomous serpent, and she guessed just as lethal if provoked. Judging by his languid expression, it would take a great deal of prodding to make him strike.

'This is where you kiss me,' she insisted, waiting for him to finish the ceremony, to claim her as his wife as he now held every right to do. She hoped the tales she'd heard of his carnal skills, the ones the maids used to bring back from Williamsburg along with the market proceeds, were true. It would make the delicate terms of their arrangement more enjoyable.

'No, I don't believe I will,' he replied in a long drawl, as if rejecting wine at dinner.

She dropped her arms, making the rosebuds brush against her ivory-silk gown.

The rector tugged at his collar. 'Sir, it's customary.'

'So is bedding the bride on her wedding night, but I have no intention of doing that either.' He arched one eyebrow at her as if he expected a challenge. She couldn't disappoint him.

'I will be your true wife.' She tossed the bouquet

on a side table, the fake pearls wound through the curls of her coiffure clinking together at the movement. He wouldn't disrespect her the way her father had disrespected and debased her mother. Nor would she fail to gain some pleasure from surrendering her freedom to this irritating and too-handsome man.

'Some day, but you're too young to risk becoming a mother just yet.'

'I'm sixteen.' Half the respectable young ladies in Williamsburg were already wedded and bedded at this age.

'And as I said, too young.' He cuffed her under the chin, and she wanted to stomp her foot in frustration. What kind of insolence was this? It made no sense.

The elder Mr Devlin, the only witness to this wedding farce besides the reverend and Mary, Arabella's lady's maid, snored from his place in the stuffed chair behind her, his long legs stretched out in front of him.

'I'll wake him and have him and your maid sign the licence,' the reverend offered, eager to leave the newlyweds to their quarrel. He stepped around Arabella and Evander, visibly relieved to have something more to do than debate their conjugal relationship.

The reverend tapped Mr Devlin awake.

'What? Who?' The older man snorted. 'Oh, it's over? Good, need to be getting on to Charleston. Congratulations, my dear, welcome to the family, such as it is.'

He touched the tip of his tricorn to her, then followed the reverend and the maid out of the room, scratching his stomach while he went.

'We're going to Charleston?' Arabella wasn't prepared to leave Butler Plantation. For all the hateful memories, there were good ones with her mother, too, and now that it would be hers again thanks to this strange marriage, there was so much she wanted to do to it.

'No. My father and I are going to Charleston. You are staying here.'

'You're leaving me? Already?' Why had he married her if he was going to abandon her minutes after the ceremony?

'I have business to deal with,' he stated as if telling her the price of cotton.

'When are you coming back?'

'Not for some time.' He withdrew two papers from his frock-coat pocket and held out one to her. 'This is the deed to Butler Plantation as I promised you when we were betrothed.' He offered her the other. 'This is the patent for the Virginia Trading Company the court awarded us to pay your brother's debts. Consider it my wedding present to you.'

She took the patent, stunned. It was unheard of for a man to give his wife a business, especially one like this. Assuming she remained his true wife.

'I'm hardly a bride if...' she flapped the papers in the air, losing her grip on her usual steadiness '...the rest doesn't follow.'

'It will, eventually, but you need a bit of seasoning first.'

'Seasoning?' If the man's rapacious business sense wasn't the talk of the county, and the whole reason she'd agreed to his proposal, she would think him a fool.

He laid his fingers along the edge of her jaw and turned her face gently from side to side, his firm skin against hers increasing the strange hunger gnawing at her insides. A rakish smile curled up the sides of his mouth, making him as tempting as a minor sin. She held her breath, waiting for more, but then he let go of her. 'I'm curious to see what you make of yourself and the business. Don't disappoint me.'

He took the tricorn from beneath his arm and tucked it down over his dark hair. He bowed, his intense gaze never leaving hers until he turned and strode out the door.

The crack of the whip as their carriage drove away snapped her out of her stupor. She stared at the deeds in her hand. It was hers, all of it, to do with as she pleased, until he came back.

She spun in a slow circle, taking in the room— her room, her house, her business.

A smile as wicked as it was determined spread across her lips. Yes, she'd make something of herself, Butler Plantation and Vincent's old business. Then, she'd find a way to free herself of this vow to Mr Devlin and never be under any man's control again.

A cool breeze drifted up from the river, the last of the summer heat and humidity having abated during the night. Autumn was crisp in the air and in the touches of brown and gold beginning to show in the leaves of the trees. Cassandra stepped on to the back porch to watch the farmers unload barrels of apples newly arrived from the cooler Shenandoah Valley. The cargo was piled up on the new dock, the one Richard had paid to construct shortly after their wedding. At first she'd objected to using his pirate money to benefit Belle View, but the dock wasn't only for their advantage. The many farmers who needed to transport their goods to other ports used it, too, as well as the new distillery Richard had also built to turn the steady supply of arriving apples into cider to ship north. She was honouring her father's memory with their generosity and helping the farmers around them the way he'd always wanted to do.

'Good morning, Mrs Davenport,' Richard called to her. He strode up the hill from the dock with the swagger of a planter, not the arrogance of a pirate. Days in the field kept his skin dark and he still favoured the same plain frock coat he'd worn aboard ship, but there was no sword fastened at his hip nor a set of pistols slung across his chest. They'd been replaced by the riding crop he carried to oversee the fields or to ride out to where the new mill was taking shape beside a tributary of the river. It was another business to protect them during the lean harvest years while helping nearby farmers survive. 'Have you taken to becoming a lady of leisure?'

'Far from it.' She caught his arm when he came up the stairs, and they strolled into the house. His boots thumped over the newly polished floors as they passed the dining room. Inside, Mrs Sween stood with Dinah and Jane arranging flowers in the silver holder on top of the table. The dust was gone and everything glistened like it used to when Cassandra was a child. Her mother would have been proud to see it. 'I was enjoying tea with Dr Abney this morning. He told me quite the bit of news.'

Richard took her in his arms, his skin hot and heady with the scent of wood and misty air from his morning activity. 'If it's about Captain Dehesa, I've already heard. He's gone to the French city of New Orleans with the hope of becoming a respectable landowner and a pillar of the burgeoning community.'

'You think he'll abide by the pardon for good? He's a man who likes adventure too much to settle for farming.'

'I hear there's more thievery than farming in New Orleans. It'll take a man like Captain Dehesa to help tame it, assuming some beauty doesn't tame him first.'

'Like I tamed you?' She slipped her arms around his waist.

'I'm fully ensnared.' He bent to kiss her, but she ducked her head.

'Do you ever miss the adventure?' She straightened his white cravat, anxious for his answer.

'No, not at all.' Richard swept off his hat, holding it behind her as he pressed his forehead against hers. 'Life with you is all the excitement I need.'

He tried to kiss her, but she turned her face so his

lips brushed her cheek, eliciting a growl of frustration from him.

'It's about to become more interesting.' She smoothed a wrinkle in his frock coat.

He pulled back. 'What else did Dr Abney tell you?'

'There'll be a new baby in the nursery come spring.'

A smile broke across his lips, as wide and deep as the James River. 'A child?'

'A little boy with your dark hair.'

'Or another girl as pretty as our Dinah.'

'Which one do you want?'

He leaned in close, his eyes holding hers with all the passion in his heart. 'It doesn't matter so long as all of us are together.'

\* \* \* \* \*

*If you enjoyed this story,*
*check out Georgie Lee's*
SCANDAL AND DISGRACE *miniseries*

*RESCUED FROM RUIN*
*MISS MARIANNE'S DISGRACE*
*COURTING DANGER WITH MR DYER*

*And check out the first book in her*
THE BUSINESS OF MARRIAGE *miniseries*

*A DEBT PAID IN MARRIAGE*